LOTTIE'S LITTLE SECRET

Debbie Viggiano

This one is for you
my lovely reader!

Chapter One

'So, when am I going to meet this new man of yours?' my bestie demanded. 'It's high time Stu and I made up a foursome with the pair of you.'

We were seated in my tiny cottage kitchen on a sunny, but cold, November morning. The weekend stretched ahead, and I knew Jen was hinting at doing something this evening. In her opinion, a Saturday night was wasted if it didn't involve company and plenty of wine.

'Soon,' I soothed.

'You said that last month.'

Jen folded her arms across her chest. Uh-oh. Her chin had thrust forward. Body language. Bad signs. Right now, I could read my mate like a book. She didn't believe my story about me having a new man in my life. Indeed, suspicion was oozing from her very pores.

Jen had every right to suspect my fella was fictitious. After all, I'd pretended before. Not that I usually told porkies. But at the time I'd been going through an arid patch in my love life. I'd been fed up with Jen bossing me about, banging on about a popular dating app. She'd joined and consequently met Stu. Naturally he was her soulmate. She'd almost ended up with Repetitive Strain Injury from so much swiping right.

'Well?' she prompted.

'It's tricky,' I said, making a see-saw motion with one hand.

'Lottie, you're repeating yourself.'

'Oh, for goodness' sake,' I huffed, pushing back my chair. I stood up. 'Do you want another coffee?'

Jen's eyes tracked me as I picked up the kettle.

'If you're having one,' she sniffed. She unfolded one arm and made a show of studying her fingernails.

'Yes, I am.'

'Okay, in which case I'll also have another doughnut,' she added.

'I thought you were on a diet and calorie counting.'

'No. *You're* the one who said she was on a diet. Instead, *I'll* count the calories that I'm saving *you* from eating.'

'You're such a thoughtful friend,' I said, giving her a smile as sweet as the sugary doughnuts we'd been tucking into.

'Anyway,' said Jen. 'Regarding this boyfriend of yours.' Her eyes swivelled back to my face. They were her most expressive feature and gave away exactly what she was thinking. Currently they reminded me of two hazel-coloured searchlights. They almost pinned me to the cupboard as I reached for the coffee jar within. As she tucked a strand of dark hair behind one ear, I pretended not to notice her scrutiny.

'What about my boyfriend?' I said casually, spooning

2

coffee into mugs.

Jen narrowed her eyes.

'I smell a rat.'

'What do you mean?' I said, playing for time. Slowly, I poured boiling water over the granules.

'I don't think this boyfriend of yours really exists. You're trying to fob me off again, aren't you?'

Flipping heck, I *knew* I'd been right about her thinking that.

'No, no!' I hastily assured. 'He's real. Promise.'

'So what's the problem about us going on a double date?'

I stirred milk and sugar into the mugs but didn't reply.

'Oh God,' Jen groaned. 'Please don't tell me you're embroiled with a married man.'

I picked up the mugs and set them down on the table, alongside the plate of remaining doughnuts.

'Ryan is *not* married,' I said emphatically.

'Hm.' Jen picked up a doughnut, all the while eyeballing me suspiciously. 'Are you certain? After all, you said he's sixty years old. No man gets to that age without some sort of track record. He must have history. Unless he's been a monk. A celibate one at that.'

'All *right*,' I snapped. I snatched up my coffee, slopping hot liquid over my jeans in the process. 'Bugger,' I muttered. Grabbing a nearby roll of kitchen towel, I tore off a strip and mopped ineffectually with one hand. 'Ryan is single, but this status is quite recent.'

'You mean it's not that long ago he was a married man. I knew it,' Jen crowed.

'He's *single*,' I said tetchily. I swapped the kitchen towel for a dishcloth, patting away at my denims. Typical. Clean on this morning. Worn for barely three hours. Now I'd have to wash them again. It was either that or smell like a Costa Coffee shop. 'Anyway' – I pointed out – 'there's nothing wrong with being newly single. Remember, we've both been married too.'

'Ah, but we only have one ex-husband apiece,' Jen pointed out. 'How many ex-wives does Relic Ryan have?'

'Don't call him that,' I tutted, ignoring the question. 'Anyway, these days, sixty isn't that old.'

'It isn't that young either,' Jen muttered.

'Sixty is the new thirty,' I said airily.

'Where did you read that twaddle?' Jen snorted. 'Probably in one of those trashy magazines you secretly read – yes, don't deny it. I extracted one from behind a cushion the other week. It was full of nonsense about Prince Harry taking up painting to supplement his income.'

'Would that make him the artist formerly known as Prince?' I said dryly.

'Ha bloody ha. And don't think I haven't spotted your attempt to evade answering my question.'

'You think Ryan is too old for me.'

'Put it this way. If you live your life all over again, you'll be ninety-six. Whereas the six for Ryan will be in relation to him being six feet under.'

'There's only a twelve-year age gap between us,' I protested.

'Never mind that for now. Spill the beans about his marital history.'

'Oh, okay,' I sighed, tossing the tea towel to one side. I leant back in my chair. 'He was married to someone called Heather for about thirty years. Prior to that, there were a couple of partners he lived with – not at the same time, obviously. Anyway, co-habitations can't be included when reviewing a potential partner's history.'

'Of course they can,' Jen scoffed. 'He might not have exchanged wedding bands with the women concerned, but they were still relationships.'

'Well they didn't last very long. Only a few months apiece.'

'That's a poor track record–'

'That can be put down to youth and inexperience,' I interrupted. 'His subsequent three decades of marriage with Heather demonstrates – to me – some serious staying power.'

'Hmm.' Jen looked down her nose. 'Who left who?'

'I don't know,' I said, trying to still the fluttering that had started in my stomach. I didn't want to tell Jen that, despite Ryan being single, he was still living with his ex-wife. Something about not yet finding suitable alternative accommodation. It was time to smartly move this conversation forward. 'Anyway, we've only been dating for a couple of months. I haven't, you know, felt able to ask any pertinent questions. Reading between the lines, I think they just got bored with each other. Ryan did divulge–'

'Oooh, yes?' said Jen, leaning forward. 'I sense juicy gossip. Don't tell me. Heather went off with the postman, and Ryan had a deep flirtation with a neighbour?'

'Nothing like that.' I shook my head. 'More… Heather being annoyed at always finding the loo seat up. Or… Ryan being irked by Heather's long hair bunging up the bathroom drains.'

'Fascinating,' said Jen, rolling her eyes. 'So, when are you next seeing him? Presumably tonight.' That was another thing about Jen. It wasn't just plenty of wine she wanted at the weekend. She expected lots of sex too. 'After all, it's Saturday. That's when lovers get together.'

'Maybe,' I shrugged. 'Ryan said he'd be in touch. Mind you, we seem to spend more time on the phone to each other than having one-to-one dates, what with the demands of his son–'

'Who must surely be grown up?' said Jen incredulously.

'Y-e-s,' I agreed. 'But unfortunately, he's still–'

'In nappies?'

'No,' I shook my head again. 'He's at school.'

'Ryan is sixty years old and has a child at primary school?'

'Of course not,' I said, doing my own eyeroll. 'Joshua is at secondary school. He's studying for his A Levels, but he seems very…' I paused, trying to find the right word. 'Needy,' I said eventually. 'He's always buttonholing Ryan to do things with him.'

'Like what?' Jen's eyebrows shot up. 'Fly kites at the local park? Go to London and visit museums for the day? Surely, if Joshua is a teenager, he's a bit beyond all that?'

I'd privately thought the same. Sally, my own daughter, had almost disowned me when she'd been a teenager. She'd found herself several jobs to pay for her social life – from babysitting to waitressing to shelf stacking – and had accordingly spent her earnings in clubs with mates or on days out with friends. The only time she'd ever freely wanted to hang out with her old mum was if I'd suggested shopping and offered to pick up the tab.

These days, I didn't see my girl as often as I'd have liked. Sally was miles away at Bristol university, in digs. Our contact was mostly confined to FaceTime or text messages. A bit like my relationship with Ryan, now I came to think of it.

'Perhaps' – my tone took on a defensive edge – 'Joshua is just a thoroughly nice boy who loves his dad's company.'

I had a sinking feeling that meeting Ryan's son was an event that wouldn't be happening any time soon. I also had a nagging suspicion that Joshua was hellbent on getting his parents back together again. I even suspected that Heather might be in cahoots with their son.

Jen would not approve of Ryan's domestic setup – no matter if it was temporary – or a woman who continued to treat her ex-husband like a spouse. Heather ensured Ryan was always at her beck and call. From putting up a shelf here. A new picture there. Changing a flat tyre. Assembling a new lawnmower. From what Ryan had let slip, such occasions involved Joshua and Heather too, whether passing a screwdriver or just idly looking on. Whenever a job was finished, they always seemed to get in the family car and take off to some local eatery or other. I'd discovered this after looking Heather up on Instagram and having a snoop. There were always lots of pictures. The three of them. Beaming away. Shoulder to shoulder. Sometimes at McDonalds. Other times, a five-star bistro. Yes, hands up, I couldn't deny it. I'd been a bit of a stalker.

My insides briefly curdled with jealousy. And why was it that whenever Ryan and I *did* manage to meet up, we'd get interrupted? Whether going for a walk together or grabbing a snatched coffee, invariably his mobile would ring. It would either be Heather or Joshua, but the outcome was always the same. Ryan being summoned to return home and attend some contrived urgent matter.

'So exactly how much time *do* the two of you spend together?' Jen now asked as she licked jam from her fingers.

'Not a lot,' I said miserably.

She gave me a curious look.

'You have slept with him, haven't you?'

I picked up a doughnut and took a huge bite, rendering speech impossible.

'Lottie?' she urged.

My jaw rotated as I eyed her silently.

'I do not believe it,' she shrieked. 'You haven't done the deed?' She rolled her eyes dramatically. 'Why ever not?'

'There never seems to be the right moment,' I said in despair.

'Don't be so ridiculous.'

'It's true,' I protested.

After all, I could hardly go back to Ryan's place. Not with Heather and Joshua in situ. I could imagine the scene now. Ryan yodelling, "It's only me. Lottie's here too. We're going to have a quick bonk, then we'll all bond together over a nice cup of tea."

Ryan had been to my place a couple of times now, but nothing had happened. On one occasion Sally had been home from uni – and no *way* was I having a romantic night with my daughter on the other side of a paper-thin wall. On another occasion, we'd just got up close and personal when, embarrassingly, I'd been caught short by a dodgy prawn from the curry we'd had earlier.

'There just hasn't been the right moment,' I despaired. 'There's always been an interruption. The last time we almost got to first base. However, Ryan's widowed mother telephoned at a crucial moment. She insisted he get in his car and drive over to her *immediately* because she'd lost her dentures. Apparently, she was fed up eating strawberry creams instead of chocolate toffees. Our intimate moments always seem to descend into a fiasco.'

'If I were you, I'd dump Ryan. You need to find someone who is properly available.'

'That's a bit harsh.'

'No it isn't. You want a guy who prioritises you.'

'Ryan is trying.'

'Ryan sounds very trying,' Jen muttered.

'Actually' – I folded my arms across my chest, a defensive gesture – 'he's suggested we go away for a weekend.' I gave Jen a coy smile. 'To *properly* get to know each other.' I followed that statement up with a meaningful look. 'Without any interruptions.'

'Then make sure it happens,' she said sternly. 'It's about time you had someone reliable in your life. Someone who gives you happiness instead of turdy nonsense. After all the hoo-ha with our respective exes, we now deserve to be cherished. Stu is coming up trumps, and I want someone in your life who does the same for you. After all, the last thing you need is another prat like that husband of yours.'

'Ex-husband,' I quickly corrected. 'Anyway, let's not talk about Rick.'

Geez, if Jen got me on to the subject of the disastrous life I'd shared with Sally's father, then I'd be exchanging the coffee and jam doughnuts for a stiff gin and tonic.

Chapter Two

After Jen had left, I went to the sink. On autopilot, I washed the dirty cups and plates.

As I stood there, swishing soapsuds about, I gazed blankly through the window at the view beyond. My eyes took in the bleakness of the narrow country lane that ran alongside my cottage.

A thorny hedgerow bordered the road. In summer months, its thorny stems were loaded with blackberries. Now winter was just around the corner and the hedge was an exploding froth of Old Man's Beard. On the other side of this rustic fence, grazing land stretched almost as far as the eye could see. A large group of shaggy cows were huddled together, as if silently communing.

I'd moved to Little Waterlow not long after the collapse of my marriage. Jen had lived in the village for the last couple of years. She'd urged me to bring Sally and live with her, kindly putting a roof over our heads while I'd sorted out my personal circumstances.

I'd been so grateful for the offer of this lifeline and taken Jen up on it. During this period, I'd overseen all manner of jobs to cover our keep and outgoings.

Despite experiencing the fallout of my disastrous

marriage, Sally had somehow managed to pass her exams and secure a place at uni. She now lived away in halls.

And then – just down the road from Jen – a house had come up for rental. I'd leapt at the chance of leasing it. Much as I loved my mate, she needed her own space, as did I.

Catkin Cottage had been offered to the market for a six-month letting. It was the perfect stopgap as I continued to pick up the reins of my new life.

I'd already discovered that tittle-tattle was a national pastime in villages like this one. Rumour had it that Sophie Fairfax, the owner of Catkin Cottage, had fallen in love with another man while on her honeymoon. There was also some gossip about the man Sophie had been briefly married to. According to someone called Mabel Plaistow – an ancient pensioner who made other villager's lives her subject of special interest – Sophie's husband had been cheating all along with the wife of an old schoolfriend. Mabel had also shared chit-chat about the bridegroom having a false leg that had fallen off at a most inopportune moment.

I'd dismissed the stories. They were of no interest to me. I had enough of my own *stuff* to contend with. Nor did I want Mabel Plaistow getting wind of my personal life and spreading tall tales. After all, everyone has secrets. Some bigger than others. And my secret was a whopper.

I picked up the scourer and removed some lipstick from one of the cup's rims. A secret was only a secret if you kept it to yourself. And up until now, I had. However, just like a nasty boil that needs lancing, this secret had started to reach epic proportions. If it ever erupted, there would be a ghastly mess. One that would be entirely of my own making.

If Jen found out, she'd probably whip off one of her size sevens and whack me over the head. If Sally ever got wind... well, it didn't bear thinking about. And what of Ryan? That would be an altogether different scenario. Bye-bye Ryan. The end of a relationship before it had even properly begun.

My hands continued to whisk through the soapy water as memory after memory started to unfurl. The latter ones were far from happy. Thank goodness for Jen. She'd been such a rock. A shoulder to cry on. Due to her own failed marriage, she'd been sympathetic about mine. She'd understood my anguish.

Jen's marriage had unravelled in the unhappiest of circumstances. A woman had unexpectedly turned up on Jen's doorstep. The woman hadn't been alone either. In her arms she'd cradled a bonny baby boy. A smiley-faced gurgling bundle. The stranger had coolly announced that Simon – Jen's hubby – had been living a double life. The baby was his. Jen had been beside herself.

'The BASTARD,' she'd later shrieked. Her cheeks had been raw from crying so many salty tears. 'It was awful discovering there was another woman, but discovering she'd had Simon's child was the absolute pits.'

Despite numerous attempts to get pregnant throughout her marriage, Jen's ovaries had refused to co-operate. There had been many fertility investigations. The results had concluded that nothing was wrong. There had then been several attempts at IVF. These had been both costly and unsuccessful.

For Jen, trying to get pregnant had been all-consuming. Eventually, it had taken its toll on her. For a little while, she'd understandably lost her marbles. It was during this period that Simon – nursing his own sorrows – had taken solace in another woman's arms. This woman was younger than Jen, and seemingly more fertile than the local farmer's fields.

Being careless with condoms had resulted in pregnancy. Simon, morally weak, but also terrified of Jen finding out, had instead tried to juggle things. This had led to him living a double life. For a while he'd succeeded – until the other woman had discreetly followed Simon home. Armed with her lover's address, she'd later returned to spill the infidelity beans.

Just like Jen, my marriage had ended on my doorstep – except my visitor had been very different.

Chapter Three

Rick Lucas had been everything my twenty-seven-year-old heart had ever desired – which just goes to show what a rotten judge of character one's heart can be.

Instead of listening to my heart, I should have paid attention to my brain. At the time, my grey matter had been screaming louder than the defunct smoke alarm in my flat.

Rick had been the drop-dead-gorgeous electrician who'd answered my emergency telephone call. He'd also been the one to come out and fix it.

'Thank goodness that racket has finally stopped,' I'd said gratefully, taking my fingers out of my ears.

'It's a common complaint with this particular brand,' Rick had said. He'd tossed the faulty alarm to one side and then set about collapsing his stepladder. 'If any dust or dirt lands on the photocell, the sensor gets triggered.' He'd paused. Glanced around my light and airy apartment. 'This is a nice place.' His eyes had rested briefly on the view beyond the lounge window. The River Thames had glistened like a strip of silver steel. 'Have you lived here long?' he asked conversationally.

'About a month.'

'Lucky you. Your hubby must earn well to have bought

one of these.'

I'd reddened. Partly out of indignation at this guy's assumption that I needed a man to pay for the roof over my head. Also, partly from the insinuation that I had a husband who was loaded.

'There is no husband and I bought this myself,' I'd retorted frostily.

'Ah, in which case you're either a high-flier' – his eyes had mocked me – 'a lottery winner or, let me guess, you've blown an inheritance.' At those last words, he'd caught the look of surprise on my face. 'Bingo. Wow, lucky you. So, who snuffed it? Don't tell me. Your ancient great-aunt Matilda? The one who had a penchant for blue rinses, lavender perfume and loved to suck – careful, Rick – the occasional pear drop?' He'd given me an impish grin. No doubt he'd believed himself to be a cheeky chappie, instead of an outspoken Cockney with a glaring lack of tact.

My eyes had momentarily brimmed. Furiously, I'd blinked back the tears, aware of two pink spots staining my cheeks.

'Actually, it was my parents who – as you so eloquently put it – *snuffed it*. One from cancer. The other from a heart attack six months later. I'd much prefer to have them back in this world with me, instead of living in this lap of waterside luxury. Money doesn't buy happiness, you know.'

There'd been a horrible, tense silence.

'I'm so sorry,' he'd eventually said. 'I've offended you.' He'd put down the ladder. 'Sorry,' he'd repeated. For a moment he'd held his arms wide, then let them drop back at his sides. A gesture of helplessness. 'My mates are always saying I speak without thinking. Please accept my condolences too.'

'Okay,' I'd said stiffly. 'Meanwhile, how much do I owe you?'

He'd backed away, hands gesturing wildly.

'Nothing.'

'Don't be silly,' I'd protested. 'You responded to an emergency callout.'

'Yes, but it's not like it was the middle of the night, or a weekend and out of hours. Anyway, as I said, I'm mortified for putting my foot in it over your parents.' He'd made to pick up the ladder. 'So, no charge.'

'Look, we all have a living to earn. Despite you thinking I'm some sort of rich bitch, I *do* go to work. After all, bills don't pay themselves. So could we please park that previous conversation to one side, and you tell me what I owe?'

'Let me see.' He'd leaned on the ladder and pretended to consider. 'It's half past six on a Friday. This is a very civilised time to be caught out by a faulty smoke alarm. It means you're my last client of the day. Ordinarily I would now slip off my overalls and enjoy a drink, like at that trendy place just around the corner.'

'Good for you. So can I now settle your invoice before you head off?'

'Well, if you're absolutely adamant–'

'I am.'

'Then my fee is' – he'd stroked his chin thoughtfully – 'half a lager.'

'Pardon?' I'd frowned.

'You heard. Buy me a drink. But there's one condition. You must have a drink with me too.' He'd winked. 'That's the fee.'

And that was how it had started.

Chapter Four

Living in Greenwich had been wonderful.

I'd thought it to be one of the prettiest boroughs in London. Also, everything had been on one's doorstep. From spectacular views – both cityside and waterside – to relaxing green spaces. There'd always been something to do. Somewhere to explore. A café for coffee. A restaurant to eat. A bar to gossip with friends and have a drink. A market to nosy around with a mate. And sometimes, a historical landmark waiting to be discovered. From river trips to guided walks, it had been impossible to ever claim boredom in such a heavenly place.

Rick and I had taken the lift down to my apartment's underground carpark. Locating his vehicle, he'd dumped his toolbox and ladder. Seconds later he'd shimmied out of his overalls, revealing a fashionably distressed pair of jeans and open-necked shirt.

He'd turned away from me to lock up the van. As he'd done so, I'd noted the brand name on the back of his denims. Also, the tiny label stitched into one seam of his shirt. Both garments had been Designer. I'd also done a double take at the sleek silver van. Mercedes. The registration plate had let me know it was only months old.

Privately I'd raised an eyebrow. Business must be good.

Together, we'd strolled to a bar two-minutes away. Having shed his overalls, Rick had immediately blended in with the locals. Many were City types who'd crowded into this watering hole to celebrate the start of the weekend.

Rick had quickly found an empty table. He'd sat down, leaving me to order our drinks. A minute or two later and I'd settled down beside him. Nearby, a group of pretty secretaries had been nudging each other. They'd constantly looked his way. However, his entire attention had been on me. I'd felt faintly uncomfortable by his focus, unused to men blatantly studying me. Despite the long blonde hair and forget-me-not blue eyes, I'd never had any delusions about my looks. I wasn't a raving beauty. My looks were very ordinary. And that was me all over. Miss Average. But I was comfortable in my own skin.

One drink had led to a second. A third. Then a fourth. The conversation had been lively. Amusing even. Certainly, on his part. Rick hadn't stopped talking. He'd told me about his family. How he'd been born in Stoke Newington. One of two boys. How his parents hadn't had – his words, not mine – a pint pot to pee in.

'My old man has been a bit of a naughty boy, Lots,' Rick had said. I'd liked the way he'd abbreviated my already shortened name. It had suggested he'd felt at ease with me. 'He still is, as far as I'm aware. He's led my poor old mum a right merry dance. If he's not blowing his wages on wine, women, and song, he's in the betting shop. Consequently, it has fallen to my mother to top up the housekeeping. In her time, she's been a cleaning lady by day and a barmaid by night. Me and my brother virtually brought ourselves up. I told myself that I wouldn't be like my dad. He never put his hand in his pocket if Kev and I needed new trainers for school. He left us to plug the holes in our shoes with newspaper. So, I vowed that one day I'd own shoes that others would envy. Same about clothes. Ditto regarding my vehicle. Instead of riding around on a clapped-out pop-pop like my dad, I told myself I'd drive a swanky car.'

'Your van is very nice,' I'd said politely. 'I noticed it's almost new.'

'Ah, but my van is a work vehicle. My other car is a Porsche.'

I'd snorted into my drink.

'Ha!' I'd giggled. 'Just like that sticker in the back of car windows.' Such labels had been all the vogue back then. Silly signs. *Toot if you're single.* Also, *The closer you get, the slower I drive.* That sort of thing. 'You're so funny,' I'd chortled tipsily.

But Rick hadn't been laughing.

'My other car *is* a Porsche,' he'd repeated, face serious.

'Blimey,' I'd said, undisguised admiration creeping into my voice. 'Are you a secret millionaire or something?'

'The Porsche is an old model,' he'd conceded. 'But one day I'll have brand new one. And one day I'll be a millionaire too. I like money. I like spending it, too. Every twelve months I go on a decent holiday with my mates. Bali

21

last year. Thailand previously. Vegas, the one before that. We haven't decided where we're going this year. However, one of the boys suggested India. I'm up for it. What about you?'

For one drunken moment, I'd thought he'd been asking if I was up for going to India too. I'd then shrugged. Faintly embarrassed by my comparatively boring life. I'd cleared my throat. Played for time.

'I've not yet thought about going away,' I'd said airily. 'But I'm sure I'll do something.' A lie.

At the time, I hadn't been able to recall the last time I'd been away. Despite being ensconced in an expensive flat, it had been my parents' estate that had paid for it. A couple of decades previously, Mum and Dad had bought a small Victorian house in a rundown but leafy London suburb. This had been at a time when houses had cost a few thousand pounds, not the huge sums of today. I'd been an only child and my parents had lived a modest life. They'd only dined out on special occasions. They'd rarely spoilt themselves. Dad had driven a twenty-year old Rover. Family holidays had taken place in England. Brighton, Cornwall, and Devon, rather than Bali, Thailand, and Vegas.

When my parents had unexpectedly demised, the area in which they'd lived had long since *upped and come*. The value of their property had left me not just flabbergasted, but surprisingly wealthy. Not wanting to squander, I'd taken a gamble on a waterside property, believing it to be an even better long-term investment. I'd ploughed everything into the Greenwich waterside apartment.

There had been a modest sum of money left over. This had been safely put away in a savings account. It had been strictly for emergency purposes. I didn't have a car – there was no need when public transport was all around me. Nor did I splurge on clothes or fancy holidays. I earnt enough to pay the bills and feed myself.

Unlike Rick, I was more than happy picking up a vintage dress for a fiver. I'd much preferred browsing the local markets, in preference to blowing a hundred quid on something that looked the same but came from a shop with posh signage.

The conversation between Rick and myself had moved to the future. He'd told me that he'd wanted children. One day. He'd also said that he would want his kids to have the type of father his never had never been.

'I wouldn't mind being a househusband,' he'd said, his mouth quirking. 'No, seriously. I'd like to be there for my child. To be the one who takes him or her to school. The one who, later, stands at the gates and receives his child's prized wet painting. I'd tape it to the kitchen cupboard for everyone to admire. I'd never miss a parents' evening. Or a sports day. Instead, I'd be standing on the side lines. The loudest father. Cheering vociferously.' For a moment, his eyes had held a faraway look.

'That sounds very admirable,' I'd teased. 'However, I thought you said you wanted your job to make you a millionaire. That won't happen if you're a househusband.'

'True. In which case' – he'd paused to neck some of his lager – 'I'll have to marry a rich woman instead.'

'Indeed,' I'd nodded. The room had momentarily spun. Drinking on an empty stomach had never agreed with me. 'Where doo yoo live?' I'd enunciated, trying hard not to slur my words.

'I rent a place in Erith. However, next year I'm looking to buy. Being self-employed, it's taken me a little longer with the accounts. That said, I shouldn't have a problem getting a mortgage.'

'Good for you,' I'd said.

Despite being hazy from the wine, a sober part of me had flagged something up. That the man sitting next to me was *a catch*. And, if I was reading the signals right – and I'd had no reason to believe otherwise – that the man was doing a decent impression of being into me too.

That night, Rick had had eyes only for me. His thigh had repeatedly rubbed against mine. His arm had been oh-so- casually slung along the back of my chair. His body had leant into mine. And then he'd mentioned the future. Being a homeowner. Becoming a dad. This had told me he'd had both financial and family ambitions. Plans to be someone. To go somewhere. Well, if all that chit-chat had been anything to go by.

Despite the Cockney accent – or maybe because of it? – he'd sounded like a man of the world. An explorer. An adventurer. And, despite him later saying he wasn't close to his brother, how lucky was he to have a sibling!

I'd felt a pang of envy as he'd chatted about Kevin. The brotherly squabbles. How Kev had once lifted a tenner from Rick's wallet. Rick had retaliated by *borrowing* a coveted pair of jeans. Except he'd snagged them on a nail, and caused a ding-dong.

How I'd have loved to have had a brother or sister to banter or argue with. Instead, I'd been left all alone in the world. Well, apart from a cousin in Scotland, who I'd barely known.

Rick had been like a breath of fresh air. He'd blasted away my grief. Made me laugh again – and it had seemed like such a long time since I'd properly belly-laughed. It had felt so good too. The previous year had been full of misery and anguish. First, I'd had to helplessly watch Mum fade. Then Dad had seemed to visibly shrink before my eyes. He'd been devastated by my mother's passing. It hadn't really surprised me when he'd suffered a fatal heart attack. It had seemed so unfair to find myself visiting the same funeral parlour. The second time in the space of twelve months.

But then… well, then the tide had turned. Rick had entered my life. He'd seemed such fun as he'd teased me about being a highly eligible single woman, before adding that he was a highly eligible single man.

'So, little Lottie.' The tone had been suddenly seductive. It had jolted me. I'd found myself staring at him. Like a rabbit caught in the glare of headlights. His hair had been dark. Tousled. As if a woman had run her fingers through it after he'd made love to her. Eyes the colour of autumn leaves had blazed into mine. 'Do you have a boyfriend?' he'd asked softly.

'No,' I'd replied. My voice had been barely a whisper.

'A beautiful woman like you?' he'd gently teased. 'I find that hard to believe.' He'd reached for my hand. Stroked the fingers. One by one. Slowly. Sensuously. I'd thought that I might faint. 'My boyfriend… we split up,' I'd gasped. 'He found someone else.'

'More fool him,' Rick had murmured. 'And talking of fools' – he'd nodded at his empty glass – 'stupidly, I've gone over the limit.' His eyes had snagged on mine again. *Come to bed eyes*, my mother would have called them. Those eyes had roved over my body. Had seemed to undress me as he'd softly delivered his next line. 'Whatever am I going to do?'

The words had leapt from my mouth uncensored.

'Do you want to stay at mine?' I'd asked breathlessly.

Rick hadn't hesitated.

'I think that's a very good idea.'

Chapter Five

After Jen's disparaging comments about my *relic* boyfriend and *prat* of a husband – I mean, *ex*-husband – I finished the washing up somewhat aggressively.

Slamming the cups upside down on the drainer, I then stacked the wet plates against them. The china could airdry. Wiping my hands on the dishcloth, I sensed rather than saw a pair of eyes upon me.

'Is that you, Audrey?' I trilled.

'Meow,' came the confirmation.

I turned and smiled. There, framed in the kitchen doorway, was the prettiest black-and-white ball of feline fluff. The cat minced towards me. Audrey had adopted me soon after I'd moved into Catkin Cottage. An apparent stray, she was looking for someone to soothe her soul. Just like me. Her affection, the constant kettledrum purr, and her demands to be cuddled – often at inappropriate moments, like when enthroned on the loo – always raised my spirits.

'Are you waiting for me to start work?' I asked. Crouching down, I extended one hand towards her. She headbutted my fingers by way of confirmation. 'I wasn't going to do any today,' I prattled. 'After all, it's Saturday. I prefer not to work at the weekend. However, I'm behind with my word count so perhaps I should sit down and crack on with it. My publisher won't be impressed if I don't deliver on time.' I scooped Audrey up into my arms. 'Come on, little one. Let's go upstairs. I'll switch on the computer, and you can snuggle down on my lap.'

Audrey, now draped over my shoulder, purred her approval.

I pushed open the door to the second bedroom. This space doubled as my study. I walked over to the desk by the window. Like a mother with a tot that didn't want to be put down, I set about multi-tasking with my one free arm. Flicking switches, I then opened a large A4 notepad, then spent a couple of minutes locating a biro that wasn't defunct. I had two mobile phones. A moment later and they were both switched off. There was nothing worse than being interrupted at a crucial writing moment. Finally, I lowered my bottom to the typing chair.

There was a moment of rearranging the cushion behind my back during which Audrey turned in two tight circles. The pair of us then settled down. Audrey collapsed like an exhausted shopper who'd finished a particularly arduous trip to the supermarket, while I leant back and scanned the screen before me.

'Okay,' I said to myself, all the while stroking Audrey's silky fur. 'Where did I leave off?' My eyes studied the handwritten summary of chapters I'd recorded so far within the notepad. 'Ah, yes. DI Denise Draper is about to discover another shocking murder. An elusive serial killer is targeting vulnerable women.' Audrey looked up at me with adoring eyes. 'This monster' – I informed her – 'is a master of deception. Just like DI Draper, I want my reader to be bombarded with red herrings. But I know how it's going to end.' I tapped the side of my nose as Audrey blinked owlishly. 'With a twist.' I nodded sagely. 'As all good thrillers do. Naturally.'

I raised my hands over the keyboard. For a moment they hovered, like a concert pianist about to launch into Shostakovitch's second piano concerto. A second later and my fingers landed on the keys, clattering away, while the onscreen words struggled to keep pace with my thoughts.

My career had changed at the same time as my divorce. Well, let's face it, my whole world had changed after Rick and I had gone our separate ways. Emotionally exhausted, I'd wanted a fresh start.

I hadn't wished to return to London for work. Having once been a fully paid-up member of the Rat Race, I'd had no desire to submerge myself again in such a lifestyle. Bad bosses. Office politics. Late nights and unpaid overtime. I'd suddenly felt too old for all that. And oh, so tired.

Not knowing what to do next, I'd sat in a Costa coffee shop nursing a hot drink. A germ of an idea had nudged at the corners of my mind. I'd always wanted to try my hand at writing, but never had a moment to put pen to paper. Not in a serious fashion. Until, that is, I'd found myself to be a newly divorced woman with a daughter at university. Suddenly the days, empty and long, had stretched ahead like an endless yawn.

Sipping my cappuccino, I'd reached for my mobile. Tapping on *Notes,* I'd outlined a novel. Three hours and one panini later, I'd emailed it off to a digital publisher who took unagented submissions. Days later, I'd been shocked to receive a response including a request to send over some chapters.

Thrilled, I'd sat down and written ten chapters in as many days. I'd nearly fallen off my typing chair when – on the strength of my submission – they'd offered a three-book deal. DI Denise Draper was now on her third case.

Meanwhile, my brain was brimming with ideas for future crime novels. Each one starred my fictitious hard-nosed investigator. Denise made Lynda La Plante's famous DI Jane Tennison seem like Holly Willoughby.

My editor, Maxine, had been thrilled with the manuscripts. She'd enthused that I should expect a lucrative career. I sincerely hoped she was right, because so far, I'd yet to earn a penny. The days of writers receiving huge advances had ceased. Meanwhile, Maxine wanted to launch the debut with Book Two and Three swiftly following. This was apparently important for maximum readership impact. So, as yet, all three books were currently awaiting their Launch Day.

'Eventually the money will roll in,' she'd assured. 'But for now, don't give up the day job.' Those last words had been delivered with a chuckle.

'I won't,' I'd assured, chortling along with her, while

trying not to feel sick.

The fact was, I didn't have a day job – or even a night job, for that matter. My lack of employment had filled me with both fear and anxiety.

I'd secured the rental of Catkin Cottage by the skin of my teeth. This had been assisted by Jen pulling some strings because she personally knew the property's owner. Jen had given Sophie a glowing reference about me.

However, bills don't wait for books to be published and royalties to roll in. It was then that I'd hit upon another idea. One that was very different to being a writer. It was a job you'd never divulge to anyone. Not your editor. Not your bestie. Not even your cat.

Chapter Six

Six hours later, I logged off, then switched both phones back on. Each instantly dinged with a message.

My private phone displayed a text from Ryan.

Hey, babe. Been trying to call. No success. Hope you're free for dinner this evening. Took a chance and booked a table at The Angel. Is that okay? Can't stay over. Ha! I rolled my eyes, no surprises there. *Joshua wants to go fishing tomorrow which means a dawn start. However, I've found a gorgeous B&B in Truro. It promises log fires, windswept walks, romantic bedrooms, and feather duvets begging to be wrapped around lovers ★winky face emoji★ xxxxx*

My second phone showed a text from someone called Mr Muppet. Yes, really.

Are you available to do a bespoke job?

I instantly replied.

I await your instructions.

Officially, I was a writer. Unofficially, I had a second job. A *secret* second job. Just like the fictitious DI Denise Draper, this other occupation involved mystery. I never knew what might happen next. If my editor had been writing copy for this second career it might have read:

Lottie's alternative job was borne through a series of twists, turns and narrative that isn't so much gripping as utterly eyebrow raising.

My editor had already told me what sort of reviews she was expecting when my detective inspector series went live. Maxine had delightedly said it would be along the lines of:

A gripping thriller that will keep you up all night…

Hooked from the first page…

I was too scared to turn out the lights…

Keeps you guessing…

Her last prediction had brought me out in a muck sweat – certainly in relation to *Mr Muppet.* You see, I hadn't the foggiest who he was, even though we'd been texting for some time.

It had all started when I'd innocently posted an online photograph of my new heels. When I say *new*, I mean second-hand. I'd found the shoes in a charity shop in nearby West Malling. There they'd been. Centre stage. Slap bang in the middle of the window display. Bright fuchsia-pink beauties in a soft suede.

The colour alone had sent me skidding to a halt, like a driver belatedly noticing a red traffic light. Slack jawed, I'd gaped at the shoes, captivated.

A small price tag had dangled from one silver buckle. Four pounds. I couldn't afford to waste money. I certainly didn't need a pair of pink peep-toes. However, telling myself I'd eat beans on toast for the rest of the week, I'd walked into the shop.

The shoes could have been made just for me. They were so comfortable, and oh-so-sexy. I'd walked out tightly clutching an innocuous brown bag. Within the paper folds had been my treasured booty.

Once home, I'd put on the shoes and paraded around the bedroom. I'd then paused in front of the long mirror to admire them. They were gorgeous. The same couldn't be said about the state of my toenails. Devoid of polish, they'd looked most unappealing. I regularly promised to give them a makeover. Preferably when I had some spare cash. If ever that day came, I'd visit one of those swanky nail bars.

Despite the unattractive toenails, I'd wanted to show off the shoes. Where better than Instagram? I had quite a few followers. So, I'd uploaded half a dozen shots with various hashtags. As you do.

A little while later I'd received a private message request. Curious, I'd opened it.

Hello! I love your new shoes. However, I love your toes even more! Before you dismiss me as a weirdo (I promise I'm a perfectly regular guy), would you consider sending me a picture of your feet with a full reveal of those tempting toes? Obviously, I will remunerate you. Would thirty pounds suffice?

Regards

Tally Toe

Tally Toe? As opposed to Tally Ho? Seriously? Was this message for real?

But then I'd given it some thought. Financially, I'd been up Poo Creek without a paddle. Thirty pounds would go a long way towards the grocery bill. Fifty pounds would go even further. Emboldened, I'd replied.

I've never been so insulted in all my life. Make it one hundred. Payment up front.

Ha! *That* would send the creep running in the opposite direction. But to my surprise, Tally Toe had messaged back immediately.

Send me your bank details.

Chapter Seven

I'd then had a bit of a wobble. The last thing I'd wanted was to reveal my identity.

Instead, I'd telephoned Jen. She'd had a PayPal account – something I'd never got to grips with. It was linked to her artistic business which used an alternative name.

'Would you be willing to receive a hundred pounds on my behalf – strictly a one-off – which I'll split with you, provided you don't ask any questions?' I'd gabbled breathlessly.

'What are you up to?' she'd asked, bursting with curiosity.

'Nothing illegal,' I'd assured. Well, I didn't think it was.

'Can't say no to fifty quid,' she'd replied, before rattling off the details.

I'd been astonished at Tally Toe's next message.

Money sent. Now please fulfil your side of the bargain.

Jen had accordingly confirmed receipt of one hundred pounds. She'd followed up and deposited fifty pounds into my bank account.

Suddenly my hands had been shaking, and I'd dropped my phone. As the device had clattered to the floor, my fingers had fluttered up to my temples. I'd rubbed ineffectually. What had I done?

Omigod. If I sent Tally Toe what he wanted, would that make me a sex worker? Surely not.

I'd rushed to the mirror. Had I morphed into a vamp? Become precociously seductive? *Lolita Lottie*? Surely, I was a bit long in the tooth to be such a female.

My reflection had stared back at me. There she was. The woman known as Charlotte Lucas. Same boring hairstyle. A smattering of freckles. Blue eyes – huge and terrified.

Trembling, I'd retrieved the phone, then tapped into a search engine.

Does selling pictures of my feet make me a prostitute?

The question had landed in a forum that had dated back some three years. Fearfully, I'd read the first answer:

Ask your boyfriend, not the internet.

Ryan hadn't been on the scene at that point. Indeed, there had been no man in my life. I'd continued scrolling.

Any sold picture of any part of yourself would – in my opinion – be "soft prostitution".

I'd given a strangled yelp and clamped a hand over my mouth. That couldn't be true. After all, I was a respectable woman. Held down responsible jobs. Been a good wife. And a great mother. I had my wonderful daughter to prove it.

At the thought of Sally, I'd emitted another sob. How would my beloved girl react if she got wind of what her mum was doing? No, no, no. I was still a decent human being. I just needed to read a few more forum comments to confirm it.

I'd scrolled further down.

Well, sorry to say this, but yeah. In my eyes it does kinda make you a prozzie. After all, you're selling your pics to people with fetishes. It's gonna turn them on. They'll likely be staring at the photo while choking the chicken.

Choking the chicken? Oh God. Were these people into bestiality too? No, wait, Lottie. Choking the… ah… yes, got it. Oh yuck. But hang on a sec. What did this next comment say?

Nope. You're not cheating on anyone, and you're not hurting anyone either.

Yes! Thank you, thank you, *thank yooo*. Finally, the answer I'd been looking for. The one that absolved me. Freed me. Put my frantic mind at rest.

The author had written more, so I read on.

After all, everyone has bills to pay, and ensuring those bills are met means you're a decent and responsible human being.

Absolutely! Decent and responsible. That was me. And this person had confirmed it. Hurrah! After all, it had been pointed out that everyone had bills to pay. And it was honourable people who paid them. Certainly, at that point in my life, there had been a stack of the blighters. But there was also another factor to this online approval – and a huge one, at that. By sealing the deal, I'd given myself some much-needed financial breathing space.

I'd duly sent Tally Toe the promised pic. Later, I'd had the best night's sleep for the first time in months.

I'd awoken the following morning refreshed and in a totally different frame of mind. One that was positive. Empowered, even. Hallelujah. At last, after everything Rick had put me through, I'd felt like I was in control again. I'd gone on to greet the day with enthusiasm, rather than dread and despair.

Madly encouraged, I'd reached for my phone. Messaged Tally Toe.

Would you like a second pic?

Chapter Eight

Tally Toe had indeed wanted another photograph. Disappointingly, he'd said it would have to wait until his next pay day.

However, he'd confided that if I wanted to have a go at making regular money, then I should give it serious consideration. He'd suggested setting up a business account on a certain platform. This would then enable me to provide… a service.

Intrigued, I'd checked it out and gone on to set up a free account. Any subsequent followers would have to pay to gain entry to my content. Everything was anonymous. My profile picture was part of my foot with a hint of toe, which apparently belonged to *Fifi Footsy*.

Without any expectations, I'd uploaded a couple of times a day. These scheduled postings had lined up with peak hours in different time zones. I'd then sat back and patiently waited, like a fisherman casting his rod and hoping for a tug on the line.

Incredibly, the fish had come along. Occasionally, I'd even land a whopper. But, more recently, I'd caught a shark. *Mr Muppet.*

This guy wanted more than the occasional pic. He had a

serious thing about tootsies. The uglier the better. Well, come on down! But, unlike the visitors I'd dealt with so far, this client liked voice notes. As he'd offered two hundred pounds for two minutes of verbal abuse, who was I to turn him away?

Trawling through eBay, I'd bought an old phone for peanuts. Then, on a pay-as-you-go basis, I'd deepened my voice and growled out what Mr Muppet liked to hear. His payments alone had enabled me to cobble together the rental deposit for Catkin Cottage.

Like repeating a daily affirmation, I'd told myself that I was a decent human being simply paying her bills and getting on with her life.

The ding of another text brought me back to the present moment. Ryan again.

Lottie? Are you there? Two blue ticks tell me you've read my text, but I've not received a reply xx

Eeeep. The time was getting on. It wouldn't do to jeopardise our booking at The Angel or to get on the wrong side of the pub's landlady. Cathy was rumoured to be terrifying. The owner of Catkin Cottage had had her wedding reception at The Angel. Rumour had it that it had turned into the biggest bar brawl in the history of Little Waterlow.

Again, I'd tried to ignore the tittle-tattle – and there was enough of it. According to nosey Mabel Plaistow, the village florist had once been a spy called Jane Pond; someone called Sadie had taken to her bed after being dumped by a member of royalty; another resident, Annie Rosewood, had run off to Dubai and shacked up with a sheikh; and then there was a tall story about someone called Wendy Walker. Her husband had apparently identified as a furry animal. While enjoying a quiet pint at The Angel, Mabel's ancient hubby had nearly had a coronary when Derek Walker had strolled in dressed as a squirrel.

I gave my head a little shake, as if to clear the image, and instead busied myself replying to Ryan's message.

Just finished work! Can't wait to hear about the proposed trip to Cornwall – windswept walks and log fires sounds blissfully romantic! Xxx

And, boy, could I do with some romance. Except for a few kisses and a brief grapple, nothing had progressed romantically with Ryan. Our last lip lock had been interrupted by his ex-wife ringing in a state of panic. Apparently, there'd been a spider the size of a spaceship in the hallway, and neither she nor Joshua had felt able to deal with it. Cue Ryan to the rescue, his Superman cape firmly in place as he'd whooshed off.

Cornwall would be a welcome break. There was the matter of arranging care for Audrey. However, Catkin Cottage had a cat flap, plus I had a very obliging neighbour who I felt sure would pop in and feed Audrey.

My second phone dinged, scattering my thoughts. I picked it up. Mr Muppet again.

Fifi, you are instructed to tell me I'm a bad boy. Make it quick.

Okie dokie.

Audrey, still ensconced on my lap, chose that moment to stand up, stretch, then jump off. Just as well. She wouldn't appreciate hearing my imminent gruff rant.

I pulled my laptop towards me and logged back on. Clicking through the document index, I double-clicked on a Word doc entitled *Sole Mates*. Seconds later, I was in. I wasn't a writer for nothing. This file contained some handy scripts.

Picking up my business phone, I pressed the microphone icon. Time to deliver an angry tirade. And… action!

'You do know you're a FREAK, don't you? It's OUTRAGEOUS that you message me demanding to know what I have on my feet. Well, I'll tell you. I've been out in the garden doing some weeding and my feet got hot. So, I took off my boots and socks and let them cool down in the mud. And, thanks to the recent rain, there's plenty of it. It felt so good I worked my toes right into the earth. Consequently, my toenails are now the colour of creosote. The soles of my feel are caked in dirt, and they look *disgusting*. And, frankly, so are you. Do you hear me? You are a DISGUSTING WEIRDO. Who, in their right mind, has a thing for dirty toenails and filthy soles? WHAT IS WRONG WITH YOU? I don't know anyone who likes the whiff of feet, especially ones that get as STINKY and SWEATY as mine. In fact, if you were here right now, I'd PUNISH you because YOU ARE A PERVERT. You need teaching a lesson… like being forced to massage, lick, and

43

kiss my gruesome feet by way of penance, you–'

My laptop battery chose that moment to die. Hell's bells. I needed my script. My brain might flow effortlessly when it came to the detective adventures of DI Denise Draper, but it tended to stumble about in the dark regarding people with a foot fetish.

Frantically, I yanked open the desk drawer. 'Where's my charger?' I said aloud.

Oh buggery-buggery-fuck-fucks. That wasn't part of the script. I'd have to wing it.

'Yes, where INDEED is my charger?' I growled. 'I suppose you STOLE IT. Along with my… my DIRTY SHOES.' What had chargers got to do with shoes? No matter. 'If I knew who you were… if I could find you… I'd stomp into your home wearing my GRIMY boots and…'

And what?

'Jackboot all over your…'

Yes?

'Willy…'

Did one say *willy* when ranting? Wasn't it a bit tame?

'I'd flatten your COCK…'

Better. Keep it going, Lottie.

'You… you… WARPED…WANKY… SWANKY… HANKY PANKY…'

Dear Jesus. Please help me. I know I don't usually pray. However, could you give me a bit of assistance with my script? I mean, you must have delivered a few choice words to Satan when you were out in that desert for forty days and nights?

'You… PRATTY… FATTY… ARTY FARTY…'

Think, Lottie, *think*. Use your imagination.

'You… PERVY WERVY CURLY WURLY' – my chest was starting to heave with such improvised insults – 'DICKHEAD.'

Excellent!

'You BEAST… of the EAST…'

Noooo, that had been the name of a storm.

'Do you know something? YOU NEED HELP.'

One of us certainly did.

'Because you are a… SOCK SUCKER…'

Shit, Lottie. You got the letters muddled up. No matter. Mr Muppet liked socks, so perhaps he wouldn't notice?

'You SUCKING SICK SOCK DICK …'

It was no good. I couldn't keep this going. Surely the two minutes was nearly up?

'Bloody fecking hell' – I swore aloud – 'I'll tell you exactly what you are. A frigging, shoe-nobbing, sodding bleeding MUPPET.'

I took my finger off the microphone icon, then collapsed down on the typing chair totally spent. There were some strange people in this world.

And then I told myself I wasn't one of them.

Chapter Nine

Leaving the laptop charging, I headed off to the bathroom.

It was time to titivate and prepare for the evening ahead. Shower first. I'd washed my hair the previous evening, so that was fine. I'd have liked to have given my feet a bit of attention, but as I knew in advance that Ryan wasn't staying over, they'd have to wait.

When I mentioned that my feet were ugly, I really did mean it. Thanks to being bonkers about ballet in my childhood, I'd spent years tippy toeing around a dance studio in *pointe shoes.* Consequently, my feet bore testament to a body weight that had regularly crushed ten little piggies.

Pointe shoes might be designed to allow dancers to stand on their toes, but they offer little protection from the impact of landing jumps and other moves. As a result, I'd often suffered injuries to the bones and joints in my feet. I can remember, as a twelve-year-old, how I'd stood up *en-pointe* for the first time. In the beginning, the class had only been allowed to do this exercise for five minutes.

It had been painful. My toes had bled. Scarlet drops of blood had seeped through the box area, bypassing the cushioning, and stained the pink satin over the arch of my foot.

Whilst I still loved ballet, these days it was to watch, rather than partake. The hobby had been abandoned long ago. However, decades later, evidence of a ballet passion prevailed. I'd been left with curly toes, and my joint knuckles were scarred with old corns and callouses.

To add insult to old injury, my left big toe had an unsightly brown mole at its base. As a child, I'd cried over this mark. My mother had told me it was a beauty spot. To me, it looked like a fairy had taken a dump. Somehow, I'd never got around to getting it removed. Ridiculously, it had attracted positive attention amongst the brigade of ugly feet lovers. So, for now, the mark remained.

Ten minutes later, towel wrapped tightly around me, I sorted out my evening attire. After an autumn comparable to an Indian Summer, the temperature had suddenly dipped. Winter was in the air. My gorgeous second-hand shoes were unlikely to have a proper outing until next year. Tonight, it would be warm boots teamed with jeans and a nice sweater. I'd glam things up with some chunky jewellery.

Slicking on some lipstick, I was just giving my hair a brush when, outside, a car gave a toot-toot. I hastened to the window. Ryan's Jag was idling in the lane, engine purring, hazard lights blinking as he waited.

Spritzing myself in perfume, I grabbed my coat and handbag and hastened down the stairs – but not too quickly. The staircase in this old cottage was lethal. Almost vertical, it required one's concentration.

Locking up, the heels of my boots click-clicked as I

hurried along the pathway towards the Jaguar. It was colder than I'd anticipated, and my breath left little clouds in the evening air.

Pulling open the passenger door, the warmth of the car's interior enveloped me. As I gratefully sunk down on the leather upholstery, Ryan gave an appreciative sniff.

'Nice pong,' he declared. 'And you look absolutely amazing,' he added gallantly.

He leant across the space between us and dropped a kiss on my cheek.

'Thanks,' I beamed. 'You look pretty dashing yourself.'

It would be rude not to return his compliment. And anyway, it was true. He was very distinguished looking.

If I hadn't gone to London to see my editor, I'd never have met Ryan. Older. Suave. Confident. Refined. He'd been getting out of the lift as I was about to step inside. Except I'd not actually moved into the tin box. Instead, I'd stood there, on the ground floor, dithering.

Several people had exited en masse. Ryan had been momentarily left behind, finger dutifully on the *doors open* button. He'd smiled, then raised his eyebrows enquiringly.

'In, or waiting for someone?'

'Trying to get in,' I'd grimaced. But I'd remained rooted to the spot.

'Are you sure about that?' he'd quipped.

'I… yes, yes, it's just …'

My voice had trailed off. I'd suddenly had to swallow down a lump the size of an Elgin marble.

'What?' he'd asked gently.

I'd put up my hands, then let them flop down against my sides. A gesture of despair.

'I hate lifts,' I'd bleated. 'They make me feel claustrophobic.'

'So take the stairs.'

'It's the twelfth floor,' I'd said, making a face.

'Tell you what. How about I escort you?' He'd given me a kind smile. I'd liked the way the lines had deepened around his temples. How his cheeks had dimpled. 'And if you faint, I promise to catch you,' he'd added.

Nervously, I'd stepped inside the lift. By the time the doors had opened again, I'd known his name. Also, that he'd worked as an accountant with the firm on the sixth floor. He, in turn, had learnt that I was Lottie Lucas and about to sign a contract with Guns & Holsters Publishing. He'd also secured my phone number. I know. Not just a lift operator but a smooth operator.

I'd floated, rather than walked, into my meeting with Maxine.

'How's my gorgeous girlfriend?' Ryan now asked.

My insides instantly went all mushy.

'I'm good.'

'Has DI Denise Draper been keeping you on your toes? I gather you've been bashing the keys for the last few hours.'

'The third and final novel is going brilliantly,' I beamed. 'It's practically been writing itself. I hope the publishers offer me another contract. I guess it depends on how the sales go.

That said, I'm quietly optimistic. Meanwhile, I have plenty of ideas for DI Draper's further gory adventures.'

'I have a good vibe for your new career,' Ryan smiled. 'You're really so very lucky to do a job that you love, Lottie.'

'I am,' I agreed.

'And thank goodness you have the means to support yourself while waiting for the royalties to roll in.'

'Indeed,' I acknowledged, as a different kind of warmth engulfed me. It was nothing to do with the hot air belching out of the car's internal heater, or the afterglow from Ryan's compliments. Rather, a hot wave of shame.

I bit my lip and stared through the windscreen at the road ahead.

Chapter Ten

'Hello, my lovelies,' said Cathy, as she greeted Ryan and me. 'Table for two, wasn't it?' She picked up a couple of menus from the bar's counter before giving me an enquiring look. 'How are you settling into Catkin Cottage, love?'

'Nicely, thank you. Sophie's house is very comfortable.'

'And pretty, too,' she nodded. 'I expect Mr Handsome here' – her eyes gleamed as they landed on Ryan – 'will be moving in with you soon, eh?'

I found myself flushing unattractively. What a personal question! Especially when we were still such a *new* couple. Ryan spotted my discomfort.

'I'm still romancing Lottie,' he quickly interjected. 'Still trying to impress her.'

'Is that so?' said Cathy, feigning surprise. 'Perhaps it would help if you weren't still living with *Mrs* Dickens.'

My mouth opened in surprise. How the heck did Cathy know *that*?

'I don't know which little bird told you that piece of info' – Ryan's smile was pleasant, but his eyes glittered dangerously – 'but I'm a fully paid-up member of the divorced brigade.'

Cathy's shrug was careless, but her face said *pull the*

other one.

'It's a small world. Sometimes too small. One of my patrons tried to view your house. The agent cancelled the booking. My customer was told that you'd taken the property off the market.'

What? I gave Ryan a questioning look. He ignored me and instead directed his answer at Cathy.

'You're quite right. The property has been taken off the market, but only temporarily. My ex-wife and I are still discussing financial matters pertaining to its sale. Meanwhile, the original agent put up their fees so we're in the process of sourcing an alternative estate agent.'

'Your private life is nothing to do with me,' said Cathy, in astonishment. Her sudden change of tack implied it was Ryan, not her, who'd mentioned the *married* word. 'This way.'

Ruffled, we followed the landlady. She led us through the bar to the restaurant area. The place was already heaving.

'Here you are,' said Cathy, indicating a table in the corner. 'What would you both like to drink?'

A barrel of beer leapt to mind. I was still smarting at the insinuation that Ryan and Heather were still an item.

'Half a lager, please,' said Ryan, already studying the menu.

'A gin and tonic would be nice,' I said. I omitted the word *please*. As far as I was concerned, I'd just witnessed Cathy delivering some character assassination. How *dare* she infer I was going out with a married man. It had left me both unsettled and rattled. Her comment had been too close to home for my liking. After all, Heather and Ryan *were* still under the same roof. Still amicable. Still going on family days out with their son. What if, one day, they giggled over some in-house family joke. Split their sides. Clung to each other as they wiped away their tears of laughter. Then paused. Stared at each other. Thought: *why are we splitting up?* And then fell into each other's arms... while Joshua conveniently melted away... leaving Heather and Ryan to thunder up the stairs... crash into the marital bedroom... rip off each other's clothes and–

'Be right back,' said Cathy, interrupting my raging thoughts.

She hastened off to greet another couple who'd just walked into the bar area.

'Well, honestly,' I huffed. 'What a flipping outrageous thing to say.'

'Hm?' said Ryan. He appeared to be deeply engrossed with menu.

'Her. Cathy,' I said indignantly. 'Suggesting I'm dating a married man.'

'Oh, that,' said Ryan. He put down the menu. 'Take no notice. We both know differently. I think I'll go for the ham hock pie with mash and garden veg.'

I stared at Ryan.

'How can you so easily let the subject go?'

'Because it's irrelevant.'

'Is it?' I questioned. An edge had crept into my voice.

53

'Yes, of course it is. Now what do you fancy?' Ryan nodded at the menu. 'If I'm honest, I could be persuaded to change my mind and have the battered cod.'

'Frankly' – I could feel myself getting upset – 'Cathy's comment has touched a nerve. Sometimes I *do* feel like I'm dating a married man.'

There. I'd said it. The whole Heather-and-Joshua thing was out in the open. Ryan rolled his eyes.

'Lottie, you're being ridiculous. Now have a look at the menu.'

'I'm not being ridiculous. Far from it. Whenever I'm with you, if it isn't Heather interrupting, it's Joshua. Neither of you behave like a divorced couple.'

'Not all divorces have to be warzones,' said Ryan mildly. 'Apart from anything else, Heather and I are making the effort to be get along for the sake of our son. Joshua has taken our split very badly.' Ryan's mobile began to ring. 'Sorry, two ticks.'

He extracted the phone from his inside jacket pocket. The caller display said *Wifey.*

Wifey?

My mouth opened again. At this rate I'd have the most gobsmacked face in Little Waterlow.

'Hiya,' Ryan chirped. 'Yes… at a pub… I'm with Lottie.'

Hang on. He'd just told Heather he was with me. Would a married man tell his wife he was out with another woman if they weren't really divorced? Probably not. I quickly closed my mouth again.

'No… I won't be late... yes… uh–huh… I'm taking Joshua fishing tomorrow, remember? You want to come too? Ah, okay. Not a problem.'

Ex*cuse* me? Let's get this straight, Lottie. Ryan's ex–wife wants to get up at silly o'clock tomorrow morning to sit, in the freezing cold, by a lake, with her son and ex–husband. Hadn't she got anything better to do? Like put on a face pack. Or wash her hair. Or gossip with girlfriends. Or make new friends – including members of the opposite sex.

I studied Ryan. He was nodding his head, but not saying anything. Perhaps he was struggling to get a word in edgeways. Having to wait for Heather to pause. Draw breath.

'Okay, sweetie,' he said eventually.

Sweetie?

My mouth opened again. Yeah, definitely the most gobsmacked village resident.

'See you later.' Ryan disconnected the call, set the phone down on the table, then looked at me. He frowned. 'What's the matter?'

'What's the matter?' I repeated.

'Is there an echo in here?'

A shadow fell across the table. Cathy set our drinks down.

'Ready to order?' she enquired.

Yes. I was. I'd start off with *One Single Man* followed by *No Rude Interruptions* with a side dish of *Zero*

Emotional Baggage finishing off with a dessert called *Sod Off Heather.*

'Ryan?' I said coolly.

Cathy caught my tone and smirked. I decided I didn't much care for her. If Mabel Plaistow was the queen of gossip around here, then Cathy must surely be the princess.

'The pie for me,' said Ryan.

I hadn't even looked at the options.

'Make that two,' I said miserably. Suddenly I didn't feel so hungry.

Cathy retrieved the menus from us, then turned on her heel. For a moment, there was a tense silence.

I picked up my gin and tonic. Took a few rapid sips. Why, when it came to men, did things always go wrong in my life? Why was I putting up with a boyfriend who claimed to be divorced but whose actions signalled anything but? Perhaps I should end this liaison now. Before it had properly begun. Before I got hurt again.

Ryan cleared his throat.

'I'd like to tell you about the place I found in Cornwall for our romantic getaway.'

A part of me instantly perked up. At the same time, another bit of me flattened any feelings of excitement.

'I think' – I said carefully – 'that there needs to be a conversation before I commit to going away with you.'

'Really?' said Ryan, looking flummoxed. 'Like what?'

'Like you telling me why Heather's number is saved to your phone as *Wifey*? Why, when speaking to her, you call her *Sweetie*? In my book, that is a loving endearment. I'd also like to know why you're playing happy families.'

'You've lost me.'

'To clarify.' I glared at him. '*We're All Going on a Fishing Holiday* starring Mrs Heather-Sweetie-Wifey-what-the-actual-feck.' I stuck up a hand to stop his attempt to interrupt. 'Finally, why have you taken your house off the market? Because frankly, Ryan, it seems to me that I'm dating a married man.'

'Ooooh, Lottie,' said a horribly familiar voice. 'You naughty girl. I had a gut feeling you weren't being truthful with me earlier.'

Aghast, I looked up to see my bestie standing beside our table.

'J-Jen,' I spluttered in horror. 'Whatever are you doing here?'

Chapter Eleven

Jen ignored my question and instead gave Ryan a glacial look.

'Hello,' she said icily. 'I saw Lottie earlier today. I told her that it was high time we met her new man. She said it was tricky.' She tossed back her hair, then stuck her nose in the air. 'After overhearing your telephone conversation, now we know why. I must say, it's awfully good of *Wifey* to let you out to play on a Saturday night. Do you have an open marriage, or something?'

'Jen!' I exclaimed, now puce with embarrassment.

'It's okay, Lottie,' said Ryan, getting to his feet. He extended one hand to Jen. 'I am indeed Lottie's boyfriend. That said, I'm probably rather long in the tooth for the first syllable of the word. You have my word that I'm *not* married.'

Jen regarded Ryan's proffered hand but didn't take it.

'Why should I believe you?'

'I have the certificate to prove it,' Ryan assured. 'Sadly, not on me. However, later, I could take a screenshot and send it to you.' He smiled. A peacemaker's smile. His hand was still extended. 'Perhaps I should also keep a couple of photocopies in my wallet. The landlady of this pub gave me the third degree too. I must say, people around here do like to know each other's business.'

Jen's frosty face suddenly relaxed. She grinned.

'They do,' she agreed, finally shaking Ryan's hand. 'So long as you're not mucking my mate about, then I will concede that it's nice to finally meet you.'

'I'm definitely not mucking Lottie about,' Ryan promised, as he pumped Jen's hand.

Jen then turned to a shy looking man standing behind her. She gave the guy a little prod and he stepped forward.

'This is Stu. My OH,' she beamed.

'Hello,' said Stu. Shyly, he shook hands with both Ryan and me. 'It's nice to meet you both.' He was pleasant looking and had a soft voice – unlike Jen, who could be both loud and raucous. Stu looked distinctly out of his comfort zone. I immediately deduced that he wasn't at ease when it came to meeting new people.

'Why don't you join us?' said Ryan magnanimously.

'That would be nice,' said Jen, answering for Stu too. 'If you don't mind,' she added, flashing me a look that silently conveyed *is that okay*. However, she'd already pulled out one of the empty chairs at our table.

'Lovely,' I said, inwardly sighing. If it wasn't Heather and Joshua interrupting my time with Ryan, now it was Jen and Stu. Was there anyone else who wanted to rock up?

Cathy chose that moment to bustle over. She looked put out.

'Oh, looks like you two have changed tables,' she said to

Jen and Stu. 'I wish patrons wouldn't do that. It mucks up our bookings.' She pursed her lips. 'Have you both seen the menu?'

'Yes,' said Jen sweetly. 'And your hubby has already dealt with our drinks and mains order.'

'Right,' said Cathy, before stalking off.

'Blimey,' Jen muttered. 'I wouldn't like to get on the wrong side of her.'

'Looks like you just did,' I said, as we all sat down and regrouped.

'Anyway,' Jen continued. She dumped her handbag on the floor, then gave Ryan an appraising look. 'I have one more question.'

'Uh-oh.' Ryan stuck his hands in the air. A gesture of surrender. 'I sense I'm not out of the woods with you yet.'

'Correct. So, regarding your list of contacts.' She nodded at Ryan's mobile. 'Why is your ex-wife saved as *Wifey*?'

Ryan laughed.

'That's an easy question to answer. In the days when Heather and I were still happily married, we used to have silly nicknames for each other. We happened to program those names into our respective phones.'

Jen's expression gave nothing away as she then asked the same question that had immediately popped into my head.

'And what did your ex-wife call you?'

Suddenly I was sitting very still in my seat.

'Hubsy,' said Ryan, giving a deprecating shrug.

'Hubsy,' Jen repeated, her lips twitching slightly. 'Well, I think it's time for *Hubsy* to change *Wifey's* contact name. Don't you?'

Cracking idea! Why hadn't I vocalised that? But... what if Ryan refused? What if he thought, "Who the flipping heck does this woman think she is? What gives any stranger the right to tell me what I should and shouldn't be doing?" Ryan's answer left me both surprised and secretly delighted.

'I agree.' He picked up his phone. A moment later and he'd brought up the list of contacts. His finger hovered over the H of the screen's keyboard. 'Heather is her name so Heather she shall be.'

'Stop,' Jen commanded. 'Time for a new nickname, methinks.'

Omigod! Jen was surely pushing the boundaries here.

'What do you suggest?' asked Ryan, looking faintly amused. 'Battle-axe?'

'Bloody Nuisance,' said Jen. 'After all, she's always interrupting things, isn't she?'

I gave a small groan before slinging some more gin down my throat. At this rate, Ryan would know I'd been gossiping to Jen about Heather being a bloody nuisance.

'Why not,' said Ryan amiably. He tapped in the two words. 'There.' He slipped the phone into his jacket pocket. 'Quite apposite, as it happens. After all, Lottie and I are planning a trip to Cornwall to escape the nuisance of so frequently being interrupted.'

Ah, this was more like it. An open discussion about Ryan's suggestion for a romantic break. Lovely!

'How wonderful,' said Jen. She suddenly looked dreamy. 'Only the other day Stu and I were saying how nice it would be to have a long weekend away. Weren't we, Chubble-Wubbles.'

Chubble-Wubbles?

'We were,' Stu agreed. He palpitated slightly, no doubt uncomfortable at being caught in the conversational spotlight.

Ryan shifted in his seat.

'Why don't the two of you come along with me and Lottie?' he suggested.

What?

'Oooh, that would be fab,' said Jen, clapping her hands together. Her face lit up with excitement as her bottom did a double bounce on the seat of her chair. She reminded me of a child who'd been told that Christmas had come early. 'I've never been to Cornwall,' she confided. 'The place is meant to be gorgeous.' She nudged Stu. 'Fancy it?'

'I'll go along with anything you want, Pumpkin Pie.'

Pumpkin Pie?

'Then that's sorted,' said Ryan happily. 'I've been wanting to meet Lottie's friends and make them mine too. This is the perfect start.'

Oh, cosmic. Whilst I was pleased that Ryan was endearing himself to my bestie, I wasn't so keen to share our weekend away with her and Stu. What if they were in a room next to ours? Jen had once confided that she was a bit of a shrieker. I wasn't averse to making a few noises myself. I had a sudden picture of Jen listening to me and Ryan. Her ear cupped against a paper-thin wall. Jen was a very competitive person, and I just *knew* she'd raise the bar on who could make the most noise.

Terrific. Much as I loved Jen to bits, right now she could share Heather's new name. *Bloody Nuisance.*

Chapter Twelve

My phone awoke me at what seemed like an unearthly hour the following morning.

'Jen,' I rasped. My voice had yet to wake up. 'What's the matter?'

'Nothing,' she chirped. 'I was simply calling to do a post-mortem on our double-date last night. It's gone ten by the way. I thought you were an early riser.'

I glanced at the clock on the bedside table. Jen was right. I'd accidentally slept in. Not something I usually did, even on a Sunday.

I swung my legs out of bed and briefly grabbed my head. Ouch. A bit of hangover. Not surprising really. I'd shipped several gins throughout dinner last night as I'd tried – and failed – to muster enthusiasm for Jen and Stu joining Ryan and me in Cornwall.

'I'm so excited,' my bestie trilled. 'Aren't you?'

'Yes, of course,' I said, standing up and testing my pins.

'You don't sound it,' she said. A huff had entered her tone. 'If you want to tell me and Stu to naff off, I'll understand.'

'Don't be silly,' I soothed, knowing fully well this wasn't an option.

'Then why do you sound so… indifferent?'

I set off for the bathroom.

'Probably because my bladder feels like it's about to burst. Also, I'm in dire need of a strong coffee.'

'Well have a wee while you're talking to me,' said Jen charitably.

'Gee, thanks,' I said, tottering over to the loo and sitting down. I could almost hear my bladder sighing with relief as it emptied. Sometimes one of the best things in the world was having a wee. Aside from eating chocolate, of course.

'Blimey, I can hear you from here,' said Jen. 'It sounds like Niagara Falls in your bathroom.'

'Charming,' I said, flushing the chain and soaping my hands. 'I need to clean my teeth and wash my face.' I reached for my toothbrush. 'So, while I'm doing that, you can go first in the *what did you think of my boyfriend* conversation. After all, I gather that's the real reason for your call.' I squeezed out some toothpaste, then stuck the toothbrush in my mouth.

'You're right,' said Jen. I could hear the grin in her voice. 'Okay, I'll concede that I was quite surprised by Ryan.'

'Why?' I asked, dripping minty froth all over the washbasin.

'Because' – she said with exaggerated patience – 'he's not too much of a relic after all. I mean, he has his own teeth. Well, as far as I can tell. The abundance of streaked hair didn't look like a toupee. His body is in good shape.

65

Okay, he has laughter lines around his eyes and mouth, but I'd still give him an eight out of ten in the Looks Department. He's actually quite distinguished looking.'

'High praise indeed,' I said, before spitting and rinsing. 'And what did you think of Ryan's personality?'

'He's very charming. Articulate. Diplomatic. First impressions, another eight out of ten. Now then' – I sensed Jen shifting her body as she huddled over her phone – 'what did you think of my lovely Stu?'

'Gorgeous,' I said. It was best to tell Jen exactly what she wanted to hear.

'Isn't he just,' she purred. 'What about his personality?'

'Ten out of ten,' I said, mentally crossing my fingers.

Stu had been more ping-pong ball than disco ball. In other words, non-descript. His conversation – if you could even call it that – had been entirely along the lines of agreeing with everything that Jen had said. I'd lost count how many times he'd said *oh absolutely* peppered with *I agree*. However, it had been obvious that he was dotty about my bestie. Also, he didn't give me the vibe of being a two-timing bastard, so for that alone he could have all the Brownie points.

Ryan had compensated for Stu's lack of conversational input. He'd made us all laugh with tall stories about his accounting clients and colleagues.

Jen had poked fun at Ryan's profession asking if he'd heard the one about the fun accountant, before adding, "Me neither." Ryan had been quick to banter back, claiming that accountants made wonderful lovers because they were great with figures. Jen had then given him a sly look and said, "I understand from Lottie that she has yet to investigate your spreadsheet." I'd given her a murderous look.

Ryan had swiftly changed the subject and steered the chit-chat to Cornwall. He'd already found a delightful Cornish inn beside the sea and wanted to make reservations for the following Friday to Monday.

'And you really don't mind us tagging along to Cornwall?' Jen now asked.

'I've already said it's fine,' I repeated. I checked my reflection in the mirror over the washbasin. Thankfully my nose wasn't imitating Pinocchio's. 'Are you and Stu able to take time off work at such short notice?' A teeny part of me hoped that Jen might suddenly say, "Oh, blast. It turns out that Stu can't get the time off work after all. Ah, well. There's no point in me going without him. The last thing I want is to play gooseberry when the two of you will be billing and cooing like a pair of lovebirds."

'Totally not an issue,' she instead said. 'Obviously, I'm my own boss, so I can take leave whenever I want.' Jen successfully ran an online shop. She sold her own artisan leather goods and jewellery. 'And Stu emailed his boss last night and received an answer this morning.'

'Which was?' I asked tremulously. Hopefully, my voice hadn't betrayed the wish that Stu's boss had told him to bog off.

'That Stu has loads of holiday outstanding,' said Jen

airily. 'His boss told him to go away and enjoy himself, and that the recruitment industry will survive without him for a couple of days.'

'That's good to know,' I said weakly.

'We'd better start packing.'

'It's not until next weekend,' I protested.

Heavens. Other than making sure I had some sexy underwear in my suitcase, I hadn't even thought about what to wear.

'What shall we pack?' Jen prompted.

'Walking boots, I suppose. Oh, and a warm coat. Maybe a hat, scarf, and a pair of gloves too.'

'I'm talking about the evenings. Do you think I could get away with a cocktail dress? Or would that be a bit OTT?'

'I think smart-casual might be more fitting.'

I wasn't sure rural Cornwall was ready for Jen in a plunging dress smothered in sequins. A mental picture flitted through my brain. That of pop-eyed farmers trying to concentrate on their pints, instead of the woman sporting huge knockers that were trying to make a break for freedom. 'I suspect this place is more *Little Waterlow* than London,' I added.

'Fair point,' she said. 'Maybe we can do this again in the future, but next time go to the capital instead. Oooh, yes!' I could almost see her rubbing her hands with glee. 'A visit to a fancy five-star restaurant before tootling off to a casino in all our finery. Mmm. I can see Stu now. Dressed in a tux. And then later, naked – except for his dicky-bow.'

Somehow, I could only see Stu in an anorak. At the thought of him not wearing a stitch underneath, my eyes bulged rather than light up.

'Are you nervous about Ryan seeing you in the nuddy?' Jen suddenly asked.

'A little,' I admitted.

This was something I'd initially fretted about. Then I'd told myself not to worry. There was an advantage to having a boyfriend who was twelve years older. I suspected Ryan might wake up with a face more creased than mine. Also, there might be one or two parts of his body that were saggier than mine. Like the knees, for example. At a certain age, this part of the body liked to cosy up with the ankles. In which case, I'd feel less bothered about my boobs cosying up with my belly button.

Jen had never had children. Consequently, she was more body confident. For me, the days of stripping off with alacrity were long over. Ever since I'd left hospital with my newborn in her carrier, my deflated bump had remained. A soft, dough-like area.

I could still remember those first weeks after giving birth to Sally. I'd worn maternity jeans for months, tucking loose skin – like shirttails – into the waistband.

Eventually, various bits and pieces had realigned. Returned to their previous locations. However, no number of sit-ups had restored a taut belly. I was now a firm believer in the missionary position. Sitting astride Ryan, tummy sagging, jowls flapping, was to be avoided at all costs.

'This is going to be such fun, Lottie,' said Jen. 'I can't wait!'

'Me neither,' I said, hoping I sounded convincing.

'Fancy going for a walk this afternoon?'

'Sure, but won't Stu be with you?'

'No, he's visiting his mother at the nursing home.'

'In that case, okay. I could do with blowing the cobwebs away.'

'Great. Walk over to mine and we'll head towards Trottiscliffe. We'll have a wander through the woods. Afterwards, we'll go to the Bluebell Café and you can buy me a sausage sandwich.'

'My turn again?' I said in bemusement. This would be the third time for picking up the tab.

'You're flusher than me,' Jen protested. 'We can't all be budding authors about to hit the bestseller ranks. Anyway, you told me that the publisher had given you a tidy advance.'

'Ah. Yes, I did tell you that,' I conceded.

Thank goodness Jen didn't know the true source of my current income.

Chapter Thirteen

Jen lived just a short stroll from me.

I set off for Sparrow Cottage, wrapped up against the cold. No matter what the season, the surroundings here were always pretty.

An abundance of trees swayed gently in the November breeze, their branches ablaze with the bonfire colours of autumn. Leaf fall was starting to edge the lane, and the wind whipped it into untidy piles. Above, a sky the colour of milk stretched out, just like the fields, their greenness extending as far as the eye could see.

I found my mind wandering. Thinking of another leafy place. One that had its own large green space. Greenwich.

I missed living in that part of London. But also, paradoxically, I didn't. That bit of my life had been neatly filed away. Put into an emotional box. Mostly, this box resided in a tucked away corner of my mind. I likened it to a storage carton stowed in an attic. It was out of the way, so didn't encroach on day-to-day living. That said, sometimes a sight, a sound, or even a smell, would trigger a memory. Like now.

Such flashbacks were always full of nostalgia. There would be many *what ifs*. What if a different electrician had turned up at my apartment? What if Rick Lucas hadn't made a faux pas about my deceased parents? What if he hadn't tried to put things right by asking me out for a drink? What if Rick had been a minger and I hadn't fancied him rotten? What if he'd not ended up over the limit, with me tipsily suggesting he stay at mine? What if he'd thought *me* a minger and declined my offer?

A person can drive themselves crackers playing the *What If* game.

Hand in hand, we'd walked back to mine. Once inside my flat, he'd kicked the door shut. Taken me in his arms. Kissed me thoroughly. It had seemed like the most natural thing in the world to snog our way down the hallway and into my bedroom. The room had overlooked the River Thames.

Rick had briefly unglued his lips. Taken in the breathtaking outlook.

'Wow,' he'd murmured. 'What a stunning view.' He'd then turned his attention back to me. His eyes had on mine. 'But not as stunning as the woman standing in front of me.'

I'd started to shed my clothes, but he'd stopped me.

'No, Lots.' That endearing shortening of my name again. '*I* want to undress you. This moment is to be savoured. Our first time.'

Something within me had expanded with joy. *Our first time.* His choice of words had left me in no doubt that there would be many more times. Of being a couple.

Quivering with excitement, I'd let Rick remove my

clothes. He'd done it slowly. Sensuously. I'd had a fleeting feeling that it was a practised move. That he'd done it many times before. It had been so skilled. However, I'd batted the thought away. And all the while, his eyes hadn't left mine. It had been a heady experience. One that had no doubt been heightened by too much alcohol.

As his head had disappeared between my thighs, I'd surrendered to those intense feelings of desire and lust. It had felt as if my very bones were dissolving. Seemingly my brain had also melted and puddled – like my clothes – across the floor. Common sense had done a complete bunk. Of that there'd been no doubt. Why else had I not stopped him, like a traffic cop pursuing a mad driver, as Rick had pushed me down on the bed and entered me?

I'd been high on happiness. No longer tipsy from alcohol, instead drunk on that first flush of love. Afterwards, he'd spooned into me. We'd fallen asleep, his arms wound tightly around me.

After feeling so alone in the world, so bereft from the grief of losing two parents in the space of one year, I'd suddenly felt *cocooned*. Protected. Like a boat, previously adrift and being tossed around on the ocean, now returned to a safe harbour.

The following morning Rick had told me that I'd slept with a smile on my face.

'How do you know?' I'd asked, grinning stupidly.

'Because I woke up an hour before you,' he'd said. 'I spent the time counting your freckles. Thinking about how beautiful you are.'

'Give over,' I'd beamed. But, secretly, I'd been delighted.

'Can I see you again, Lots?'

'Yes,' I'd smiled.

'I have a good feeling about us,' he'd said, stroking my hair.

I'd kissed the palm of his hand and nestled into him.

'I'll call you,' he'd later promised, before letting himself out of the apartment.

After he'd gone, I'd lain back against the sheets, content and happy. I'd been blissfully unaware that he'd left something behind. Something growing within my womb.

Chapter Fourteen

For the next six weeks, Rick and I were almost inseparable.

I wouldn't say he moved into my apartment. However, he might as well have done. For aside from going to work, we were almost joined at the hip.

At the end of a working day, we'd hook up at mine. I'd then cook for the two of us. Sometimes we'd opt to eat out. Enjoy candlelit dinners.

If it was me picking up the tab more than him, I didn't notice. Nor did it register that he never suggested I stay at his. I was too busy looking at life through my newly acquired rose-tinted spectacles. And, oh! How rosy everything looked. Life was suddenly gorgeous. Wonderful. You see, Creator… God… Universe… whatever you wanted to call the energy that had dressed my essence in skin, blood, and bone, had spoken. The voice had quietly whispered into my brain: *Enough sadness, Lottie. After a testing period – one of double bereavement, loss, grief, and intense loneliness – it's time for your reward. Let there be joy!*

Rick Lucas might not have been Jesus, but he'd lit up my life like a host of angels with neon halos. I'd been dazzled. He'd been my own personal miracle.

Every day, I'd floated into work. Nothing had seemed impossible. No challenge insurmountable. Everyone had noticed the difference in me. My boss had given me a benign smile. "If I didn't know better, Lottie, I'd say you'd fallen in love." I'd made a *harrumph* noise. Protested otherwise. But my heart had known the truth.

It was two weeks after my missed period that I'd felt a flash of concern. Only a smidgen, mind. It wasn't the first time in my adult life that I'd experienced a blip in the menstrual cycle. It had sputtered all over the place after Mum had died. When Dad had followed in her heavenly footsteps, I'd missed a period completely. The doctor had put it down to stress. I'd had some blood tests, and all had been well. A little while later, my ovaries had resumed normal service.

Also, I'd hit on a theory about sputtery periods. If stress had the power to cause a hormonal blip, might not the opposite do the same? After all, I'd spent weeks experiencing over-the-top elation. Back then, joy hadn't been my natural default mode. It was, I'd reasoned, no wonder my cycle had gone haywire.

Apart from anything else, Rick and I had taken great care to use contraceptives. Only one chance had been taken. That first coupling. I'd also silently argued that loads of people took chances. And loads of people got away with it.

When the second period had failed to arrive, I'd bought a pregnancy test. Even as I'd piddled on the stick, I'd not expected to see two blue lines. Mentally, I'd been elsewhere. In the doctor's surgery. Saying, "Yes, I've done a pregnancy test. It was negative. What can possibly be wrong, Doctor?"

That imaginary conversation had evaporated the moment I'd stared at the stick. Such shock. Utter disbelief. Pregnant. Oh no. Oh God. Oh help. Oh how wonderful. All those emotions and more. From panic and horror to elation. God had taken away people I'd loved. Now he'd given something back. A new life. Growing within me.

It hadn't mattered that Rick and I weren't married. Nor that we weren't even *official*. In a nano-second I'd made the decision to raise the child alone. I'd planned to tell Rick. Of course. But I'd also intended to make it clear that he didn't have to stick around. I hadn't wanted to burden him with unplanned parenthood. Or being shackled to me.

I'd sent Rick a text and invited him over to dinner.

Can't do tonight, he'd replied. *My landlord wants to see me.*

So we'd arranged to meet up the following evening.

Rick had arrived at the flat not quite his exuberant self. Apparently, his landlord had wanted to put the rent up, but was in breach of contract. Something like that.

'Anyway' – Rick had swiped the matter away with a gesture of one hand – 'enough of that stress. Let's change the subject.'

'Sure,' I'd said. Smiling nervously, I'd dished up dinner. 'I apologise in advance if what I tell you causes further stress. It's not meant to.'

'What do you mean?' Rick had frowned.

Together, we'd sat at my small dining table. However,

our meals had remained untouched.

'I'm so sorry, Rick, but–'

A shadow had flickered across his face.

'You don't want to see me anymore?'

'Not at all.' I'd almost laughed at the question. 'Rather, it might be you who no longer wants to see me.'

'I'm not following.'

I'd taken a deep breath. Dived in.

'I'm expecting your baby.'

He'd stared at me for a moment, evidently processing my words. Then his whole face had lit up. His mouth had split into a huge banana grin.

'You're pregnant? Truly? Are you sure?' he'd gabbled.

Silently, I'd reached into my handbag. Removed the used pregnancy stick from its cardboard box. Wordlessly, I'd passed it to him. He'd looked at it. Then he'd looked at me. Finally, he'd pushed back his chair and pulled me into his arms.

'Marry me, Lots,' he'd whispered.

Startled, I'd pulled away. Studied his face. He'd looked so sincere. Desperate even.

'Do you really mean that?' I'd quavered.

'I do. You're the answer to all of my prayers.'

At the time, those words had made my heart burst with happiness. It was only much later that I'd realised he'd meant something quite different.

Chapter Fifteen

The black door knocker was shaped like a bird. Lifting one iron wing, I delivered several firm *rat-a-tat-tats*.

Jen had lived at Sparrow Cottage ever since her divorce. We'd known each other since school days. Ironically, she'd not been my bestie until our last year at secondary. I have no idea why our friendship didn't bloom earlier. However, by the time we were school leavers, I'd felt Jen to be the sister I'd never had.

The door swung open.

'Wotcha,' she now said, before peering up at the sky. She frowned. 'Do you think it's going to rain?'

'Not sure. However, I'm not bothered if it does because I have a hood on my jacket.'

'I haven't.' She grimaced. 'Let me grab a hat, just in case.'

Jen briefly disappeared. She returned with what looked like a woolly tea-cosy topped with an exploding pompom. She tried and failed to stuff the hat into her pocket.

'You might as well wear it,' I said. 'It's cold enough.'

'True,' she nodded, pulling the hat down over her ears. 'Let me lock up, and then we'll set off.'

Inevitably, throughout the stroll to the woods, our

conversation turned to the upcoming trip to Cornwall.

Negotiating a stile, we then took a public footpath through a field of grazing ponies. Most of them were rugged up against the elements. A small one started to follow us, perhaps hoping we had a pocket full of carrots.

'Shoo,' I said nervously.

'He won't hurt you,' Jen assured. 'This little chap is more Thelwell than racehorse. His name is Snowdrop. He belongs to one of my neighbours. Their daughter rides him. She's only seven. I don't think they'd let her get on a pony that wasn't bombproof.'

My mobile chose that moment to ring. The shrill noise startled Snowdrop. He let out a whinny of surprise. Eyes rolling, nostrils flaring, he galloped off, delivering a couple of bucks along the way.

'Hmm,' I mused. 'I think that might be the equine equivalent of two fingers.'

'Possibly,' Jen laughed.

I glanced at the still ringing handset. The caller display informed me it was Ryan.

'Hello?'

'Hi, Lottie.' My boyfriend sounded extremely chipper. 'Just to let you know, I've successfully booked–'

'Hang on a mo,' I interrupted. 'Let me put you on loudspeaker. Jen is with me. I'm sure she'd love to be in on the conversation.'

'You bet,' said Jen. She leant in, so Ryan could hear her. 'Morning, Ryan.'

'Hiya,' he said.

'Are you still on the fishing trip?' I asked.

'No. Joshua and I are back home now, but we had a great time. We checked out Basil Lake. It's over at Darenth, and fabulous for catfish and carp. Joshua caught a whopper.'

'Amazing,' I said, endeavouring to inject enthusiasm into my voice.

'It was indeed amazing, although Heather wouldn't agree. She screamed at the sight of it. She said she didn't like to see a fish wiggling on the end of a line. Anyway, we put it back.'

Jen pulled a face at the mention of Heather's name. I must confess, I was tempted to do the same.

'Meanwhile' – Ryan swept on – 'Let me tell you about Cornwall. All good news. I've paid the deposit. We're booked to stay at Penwern Lodge, near Falmouth. We check in next Friday. I have the website in front of me. I have to say, girls, it looks amazing.'

'Oooh, tell me more,' said Jen.

'Well, apparently Penwern Lodge was a manor house. It was subsequently converted into a hotel and now sits in sixty-five acres of private Cornish countryside. The blurb waffles on about the delights of unspoilt bays around the Helford River. Penwern Lodge has its own private foreshore with direct access to the Southwest Coast Path. This means it's a terrific spot for some serious walking.'

'Ah, so I won't be packing my sexy stilettoes,' said Jen wistfully.

'For the daytime I recommend a pair of strong, sturdy lace-ups,' Ryan chuckled. 'It will probably be quite muddy in places, but that's all part of the fun.'

'And you're quite sure' – I interjected – 'that Heather is okay about you going?'

'Er, excuse me,' said Jen, butting in. 'Ryan doesn't need to ask Heather's permission to go away. He's a divorced man, remember?'

At the other end of the line, Ryan let out a chortle of laughter.

'Absolutely. Anyway, Jen, I've already adopted that new name you gave her – *Bloody Nuisance*. Although I might refer to her as *BN* for short. Just in case she overhears. There's no point in ruffling feathers unnecessarily. And, to answer your question, Lottie, I don't need *anyone's* permission to go anywhere. Okay?'

'Good to hear,' I said, instantly perking up. 'Do you fancy coming over this evening? I could cook us a roast dinner.'

'Ah, I'm going to have to pass, darling. I'm afraid Heather… I mean, BN… has booked us a table at our local. Joshua said he was ravenous after the fishing trip. He's requested a roast beef dinner with traditional Yorkshire puddings. I won't be able to eat two huge meals so close together.'

'No, of course not,' I agreed. As I swallowed down the disappointment, I studiously ignored the outraged expression on Jen's face.

'Anyway,' Ryan continued. 'This whole situation won't last for much longer. We've found another estate agent. This one has promised not to renege on their fees. I can also share the news that BN is actively looking for two-bedroomed properties for Joshua and herself. Earlier, I saw her scrolling through *Rightmove*.'

'Oh that *is* good news,' I agreed, my spirits lifting again.

From the background came a female voice.

'Ryan? Are you ready to go, darling?'

An invisible hand immediately squeezed my heart. Another woman had just called *my* man *darling*. It didn't matter how many times Ryan assured me that he and his ex were amicable for the sake of their son, it nonetheless jarred to overhear Heather using such an endearment.

'Coming,' he called. At least he hadn't called her *Sweetie*. 'Going to have to go, Lottie.'

'So I gathered,' I replied coolly.

I was immediately aware how my emotions see-sawed with Ryan. It happened a lot. Sometimes within seconds. Like now:

Want to go to Cornwall? Woohoo!

Want to have dinner? No, sorry, I can't!

It was a constant yo-yo effect – one where my feelings either rode high, or miserably low.

Ryan had detected the frost in my voice.

'Oh, don't be like that,' he now cajoled. 'Just think. This time next week you'll have me all to yourself. No interruptions. Oh, and one more bit of good news.' He lowered his voice, as if to share a confidence. Jen leant in closer, keen to catch every word. 'I've been looking at properties online too. There's a couple I'd like to check out.' Ryan cleared his throat. A nervous gesture. 'I wondered, Lottie–'

'Yes?' I said breathlessly as my heart suddenly sped up.

Wondered what? Wondered if I'd move in with him?

'Would you be prepared to check them out with me? Only I'd really appreciate your opinion.'

'Oh, right.' My heart resumed its normal pace. How silly to have suspected he'd been thinking of us moving in together. After all, we hadn't known each other that long. Certainly not long enough to go anywhere near such an idea. Even so…

'I'd love to,' I said warmly.

'Good, that's settled then. Meanwhile, darling, I have one hell of a week coming up at work. Do you mind if we don't see each other until Friday morning, when I pick you up? I want to be able to stay late at the office. Clear my desk. Tie up all the loose ends. It would be good to leave the office knowing that the only dark clouds on the horizon might be one or two rainclouds in Falmouth.'

'Sure,' I said.

'What are the travel arrangements?' asked Jen. 'Are we going in one car, or taking two?'

'I'm happy for us all to go in mine,' said Ryan generously. 'I can wangle the petrol costs through expenses.'

'Cool,' said Jen. 'I'll let Stu know.'

'Okie dokie,' said Ryan. 'Meanwhile, Lottie, we'll talk during the week. Sending lots of love.'

'Sending it back,' I replied, before ending the call.

We were entering the woods now. Jen let out a sigh before giving the smallest shake of her head.

'What?' I said, at the same time ducking under a low branch.

'Nothing.'

I sighed. Why did people always say *nothing* when you knew they wanted to offload *everything*?

'Go on.' I pursed my lips. 'Spit it out. You know you want to.'

'He's a nice guy, Lottie…' Jen paused. Her hesitation told me she was choosing her words carefully. 'I can see the attraction. However, you must admit that his situation takes a lot of…' She trailed off again.

'A lot of what?' I prompted.

'Patience,' she said eventually. 'I mean… Ryan's circumstances. It's quite a big ask. Don't you think? You're his girlfriend, yet you've just overheard his ex call him *darling*. And then, he turns down your dinner invitation because he's off to have a roastie with his family. *And* they're all still living together. Under one roof. I couldn't put up with it.'

'He's not married, Jen,' I protested.

'Yeah, I know,' she conceded. 'But it doesn't half seem like it.'

'Don't be silly,' I said, stumbling over a snaking tree

root. I didn't like to admit it, but her words had rattled me. 'If Ryan were a married man, he wouldn't organise a weekend away with another woman *and* with his wife's knowledge.'

'I know, I know,' she said, flinging her hands up in the air. 'Ignore me. I'm just an embittered and negative old harridan. Ryan's great. And so is my lovely Stu. We're all going to have a fabulous weekend together.'

'Absolutely,' I agreed. 'And nothing is going to spoil it.'

Although a fortune teller might not have agreed.

Chapter Sixteen

'Flipping heck,' grumbled Jen. 'My legs are aching so much.'

'Hardly surprising,' I answered. We'd left the woods and were now entering a clearing. The Bluebell Café was located nearby. 'We've done the best part of a two-hour walk, which included a horrendously steep hill. Such is the joy of living on the North Downs. Shall we eat inside?'

'No, outside,' said Jen. She collapsed down on a bench and momentarily slumped over a trestle table. 'I can't take another step.' She rolled her eyes dramatically.

The café's outside area was mostly occupied by dogwalkers. Pooches were banned from entering the restaurant itself. However, you didn't have to have a four-legged friend to enjoy some al fresco woodland dining.

'I must be terribly unfit,' Jen groaned, massaging her legs.

'It was a hard walk,' I pointed out. 'Think of it as a workout.'

'That's putting it mildly,' she said. Her fingers worked at her calf muscles. 'Sometimes I think I should stick to the gym. Do a bit of stationary cycling. A few months ago, I was really into that.'

'Yeah, I remember.' I gave her a look. 'You became a

bit of a *cyclopath.*'

'Ha funny ha.' Jen pulled a face.

'Anyway, we've burned loads of calories thanks to that steep hill and the bracing cold.' I pulled up the collar of my jacket. 'We've definitely earnt a toasted sausage sandwich.'

'Your shout, remember?'

'Actually, *your* shout' – I corrected – 'but I said I didn't mind paying.'

'Oh, now you sound peeved.' Jen stopped rubbing her legs. 'Are you? If so, you can be honest. I don't want you being annoyed with me.'

'It's fine,' I sighed.

'Are you sure? It's just that – now I've committed myself to the Cornwall trip – I must be even more careful with my spending. Stu said he can't pay for me. He's waiting for outstanding commissions to come in. He's also asked if we can split everything down the middle. You know, meals and drinks and whatnot. Anyway, you told me you'd received a healthy payout from your publisher.'

Ah, yes. The fictitious advance. I sighed again.

'Look, I said it's fine, and it is. It's just that my own finances have recently taken a battering. What with the deposit on Catkin Cottage *and* a month's rent up front.'

'I'll definitely get the next one,' Jen promised.

'Shut up,' I said good-naturedly. 'Now then, are you having a cappuccino too? And if so, do you want chocolate sprinkles on the top?'

'Yes and yes,' Jen smiled. 'Oooh, and can I have a

shortbread cookie too?'

'Coming right up.'

Flaming Nora. At this rate I wouldn't have much change from twenty-five quid.

As I walked into the café and joined a short queue, my phone pinged. I reached into my jacket pocket. A text from Ryan.

By the way, darling. Sorry not to have mentioned this earlier – it wouldn't have been good form in front of Jen. I know it was my suggestion to go to Cornwall – and I fully intended to treat you. However, this month I've had some unforeseen expenses, including a stonking solicitor's bill. Would you mind sharing the cost of our long weekend?

I groaned aloud. If Ryan had mentioned this earlier, I wouldn't have agreed to go to Falmouth. However, I could hardly tell him to cancel the trip. Not when Jen and Stu were now included and looking forward to it. Nor could I give Ryan a hard time over this last-minute bombshell. After all, it wasn't his fault that his lawyer had invoiced him. A divorce cost money. Ending a marriage wasn't cheap. I should know.

Okay, I typed back. *Will make sure I eat only beans on toast for the next few weeks!*

There. A light reply but, at the same time, gently informing that I hadn't been expecting additional expense.

Attagirl! he replied. *And should you wish to extend a future dinner invitation, rest assured I LOVE beans on toast xxxxxxxx*

Good to know, Ryan.

The queue moved forward, and I slipped the phone back in my pocket. My brain whirred and I chewed on my lip thoughtfully. Of course, there was another way to top up my battered finances.

Earlier, just before I'd left to go to Jen's cottage, a message had come in on my *other* phone. Mr Muppet again. He'd told me how much he'd enjoyed my voice note – a relief after all the frenzied improvising. He'd also asked if I would consider something else. Going a little further. Upping the financial reward, so to speak.

Mr Muppet was after a video. In his message, he'd praised my *perfectly fleshy soles*. He wanted a five-minute film to include bending and flexing the arches of my feet, rotating the ankles, and lots and lots of toe wiggling.

The offered fee had been astronomical. Three hundred pounds. *Three. Hundred. Pounds.* I'd gasped when reading his text. The suggestion was shocking. Obscene. And yet… and yet… what harm was it doing? It would certainly take care of this unexpected blip in finding the wherewithal to fund Cornwall.

I hadn't yet replied to the message. There was a concern about how to film it and, more importantly, where. I didn't want anyone – no matter how slim the possibility – potentially identifying me from my surroundings.

However, I'd now have to give Mr Muppet's latest request some serious consideration. After all, so long as I was careful, what were the chances of anyone ever finding out?

Chapter Seventeen

The moment I was back home – alone – I went upstairs to the bedroom and retrieved my second phone. I then clicked on Mr Muppet's message.

Okay. I've had a think about it. The answer is yes. However, the fee is four hundred pounds.

Was that greedy? Yes, of course. But needs must. And right now, I had a need to pay for visiting a stretch of Cornish coastline.

Seconds later, my phone dinged with a reply.

Sorry, Fifi. I'll have to cancel the order.

What? No, no, no. That mustn't happen. I tapped out a swift response.

Why?

The reply arrived in moments.

I've overspent this month. Must rein in my finances. Apologies.

Yeah, well, what about my finances? Unlike most people, I didn't have the luxury of an arranged overdraft with my bank manager. In fact, me and my bank manager were on distinctly chilly terms – thanks to matters I didn't want to dwell upon.

Think, Lottie, *think*. And make it snappy. I began to type again.

I have a proposition – should you change your mind. What about a two-for-one deal? A video AND me speaking?

Oh, help. What was I doing? Leading someone financially astray? His reply was immediate.

Fifi, you are incorrigible. Three hundred and fifty and you have a deal.

Three hundred and fifty pounds wasn't as good as four hundred, but it was still better than his original offer.

You're on. Give me your instructions.

I watched the screen. Mr Muppet was typing.

As per my previous request but to include smelly socks. Also, mud. I want to see those soles covered in muck. Insult me, too. I'm transferring the money now. I await in anticipation.

I sighed with relief and moved over to my laptop. Time to pull up a script. Except, a few minutes later, I realised there wasn't a script that fitted Mr Muppet's demand. I'd have to do some more improvising. Fulfilling the request for mud wasn't too tricky. If nothing else, his strange requests were easy to deal with.

I went to the bathroom, located my Ali Baba laundry basket, and dug deep. Somewhere within were several socks awaiting the washing machine. The pair I was after were stripy. Also, one sock had a hole in it. Over the big toe area, which I knew Mr Muppet would appreciate.

It was important to get properly into the role. As I extracted the socks, I knew my client would be thrilled to bits.

I went downstairs, through the kitchen, and opened the back door. After the walk with Jen, my hiking boots were plastered in thick mud. Consequently, I'd left them on the back step. The state of the shoes would make Mr Muppet very happy.

I bent down to pick them up, then paused. Where to make the video? I didn't want to bring all that mud into the house. Nor did I want to film in this garden. The small space was stuffed with gaily coloured pots, shrubs, and plants. Paranoia ambushed me. What if Catkin Cottage's patio inadvertently led to me being identified as Sophie Fairfax's tenant? It wasn't part of my game plan.

I blanched. Don't mention the word *game*, Lottie. It makes it sound like you're on it. A whimper escaped my lips, and I had to resist the urge to stuff a fist in my mouth. Instead, I busied myself with changing into the whiffy stripy socks, then laced my feet into the hiking boots.

Now, I still had to think about where to do the filming. And then it came to me. Further down the lane was another row of cottages. Directly opposite, a public footpath snaked through open farmland. The fields were bordered by trees and bits of hedgerow. Both could act as excellent screens from prying eyes.

Round here, one field looked much like another. Well, that was my reasoning anyway. Certainly, this chosen location would provide protection in maintaining my anonymity.

Decision made, I locked up and set off. Walking along

93

the lane, I had to force myself not to break into a run. The urge to keep stopping to look furtively over my shoulder was huge – which would be a giveaway of suspicious behaviour. Feeling like a dodgy member of the Secret Service, I scampered on.

I eventually reached the second row of cottages. My heart had started to beat in an erratic fashion. Come on, Lottie. Calm down. Otherwise, you might as well be carrying a placard that declared UP TO NO GOOD.

My eyes flicked from left to right. Hurrah! There was the footpath. But… oh no… one of the cottages had someone lurking at the downstairs window. Net curtains had started to twitch violently.

I broke into a jaunty whistle, mainly to keep my pecker up. My stomach was now doing somersaults. Adopting a carefree gait with an air of contrived insouciance, I tried to look like someone minding their own business – unlike the busybody who was still watching me. Unable to bear being spied upon for another second, I broke into a guilty run and disappeared through the overgrown opening to the public footpath.

Exhaling gustily, I ground to a halt and looked wildly about. Ploughed fields stretched out around me. A single scavenging seagull, far from the coast, was picking over the brown earth. It let out a shrill screech before shaking out its wings and taking to the air.

I was alone. For now. But who knew for how long? A dog walker or rambler might appear at any moment. There wasn't a moment to lose.

Holding the phone in one hand, and taking great care to avoid showing my face, I pressed the record button and got to work.

'You wanted mud, Mr Muppet,' I growled. The camera lens zoomed in on my caked footwear. 'Well, I have it in spadefuls. After a long, arduous walk, my boots are covered in the stuff. Consequently, my feet are HOT and very, *very* SWEATY. In fact, my favourite SOCKS are so damp and RANK, they're practically stuck to my soles and positively STINK!'

I lifted up one foot. Zoomed in closer still. Grabbing hold of some hedgerow to steady myself, I began to rotate my ankle this way and that.

'I bet you'd like me to get these off, eh?' I rasped into the microphone.

Careful, Lottie. Try not to sound like Darth Vader. I cleared my throat. Concentrated on making my voice more Fenella Fielding.

'Here goes,' I said hoarsely.

That was awful. Forget Fenella. Now I was sounding like Albert Steptoe. Oh, get on with it, Lottie. Stop worrying about sound effects and concentrate on the visuals.

Using the toe of my left boot, I worked off the right hiking shoe. A stripy-socked foot was revealed in all its glory.

'Oooh, PHOOEY,' I said in disgust, as my big toe popped through the frayed hole. 'Oh, geez, YUCK.' I made some sniffing sounds. 'What a horrifically, horrible CHEESY

SMELL. But I bet you'd like to sniff my smelly feet, eh, Mr Muppet. Because we both know you are absolutely DISGUSTING when it comes to DIRTY feet.'

Wobbling slightly, I grabbed another bit of hedgerow, endeavouring to stabilise myself, all the while keeping the camera trained on my foot. Taking a deep breath to psyche myself up, I then pressed my sole down to the freshly ploughed earth.

'*Ewww*,' I groaned.

The ground was cold and wet. Moisture seeped through the thin cotton. I momentarily closed my eyes and tried to ignore the unpleasant sensation. Instead, I concentrated on flexing my arches a few times then zoomed in on my naked big toe. It was time to use it to ease off the other boot.

'Oh God,' I declared. 'The SMELL is now truly awful. In fact, PUTRID.'

I flexed my left foot up and down. Slowly. One thing I'd learnt from *Fifi Footsy's* platform was that clients were attracted to the visual nature of ankles, toes, and soles. For them, it was captivating. Playing on that appeal, I did some more toe wiggling and ankle rotations.

'And now… I suppose you want to see my feet NAKED, eh?' I growled. 'Because, let's face it, that's what weirdos like you want, and make no mistake, YOU ARE A TOTAL WEIRDO.' Mr Muppet had requested some insults. Well, bring 'em on. 'I know what you're now thinking. You're fantasising about SUCKING MY TOES. Outrageous. If my feet were able to talk, they'd tell you how utterly REVOLTING you are for even *considering* the thought of putting one of my muddy toes between your lips. *Bleurghhh.*'

It was time to remove both socks and go barefoot.

Hmm. This was going to be tricky. I really needed to use two hands. However, I hadn't thought to bring a pair of gloves, and was reluctant to reveal any other part of me – not even a thumb and index finger. Never mind. Somehow, I'd manage without. It might take longer to achieve, but I could always eke it out with some panting for effect.

Slowly, carefully, I worked my right big toe into the top of the left sock. Clumsily, swaying about somewhat, I managed – bit by bit – to slide the top of the sock from calf to heel, before wiggling it over the arch. I then repeated this all over again until both socks lay abandoned on the earth.

'Et voila!' I declared.

My ugly feet were now revealed in all their hideous glory, including the large mole at the base of my big toe.

I wiggled my little piggies about. Curled them backwards and forwards. I then attempted doing a Mexican Wave with them. Oooh. That was harder than it looked. Eventually, I lifted one foot at a time and revealed the soles. They were grim beyond belief. And – oh yuck – a worm was stuck to the ball of one foot. Hastily, I shook it off.

'So, Mr Muppet,' I exhorted. 'No doubt you'd like my feet to trample all over your body. I'd gladly do it, too, because nutters like you need punishing. Right now, if your body was under my soles, I'd do THIS!'

I began pounding my feet up and down on the cold earth, effectively marching on the spot.

'YOU' – stamp, stamp, stamp – 'CRAZY – stomp, stomp, stomp – 'CRINGE-MAKING, BIG-TOED, FLAT-FOOTED, SOLE-LICKING' – the seagull returned and took a mid-flight crap which landed on my my left foot's mole – 'PONGO-MAKING, WHIFFY-WANKING, DASTARDLY DUMPSTER!' I shrieked at the top of my voice.

Exhausted, I released the recording button. I then screamed aloud as a wrinkled face popped through a gap in the hedge.

'What the bloomin' 'eck is goin' on 'ere?' demanded a familiar voice.

I inwardly groaned as, one second later, the entire person came into view. I'd heard much about this octogenarian. It was Mabel Plaistow. The number one village gossip.

'I-I-I was just…' I stammered.

'I 'eard what you was doin',' she roared, glaring at me.

'P-Please don't tell anyone,' I begged.

Oh, help. This was it. My life in Little Waterlow was over. I'd have to move.

'You should be ashamed of yerself,' she declared, wagging a gnarled finger.

'I am, I am, I am,' I gabbled.

'Don't ever let me catch yer again shoutin' at a poor defenceless little seagull.'

Chapter Eighteen

Scooping up my soggy socks, I stuffed my mud-encrusted crapped-on feet into the hiking boots, shot past Mabel and, on rubbery legs, pogoed home.

People with foot fetishes might be intoxicated by grubby feet, but all I wanted to do was get in the shower and scrub mine with a scouring pad.

I burst into Catkin Cottage – filthy boots and all – and slammed the door after me as if the devil incarnate were snapping at my heels.

A shadow fell across the hallway and a fresh wave of terror filled the space around my hammering heart.

'Meow,' came a cry.

'Audrey,' I gasped, and closed my eyes. Relief washed over me. Audrey minced over. Her expression told me that she was perplexed by such kerfuffle. 'You'll never guess what's happened?' I burbled, wiping one hand across my damp brow. 'I nearly blew my cover. Down the lane. In a field. I was doing a video. For that ridiculous Mr Muppet. Mabel Plaistow caught me at it. Fortunately, she thought I was berating a seagull. *Un*fortunately, she's a massive gossip. I dread to think what rumours she'll spread.'

I slid down to the floor and landed on my bottom. Legs

sprawled out in front of me. Right now, my pins couldn't even bear the weight of a feather.

'Thank goodness Mabel didn't know what I was *really* up to,' I confided.

Audrey sat down and curled her fluffy tail over her front paws. She blinked at me languorously. Then yawned. For a second, I was privy to a very pink tongue and some sharp teeth.

'Is that all you have to say about the matter?' I said.

There was a sudden frenzied hammering at the front door. Startled, Audrey shot upstairs leaving me alone with a sky-high heart rate. All these adrenalin rushes couldn't be doing my health any good.

'Who is it?' I croaked, still unable to move.

The letterbox peeled back on its hinges revealing a pair of bemused brown eyes.

'It's me,' said a familiar voice.

'Jen?'

'Who else?'

'What do you want?'

'To come in, of course.'

'I can't do that right now.'

'Lottie, stop behaving weirdly and let me in.'

'Just a sec.'

I groaned. Shifted my body. Finally managed to manoeuvre onto all fours. However, my body was racked with the shakes. I was vibrating from head to toe and didn't quite trust myself to stand up. Instead, I crawled to the front door. From her position at the letterbox, Jen monitored my progress.

'What on *earth* are you doing?' she asked, as I shuffled along the hallway.

'What do you think I'm doing?' I said sarcastically. 'Baking a cake?'

'Stop fannying about,' she said bossily. 'Hurry up and open this door.'

Her no-nonsense tone let me know that I should get on and do her bidding. My knees cracked as I stretched upwards. Reached for the catch. Released it. I sank back to the floor again just as Jen pushed her way into the cottage. At the sight of my mud-splattered legs and footwear, her mouth dropped open.

'Omigod. Is it true?'

I looked up at her warily.

'Is what true?'

'I've just had Mabel Plaistow on the blower. She was beside herself. Absolutely livid. She said, "That friend of yours is no friend of mine. She woz usin' 'er socks as a makeshift catapult. She tried to pelt a seagull with 'er boots. We don't need the likes of 'er in this village."'

I let out another groan.

'It wasn't like that.'

'Look at the state of you.' Jen's eyes were wide as she pointed at my legs and feet in disbelief. What's going on?'

'I went for a walk.'

Jen looked puzzled.

'But we've just been for a walk.'

'So I went for another one,' I cried.

'Whatever for?'

'Because… because… after eating that toasted sausage sandwich, I… I felt fat.'

'Oh don't be so ridiculous.' Jen plonked her hands on her hips. 'Stop lolling all over the floor and get up.'

'I don't think I can,' I bleated. 'I've gone all weak-kneed, but not in a romantic way.'

'For heaven's sake,' she tutted. Jen hooked her hands under my armpits and hauled me upright. 'You do realise Mabel Plaistow is going to have a field day. She's going to tell everyone what you've done. It wouldn't surprise me if the local rag pays you a visit.'

I let out a low moan. I could imagine the headline.

BIRD BRAINED

And – omigod – what if Mr Muppet turned out to be the journalist? Everyone always said it was a small world. He'd dish the dirt on me for sure.

SOCK STRIPPER SUSSED

Budding crime-writer Lottie Lucas's career is over before it has even properly begun. Miss Lucas, whose alter ego is known as Fifi Footsy, provides toe-tally titillating pictures of her tootsies to those who are sweet on feet. Neighbour Mabel Plaistow was eyewitness to Miss Lucas making a lewd film involving a seagull wearing socks. When asked to comment, Miss Lucas said, "I wish I could pass this matter over to my fictional character, DI Denise Draper, because she always knows when something is afoot." Miss Lucas was then arrested and taken away by police officers. Her expression was one of de-feet.

'Lottie, I'm talking to you,' Jen prompted. 'Would you answer me, please? This is serious. Now tell me what the heck is going on?'

Chapter Nineteen

Jen had eventually left, but not until I'd given her a reason for being found barefoot in a field. I'd said that I'd had stones in my boots and had simply stopped to shake them out.

'You had stones in *both* shoes?' she'd quizzed. Her expression had indicated disbelief.

'Yes, both shoes,' I'd said glibly.

'So why were your socks off?'

'Because it had felt like… there were stones in them too,' I'd added lamely.

She'd folded her arms over her chest. So far, she'd not bought any of my explanations.

'And why were you ranting at a seagull?'

'Because it crapped on me.'

'Hmm. Why do I get the feeling that something is off?'

'Nothing is off,' I'd promised.

'Well your shoes and socks certainly were.'

I'd been red-faced with shame. What a pity Mr Muppet hadn't been there with me, in the hallway. He'd have had a free session at being humiliated thanks to Jen launching into a rant. Eventually, I'd stuck my hands in the air. A gesture of surrender.

'I'm going to the bathroom to get cleaned up,' I'd told

her.

Jen had shaken her head, at a loss to make sense of my behaviour. Her parting remark had been to sort my head out.

'If I didn't know better, I'd say you're up to something, Lottie,' she'd exhorted. 'I've never heard so much nonsense about being fat after eating one sausage sandwich.'

'It's okay for you,' I'd said flippantly. 'You burn calories simply by jumping to conclusions.'

She'd shaken her head and rolled her eyes. Muttering something about outstanding work commissions, she'd then taken herself off.

'See you Friday,' she'd called over her shoulder. 'Until then, try and stay out of trouble.'

If I'd been a dog, my tail would have been jammed between my legs.

'Hey' – I'd called after her – 'not a word about this to Ryan, okay? I don't want him thinking I'm a bit, you know…'

'Bonkers?' she'd suggested, one eyebrow raised.

I'd nodded weakly.

'Don't worry,' she'd assured. 'Your secret is safe with me.' She'd then spoilt it by adding, 'And the whole of Little Waterlow.'

I now lay in a cooling tub, reflecting over *Bird Gate*. I turned on the hot tap, added some more bubble bath, then swished it about with my hands. The water turned to foam, and I sank beneath it.

Enough was enough. It was one thing to earn a bit of cash via pics of my feet online. It was quite another to be making voice notes and videos for some nutcase. If Mr Muppet's pseudonym was anything to go by, he probably had a thing about Kermit and Miss Piggy too.

This was all Rick's fault. Rick with his charm. His smarm. Rick who'd come into my life thanks to a faulty smoke alarm, got me up the duff, and then later exited, leaving me as a single parent desperately trying to hold the fort.

Except the fort had collapsed.

Chapter Twenty

Rick had moved into my Greenwich apartment in a whirl of black sacks and cardboard boxes.

As the sheer volume of *stuff* had piled up in the hallway, then overflowed into the spare bedroom, I'd looked on in bemusement. How many clothes, jackets, coats, boots, trainers, and shoes could one man possibly own? And whatever was in all those heavy boxes?

Tentatively, I'd peered inside one of the cartons. It had been full of tools. Power drills. Umpteen screwdrivers. Assorted plugs. You name it. Not forgetting reels and reels of electrical cable.

'Can't these stay in the van?' I'd asked, staring at the clutter.

'No way,' he'd replied. 'A workman never leaves his tools in his vehicle. That's asking for trouble. If this lot got stolen it would cost a fortune to replace.'

Wasn't that the point of insurance? I'd tried again.

'I've seen vans with special reinforced locks. What about doing something like that?'

'Not a chance. Now then, where am I going to put my clothes?' He'd looked about vaguely. 'They're not all going to fit in the master bedroom's wardrobe. I'll have to buy a temporary rail and some of those stacker-drawers. It can all go in the spare room.'

'You can't put your belongings in there,' I'd protested.

'Why ever not?'

'Because it's going to be our baby's nursery.'

His reply had been immediate.

'Don't be silly, Lots. We can't carry on living here. There's not enough space. We'll have to move.'

'Move?' I'd repeated stupidly.

'Yes,' he'd smiled. 'Buy a house. You don't want to raise our kid in a flat, do you?'

I'd stared at him uncomprehendingly.

'I don't see why not. It's a lovely flat.'

'It's a rabbit hutch. Trendy enough, I grant you. But this place is totally unsuitable for a child. He or she will need space. A place to run around and let off steam.'

'There's a huge space just a stone's throw away,' I'd pointed out. 'You won't find any house with a garden as big as Greenwich Park.'

'Not the same,' he'd said, pursing his lips. 'Anyway, I need a place with a garage. For my tools. I can't keep lugging them up and down the stairs to this apartment.'

'There's a lift,' I'd pointed out.

Rick had screwed up his face. A *don't-be-daft* expression.

'Nope, I can't go backwards and forwards in a lift either. It will take an hour to load up the van. Then I'd have to repeat it all over again at the end of the day. Anyway, what about my Porsche?' Rick's chin had jutted.

'What about it?' I'd frowned.

'This flat only has one allotted parking space. Right now, my van is in it. There's nowhere to park the Porsche. I've had to leave it at my mum and dad's place. They weren't too happy about it either. So, sorry, Lots. We're moving. We need to sell this place and buy a house.'

We'd not exactly gone to bed on a row, but the initial joy of having Rick under my roof had… well, let's just say that if my excitement had been a balloon, it hadn't exactly popped, but it had definitely deflated.

However, when contemplating any lifechanging decision, there is a saying. *Sleep on it.* And that was what I did. When I'd awoken the following morning, I'd been greeted by a gorgeous man who'd thoughtfully made me tea and toast. And I'd come round to his way of thinking.

Rick was right. We did need more space. I was disappointed about the spare room never becoming a nursery. You see, in my mind, I'd already decorated it. Beatrix Potter wallpaper. A wardrobe full of sleepsuits in one corner. A crib – with a Flopsy Bunny and Peter Rabbit quilt – in the other. However, as I'd munched on my toast, I'd told myself that I could still have that pretty nursery. It just wouldn't be in Greenwich.

I'd quickly learnt that Rick was a man who, once his mind was made up, acted upon it. That morning, before kissing me good-bye, he'd told me to check my WhatsApp.

'I was awake before you,' he'd chirped. 'I spent a happy

half hour online looking at houses in Erith.'

'Erith?' I'd said, aghast.

I'd had nothing against the place, but not wanted to live there.

'What's wrong with Erith?' he'd said, suddenly on the defensive.

'Nothing, I suppose,' I'd shrugged. 'But it's not a great place for me to commute from. My job is in London.'

'Erith does have a train station,' Rick had pointed out. 'You're carrying on like the place is in the back of beyond. Anyway, don't you want to give up work when our baby is born?'

At the time, I'd not thought that far ahead. The situation had been so new. Everything had been happening at warp speed. At that point, I'd not even told work about my pregnancy, never mind discussed maternity leave, or thought about childcare.

'Can we afford for me to give up work?' I'd asked cautiously.

'Well, I think so. We'll get loads of money for our flat. If we buy a house in Erith, we'll have a stack of change in our bank account. Anyway, if you want to go back to work, that's fine with me. However, there will be no splashing out on those fancy daycare places. It won't be required. Not when Mum is just around the corner. She can look after our baby without us having to dip in our pockets.'

I'd looked at Rick, but kept my mouth shut. Mainly on account of not being able to speak. His little speech had set a whole spectrum of emotions at play. I was struggling not just to absorb his words, but also to *innerstand* how those words were making me feel.

our flat …

our bank account…

The Greenwich apartment wasn't *ours*. It was mine. Any spare cash in the bank wasn't *ours*. It was *my* money. Wasn't it?

Well, yes, at that point it *had* been my money. But then I'd reasoned that if we were going to have a life together… get married… buy a house together… then one could say that, by definition, everything would eventually become *ours*.

My mind had wandered to marriage vows. I'd tried to remember the last wedding I'd attended. It had been a church gig. I'd then recalled the bride's words:

With this ring, I thee wed, with my body I thee worship, and with all my worldly goods I thee endow…

I realised that Rick's possessions would therefore become mine too, and mine would also become Rick's. Right.

The idea had made me slightly uncomfortable, but then I'd reasoned that this was what marriage was all about. Sharing. And who better to share it with than the father of my unborn child?

Chapter Twenty-One

That weekend, we'd visited Erith. The sky had been grey, and the town had matched its drabness.

Like Greenwich, Erith lay on the banks of the River Thames. The name dated from Saxon times meaning *muddy harbour* or *gravelly landing place*. Although, from what I'd glimpsed that day, mud had seemed to be the more accurate description.

Due to the presence of the docks, Erith had presented itself as predominantly industrial. There had been many wharfs. Several gasworks. Lots of railway bridges. Narrow streets were everywhere. All had been lined with nondescript terraced houses.

As we'd driven down one such road, litter had decorated the pavements and gutters. A pack of suburban foxes had ransacked several dustbins. Every now and again little gusts of wind had sent empty drink tins rolling along the pavement. Newspaper, previously used to wrap battered cod from the local chippy, had also been blown by the same wind. Printed sheets of *The Sun* had been lifted into the air, and a grease-stained picture of a *Page 3 girl* had ended up on someone's doorstep.

Back then, major regeneration of the area had yet to

take place. That said, there had been small glimpses of the change to come. The bit we'd visited had been tacked on to the back of Dartford and had included a new development only a stone's throw from Dartford Station. The station, at the time, had been having an update.

'See,' Rick had said triumphantly. He'd been driving through some temporary traffic lights, taking the van on to a new road layout. 'This place *is* civilised. You can easily commute to London from here.'

We'd rounded a corner, dipped under a railway arch, crossed a roundabout, and then turned into a new road. At its entrance, a vast hoarding had been emblazoned with the words *New Homes*.

A local builder had bought a plot of wasteland. He'd not lost a moment in transforming it into a cul-de-sac. Several half-built properties had been dotted about. There had been a handful of detached houses, a few semis, and half a dozen terraced starter homes.

The showhouse – a detached – had been finished and was *dressed* for viewing. It had been very attractive. Pretty curtains had hung at the windows. Outside the front door, several pots of flowers had been in full bloom. This mini explosion of colour in an otherwise grey town had lifted my spirits.

Once inside the showhouse, I'd further warmed to it. The kitchen had been smart with plenty of cupboard space. There had been three reasonably sized bedrooms, although the fourth had been little more than a box room. In my mind, I'd seen it as a playroom for our child. Unlike the Greenwich apartment, there was no waterside outlook. The view from the kitchen had been of a busy road. A bus had rumbled past, and I'd wondered if one would ever get used to the endless noise of traffic.

In the lounge, French doors had issued into a small garden. So much for a child being able to let off steam. Still, it had been big enough to permit a paddling pool in summer and a sandpit in autumn.

Rick had been keen to pay the holding deposit there and then.

'We want one of the detached houses,' he'd informed the sales assistant. Rick had been full of self-importance. 'I absolutely *have* to have a double garage.'

The saleswoman had suggested Plot 10. Located at the far end of the cul-de-sac, it had been the furthest from the main road with its traffic noise. The lady had gone on to tell us when it would be ready for completion.

'That works well for us,' Rick had said. 'My partner is pregnant,' he'd added.

'Congratulations,' she'd beamed. 'You'll be able to move in and immediately get nesting.'

'Yes,' I'd agreed, finally feeling a flutter of excitement. Instinctively, my hand had covered my belly area with its tiny swelling.

'Let's seal the deal, Lots,' Rick had suggested.

So, we'd sat down at the saleswoman's desk. Together, we'd filled in the paperwork. As we'd each signed our names at the bottom of the form, I'd felt a flicker of apprehension, but then dismissed it.

The saleswoman had then glanced expectantly at Rick. He'd turned to me and given the same look.

'Get your chequebook out, Lots.'

'O-Oh. Aren't we splitting the deposit?'

'I'll let you sort it out, darlin',' he'd chirped.

I'd not wanted to embarrass him in front of the saleswoman but, once back in the van, I'd touched his arm before he'd started the engine.

'What?' he'd asked, snapping his seatbelt together.

'Er, the deposit.'

'What about it?'

'Well, I've just written out a cheque for one hundred pounds. However, when the conveyancing gets underway, there will come a point where we will be required to pay ten per cent.'

'And?'

'Will you be taking care of that?'

'Me?' Rick had looked startled. 'I don't have that sort of money.'

'But... a little while ago you mentioned you'd been saving up. You will be contributing, won't you?'

'Oh, *that* money,' he'd said, sucking on his teeth. 'That money has been set aside.'

'Really?' I'd frowned. 'Whatever for?'

'For our wedding, of course,' he'd grinned. 'And a nice engagement ring. You want something sparkly on that left hand, don't you?'

Fair point. Weddings and diamond rings weren't cheap.

'Come on.' He'd rubbed his hands together. A gesture of excitement. 'Let's go and celebrate with a cup of tea at Mum and Dad's. They're dying to meet you. Plus, I can't wait to see the look on their faces when I tell them we're moving to Number 10 Sandpiper Close. Their reaction is going to be epic.'

It certainly was a moment to remember, but not in the way I'd anticipated.

Chapter Twenty-Two

My parents had passed away at a time when they should have had decades left to live. They'd been deprived of meeting their grandchild, of having a happy retirement, and of going on to embrace their golden years. Their absence was keenly felt.

Having lost both parents just months apart, I was ready to welcome Rick's mum and dad not just into my life, but also into my heart.

Rick had driven into a road rammed with cars. He'd parked the van outside a scruffy house and directly behind an ancient car without wheels. The vehicle had been jacked up on bricks. It had taken me a moment to realise that this was the Porsche he'd talked about.

He'd caught my look of incredulity and had had the grace to look sheepish.

'I've decided to scrap it.'

'I think that might be a good idea,' I'd replied carefully.

As Rick had pressed the doorbell to the home of Doreen and Neville Lucas, I'd had a sense of anticipation. Optimism. Who better to fill the yawning hole my parents had left behind, than the future grandparents of my unborn child?

As we'd waited, it had started to rain. We'd huddled

into our coats. Eventually, Rick had pushed the doorbell for a second time. From within, someone had shouted.

'Someone answer that feckin' door.' This from a female.

'I'm in the bleedin' bog,' had come a man's indignant reply.

'Well, I ain't movin' me backside. I'm watchin' telly, an' it's got to a good bit.'

I'd given Rick a dubious look. He'd shrugged his shoulders.

'Heads up,' he'd said. 'Best to get used to this. They're always bickering.'

We'd waited a bit longer, steadily getting soaked. Eventually a downstairs loo had been energetically flushed.

Moments later, the front door had opened to reveal a man in braced trousers and a string vest. In his hands he'd held a newspaper. An ominous smell had drifted through the open doorway.

I'd been taken aback. Rick had mentioned his father being a hit with the ladies. A bit of a naughty boy, he'd said. I'd had a sudden vision of this man chatting up a woman at the local pub.

Him: *You've 'ad two pints off me, darlin'. Am I yer dreamboat yet?*

Her: *Gimme a third an' then I'll 'ave me beer goggles on.*

Neville Lucas had glared first at me, then Rick.

'What'd'ya want?' he'd demanded.

'Dad,' Rick had smiled. 'I want you to meet Lottie.

We're getting married.'

If Neville had been surprised to hear this, he hadn't shown it. Instead, his expression had changed to one of resignation. He'd shaken his head as he'd looked me up and down.

'I suppose yer up the duff, eh?'

I'd been too stunned to reply.

'Thought so,' Neville had tutted. 'This feckin' family.' He'd raised his eyes to the ceiling before blowing out his cheeks. 'Yer brother has just told us that Shannon is expectin'. That said, Kev's made it quite clear he don't wanna know.'

'I'm not Kevin,' Rick had muttered.

'Yer not that different,' Neville had snorted, before turning to me. 'I suppose I'd better pretend I'm delighted to meet yer.'

He'd folded up his newspaper and stuck out one unwashed hand. Reluctantly, I'd shaken it.

'I'm Charlotte,' I'd said. 'But everyone calls me Lottie.'

'You should be renamed *Potty*.'

'Pardon?'

'Well you must be potty wanting to marry this waste of space.' Neville had jerked his head at Rick.

'Leave it, Dad, eh,' Rick had mumbled.

'Well… obviously… I mean' – I'd twittered, searching for the right words – 'we're madly in love. Our baby, although unexpected, will be a huge joy. We're over the moon about becoming parents,' I'd gabbled.

'Really?' Neville had looked scornful. 'Rick wasn't so over the moon the last time it 'appened. What was 'er name? Oh, yeah. Karen. That was only three months ago.' Neville had then leant in. Peered intently at me. 'Hmm. Karen was more of a looker than you.'

'I beg your pardon?' I'd spluttered.

Evidently this man had never got to grips with the definition of *tact*. For a split second I'd been tempted to walk away from Neville Lucas, his string vest, his unsavoury attitude, and the hideous stink in the hallway.

'Take no notice.' Rick had grabbed my hand. Squeezed it hard. 'Karen was a one-night stand, and she looks like a total dog. Anyway, she was before I met you.'

'Good to know,' I'd said, teeth clenched. 'And what about the baby you're expecting with her?'

'There isn't one. She did the necessary.'

'I see.'

In that moment, an awful lot of thoughts had tumbled through my head. What of this Karen woman? Did she live in Erith? Was I likely to bump into her? She might have been a one-night stand, but she'd ended up pregnant. As I had with Rick. The similarities hadn't been lost on me. I'd also wondered why he'd stuck with me but walked away from her. Especially as Neville had thought Karen a glamour puss, and me nothing more than a Plain Jane.

'She meant nothing.' Rick had interrupted my thoughts. 'And I meant nothing to her. That's why we went our separate ways.'

'Right,' I'd said, nonetheless reeling.

'Look, Dad. Can we come in? It's pouring with rain, we're wet through, and this isn't a conversation to have on the doorstep.'

As if on cue, Rick's mother had shouted from the lounge.

'Shut that bleedin' door. It's bringin' a right draft in 'ere.'

'It's our Rick,' Neville had shouted back.

'If yer after money, I ain't got none. Yer took what I 'ad to pay yer rent and get that landlord of yours of yer back.'

'Don't be silly,' Rick had said, turning a bit pink.

As we'd finally stepped into the hallway, a woman had appeared.

'Who's this?' she'd asked, narrowing her eyes suspiciously.

'Mum, I want you to meet my fiancée. This is Lottie.'

'Oh fer feck's sake,' she'd said, rolling her eyes. 'Are yer pregnant?'

I'd had enough.

'How very nice to meet you,' I'd said sweetly. My voice had dripped with sarcasm. It hadn't gone unnoticed.

'Don't yer get hoity-toity with me, love,' Doreen had snapped. 'Yer might 'ave a posh accent, but that don't mean yer better than us.'

I'd stared at Doreen, wondering what the heck was wrong with this family. My parents wouldn't have carried on like her and Neville. Whatever reservations they might have had about me rushing into marriage with Rick, they would never have been so rude and unwelcoming. And to think Rick had suggested his mother being willing to look after our baby.

'Please, can we just stop and take a breath,' Rick had implored. He'd then turned to me. 'This is my kith and kin, Lottie. They say it how it is.' From upstairs, a door had creaked back on its hinges. Rick had paid the sound no attention as he'd attempted to lighten the atmosphere. 'If I shook my family tree' – he'd given me a deprecating shrug – 'a bunch of nuts would fall out.'

At that moment, a young man had appeared at the top of the staircase.

'I disagree,' the lad had grinned as he came down the stairs. 'This family is more like a cactus. Full of pr–'

'Shut yer gob, Kev,' Doreen had interrupted. 'Make yerself useful. Put the kettle on.'

'Pleased to meet you,' Kevin had said, initially ignoring his mother. He'd given me a hug. 'Welcome to Erith's most dysfunctional family.' He'd given me a cheeky grin. 'And now I'd better make you that cup of tea before my mother gives me a clip round the ear.'

We'd all followed Kevin into the kitchen. As he'd stuck the kettle under the tap, I'd come to a decision. After the birth, I'd be a stay-at-home mum. Hell would freeze over before Rick's mother ever had charge of my baby.

Chapter Twenty-Three

After *Bird Gate*, I spent the remainder of Sunday keeping a low-profile. I stayed indoors. I was all set to do the same on Monday, until realising I'd run out of both bread and milk.

Rather than stock up on a few groceries locally, I travelled into West Malling. This meant I could avoid certain nosy villagers who might stare and whisper behind their hands.

Mabel Plaistow had been exceptionally busy spreading a variety of rumours. I discovered this when I bumped into a previous Little Waterlow resident by the name of Sadie Farrell. We'd both been in Tesco, on West Malling's high street.

Sadie had once lived at nearby Clover Cottage. I'd met her a few times previously when out walking with Jen. At the time, Sadie had been exercising her dogs. One of them, William Beagle, was a bit of a character.

Sadie now gave me a mischievous grin.

'Hello, Lottie. I hear you ran into a spot of bother with a seagull.'

'Oh, no,' I said warily. 'What have you heard?'

'That you were picnicking in a field when a seagull snatched your sausage sandwich, and you went bonkers.'

I rolled my eyes.

'That isn't true.'

'I thought not.' She nudged me. 'Otherwise, it would have been a *tern* for the *wurst*.' She nudged me as she giggled.

'Very droll. I was simply minding my own business–'

'That's something nobody does in Little Waterlow,' she snorted.

'You can say that again. Anyway, this seagull crapped on my foot and, well, I might have let loose with a few expletives.'

'So you didn't wrap your picnic blanket around you like a superhero's cape, then leap into the sky, and wrestle the gull to the ground? Mabel said there were feathers everywhere.'

'Not this time,' I said, suddenly seeing the funny side.

'Good to know,' she grinned. 'How's the writing going?'

'Very well,' I said, nonetheless relieved at the change of subject. 'I might put Mabel Plaistow in one of my books.' My mouth twitched. 'Now there's an idea. I could have her stalked by a serial killer. Shake her up a bit. Rattle her dentures. Then I'll have my character – that's DI Draper – arrest Mabel. The charge will be for spreading false rumours and perverting the course of justice.'

'Revenge is sweet,' Sadie agreed.

Once home, I put away the shopping, then went to the study and fired up the laptop. There weren't many more chapters to write and currently I had no distractions. Jen was spending the week finishing a flurry of commissions. Ryan had his head down working late at the office while he cleared his desk. I might as well do the same. It would be good to finish my third work-in-progress before heading off to Cornwall.

I settled down and got stuck in. By midnight I was bleary-eyed but satisfied things were coming to a twisty, exciting conclusion. I'd created three possible outcomes. However, I'd yet to decide which one to conclude with. It was important to surprise the reader.

By late Thursday afternoon, Book Three had been wrapped up and emailed off to my editor.

Heaving a sigh of relief, I'd enjoyed a hot soak in the bath before packing my case for Cornwall. As an afterthought, I'd chucked my *other* phone into the suitcase. I'd then fished it out again and instead zipped it, out of sight, within an internal flap by the lining.

I couldn't bring myself to leave the phone behind at Catkin Cottage. My paranoia wouldn't let me. I'd already had a nightmare about a burglar breaking in and stealing the phone. The thought had made me go hot and cold. A crook could blackmail me forever over the content within.

Meanwhile, Ryan had since texted saying he wanted to be on the road by eight o'clock the following morning.

That night, as I slid under the bedcovers, Audrey jumped up to join me. Her paws paddled the duvet as she purred with happiness.

'I'm going away for a long weekend,' I told her. 'Our neighbour will feed you. Be a good girl. Don't bring home any relations belonging to Micky Mouse. The cat flap is for you and you alone – not rodents, be they dead or alive.'

'Meow,' Audrey agreed, as I rubbed her head.

'I'll be back before you know it, and I'll tell you all about Cornwall. Who knows, maybe Ryan and I will fall in love with the place. Perhaps he'll say, "Lottie, we simply *must* move here." Don't worry' – I added – 'you'll be coming too, darling. I'd never leave you.' Audrey extended her neck, allowing me to gently scratch the area under her chin. 'Moving to Cornwall might be rather nice,' I mused. 'Heather would no longer be able to boss Ryan around. There would be no more charging off to do her bidding. Mind you, I'm not sure Ryan would want to move so far from Joshua. But then again, Joshua isn't a kiddie. He's perfectly able to get on a train and travel to Truro, or wherever we might end up.'

For a moment I brooded over the dynamics of it all. But I didn't ponder for long. Audrey had now curled herself into a tight ball and flicked a fluffy tail over her face. Moments later, sleep had claimed me too.

Chapter Twenty-Four

'What do you mean, you've been delayed?' I said into the phone.

It was ten past eight on Friday morning. Jen, Stu, and I were sitting in the lounge of Catkin Cottage. Three suitcases were taking up much of the floor space.

'Sweetheart, it can't be helped,' Ryan cajoled. 'Joshua isn't well, and Heather is panicking. His temperature is sky-high. She's currently bundling him into my car. I've been instructed to take him to A&E.'

'Okay,' I nodded. This wasn't good. Not good at all. 'So, you'll drop Heather and Joshua at the hospital and then come over Catkin Cottage in, what, about an hour?'

'No, Lottie. Heather is scared that it might be' – he lowered his voice – 'meningitis.'

'What?' I squawked, my voice rising an octave.

Jen and Stu flinched. They were trying to read my body language as I talked to Ryan. They gave each other a snatched worried look.

'What are his symptoms?' I asked.

Years ago, one of Sally's classmates had come down with meningitis. The lad in question had spent almost two weeks in hospital. His symptoms had started with a blinding headache swiftly followed by a purple rash. It had been a worrying situation, but thankfully he'd made a full recovery.

'Joshua says he feels hot and bothered. Lottie, I can't take any chances. I'm going to have to go with Heather.'

'Of course,' I said, trying to ignore the sinking feeling in my stomach. After all, it was the right thing to do. One's child came first. End of. 'Shall I ring the hotel and cancel the booking?'

Jen inhaled sharply while Stu looked aghast.

'No, don't do that,' said Ryan. 'Look, I have a suggestion. Tell Stu to drive you and Jen to Cornwall. I'll join you all later. Meanwhile, let me get Joshua to hospital. I anticipate a six hour wait but reckon, by mid-afternoon, he'll have been seen and diagnosed. If it isn't anything serious, I'll drive down immediately afterwards. I might not get to you until midnight, but we'll still have three days together. How does that sound?'

I swallowed down the disappointment but quickly rallied. If the boot were on the other foot, I'd do the same. If Sally needed urgent medical attention, there was no way I'd leave her. It was just Sod's Law that these things happened when you were *soooo* looking forward to something.

'What's going on?' Jen whispered.

'Two ticks,' I mouthed, before talking to Ryan again. 'Okay, that sounds like a good idea.'

'That's my girl,' said Ryan. 'I'd better go. Heather's calling me.'

'Keep me post–'

But he'd already hung up.

'Are we going or not?' said Jen. She sounded extremely put out.

'We're going, but without Ryan. For the moment,' I hastily added.

Jen rolled her eyes.

'It's that wife of his again, isn't it? Heather Bloody-Nuisance. I'll bet my last five pence that she's deliberately trying to sabotage things.'

'Jen, *please*,' I implored. 'It's their son.'

'Okay, so its Bloody-Nuisance Junior disrupting our weekend.' She folded her arms across her chest. 'I don't know how you put up with it, Lottie. I really don't. It's–'

'Joshua is ill,' I interrupted, before she could launch into a full scale rant.

'How ill?'

'Enough for both parents to be concerned it's meningitis.'

Jen shut up, although her mouth remained pursed like Audrey's backside. However, she couldn't stay quiet for long.

'So, let me get this straight,' she said. 'Stu and I are going to Cornwall for a romantic weekend, and you're coming along without Ryan. Isn't that called *third wheeling*?'

'I wouldn't dream of doing that,' I cried.

'But you will be,' she said. Jen was never backward in coming forward.

'D-Darling,' Stu stuttered. 'I don't mind Lottie coming with us.'

'Well, I flipping do,' said Jen. 'No offence, Lots. But what's it going to look like when Stu and I sit down for a candlelit dinner? I will want to hold Stu's his hand across the table but won't feel able to do that if you're on your tod.'

'I'm not going to stop you holding hands,' I said, rolling my eyes. 'And anyway, it's only for this evening.'

'Oh?'

'Ryan said he'll drive down later. He won't arrive until around midnight, but he *is* coming.'

'Ah. Well, that puts a different complexion on it,' Jen conceded.

'And don't worry about your candlelit dinner for two,' I said. 'I'll have my meal in my room.'

'There's no need for that,' said Jen. She could afford to be magnanimous now she knew I wasn't playing gooseberry for the entire weekend. She got to her feet. 'Right, come on. Let's get going. Stu, you put the cases in the car.'

While the two of them went outside with the suitcases, I did a final check around Catkin Cottage. I dropped a kiss on Audrey's furry head, then left the spare key with my neighbour.

When I got into the back of Stu's car, I found my bag on the seat beside me.

'Sorry, Lots, but Stu's car isn't as big as Ryan's. There was no room in the boot for a third case.'

'It's fine,' I said, squeezing my rather ample bottom into

the small space.

I really should go on a diet. Months of being immersed in murder with DI Denise Draper had seen me skipping proper meals and stifling hunger pangs with too many chocolate biscuits.

'We're off,' said Stu, putting the car into gear.

'Cornwall here we come,' grinned Jen.

'Yayyy,' I added, attempting to muster up some cheer.

I quietly told myself that all would be well. Joshua would make a miraculous recovery. Heather would be reassured. Ryan would be with me later. And then, finally, *finally* the pair of us would snuggle down together under the duvet. Naked.

Bring it on.

Chapter Twenty-Five

The car journey took nearly eight hours. This included one stop for refuelling. Three for caffeine top-ups. One for a cardboard sandwich. And three emergency wees. Two for Jen and one for me.

Stu drove like someone who'd only recently passed their test. As soon as the speedometer edged past fifty, he broke out in a muck sweat. The car stayed firmly in the inside lane throughout the entirety of the journey.

The radio played throughout. Stu and Jen sang along to old pop songs. Periodically, they duetted to slushy lyrics. The pair of them had looked directly into each other's eyes over the handbrake, which had been somewhat unnerving. Consequently, a part of me had been relieved at Stu's lack of speed, especially when they'd reached the crescendo of *Total Eclipse of the Heart.* Occasionally the car had drifted. At one point, an HGV had made everyone jump by blaring its horn. It hadn't helped that the car had slowed to twenty-five miles per hour on the A30. This while Stu had warbled that every now and then he fell apart.

Ignoring their racket, I'd sent several texts to Ryan, each time hoping for an update on Joshua. However, my messages had gone unanswered. I'd told myself that mobiles were usually switched off in hospitals, and that Ryan would be in touch when there was any news.

Sighing, I'd zoned out from Jen and Stu's caterwauling. Instead, I'd outlined a fourth novel for my editor to put forward to the submissions team.

DI Denise Draper was having her work cut out. An unknown killer had strangled the male singer of a famous rock band. An unsigned note had been left on the corpse's chest. It had been addressed to the dead musician's wife with a two-word warning: *You're Next.*

It was no coincidence that my characters bore a striking resemblance to my bestie and her boyfriend.

When we finally rocked up at Penwern Lodge, a bank of purple-black clouds were chugging ominously across the sky. Despite it being not quite four o'clock in the afternoon, the November light was dramatically fading. The air held a strange stillness. One that signalled calm before a storm.

The car's wheels crunched over gravel as we headed towards the hotel's private carpark. I craned my neck to properly see Penwern Lodge and glimpsed a stone building with gabled windows and a Rapunzel-style turret. How lovely. I wondered if Ryan and I might soon be sleeping in a bedroom at the top of that tower. Isolated. Away from the world – and Heather and Joshua. I instantly felt guilty at such a thought. It wasn't right to feel that way. Not when a teenager was poorly and in hospital.

Meanwhile, we were here. Cornwall at last! Okay, Ryan wasn't with me. But it wouldn't be long before he was.

Maybe he'd do something exciting upon arrival. Like… instruct Room Service to deliver a bottle of their finest champagne. Then he'd raise his glass and declare, "To us, Lottie. Now get your clothes off." I'd certainly drink to that.

'Oh, it's so good to be out of the car,' said Jen. She stretched her arms high above her head as Stu unloaded their cases from the boot.

I dragged my suitcase off the rear backseat, then straightened up. Unkinking the knots in my shoulders, I yawned widely. There was something exhausting about sitting in a confined space for hours on end.

'Tired?' asked Stu, giving me a sympathetic smile.

'A little,' I acknowledged. 'I shouldn't be. Not when it was you who did all the driving.' Even if it had been at a snail's pace.

'I feel as fresh as a daisy,' Stu assured. 'Jen's singing did wonders for me.'

Jen smirked.

'I propose we unpack and have forty winks before getting ready for dinner,' she said. 'And if you're feeling so skippy' – she gave Stu a playful tap on the nose – 'you can do something else for me too.' She winked lasciviously at him.

Stu flushed with pleasure and promptly tripped over his suitcase. He only narrowly avoided face-planting down on the gravel.

Once inside the hotel, a receptionist greeted us warmly.

'Welcome to Penwern Lodge,' she smiled. 'Let's get you

all checked in.'

As she busied herself at the computer, I discreetly glanced about.

The reception area was tucked to one side of a large square inner hallway. It was almost a room in itself.

Ahead was a vast inglenook hearth. It contained a lit woodburning stove. Logs crackled and popped away, occasionally discharging bright orange embers. The sound was both cosy and comforting.

In front of the hearth was a large occasional table. Squashy chairs and sofas, including a statement wingback, were grouped around it. To the left of this was a grand sweeping staircase to take patrons to the upper floor. To the right, an ancient grandfather clock steadily ticked away, adding to the relaxed ambience.

Despite the day getting off on the wrong foot, I could feel myself starting to unwind.

'Okay,' said the receptionist, handing Jen a key. There was a metal tag imprinted with lettering. *Room 2.* 'You're on the first floor.'

'Fabulous,' said Jen, pocketing the key. 'Come on, Stu. Pick up those cases. See you in a bit, Lottie.'

I stepped up to the desk to collect the key to my room. However, the receptionist gave me a quizzical look.

'Was there something else?'

My smile faltered.

'Um, yes. I'd also like to check in.'

The receptionist frowned.

'You have. I've just given your friend the key.'

'Sorry?'

Jen, about to go up the staircase, stopped in her tracks. She swung round, just as the receptionist repeated herself, more slowly, as if I might be hard of hearing.

'Your. Friend. Has. The. Key.'

I blinked.

'I. Want. One. Too.'

The receptionist raised her eyebrows.

'Madam, I'm very sorry, but we only hand out one key per room.'

'But I'm in my own room,' I countered.

Now it was the receptionist's turn to blink.

'I don't think so. I have four guests booked into the family suite.'

Jen's nostrils flared as she marched back to the desk.

'The family suite?' she repeated, aghast.

'That's right,' the receptionist nodded. 'Two double beds in one room.'

'That can't be right.' I shook my head. 'My boyfriend booked two double rooms.'

'Not according to our computer system,' said the receptionist.

'But… but… we can't all stay in one room,' I spluttered. 'This is a romantic break.'

My expression said it all: *There will be shenanigans. And no. We won't be doing it in front of each other.*

'Where is the gentleman who made the booking?' asked

the receptionist.

'Otherwise detained,' I said. 'Ryan will be along later tonight.'

'Well, as Mr Dickens is the lead name, and the one who made the reservation, it will be Mr Dickens who has had confirmation of the same. I suggest you get in touch with him.'

'Right now, he's unavailable,' said Jen irritably.

'Look, there's obviously been a mistake,' I said. 'Can we not simply rectify it? I'm sure my friends will be happy to take the family suite, but Ryan and I would like a double room.'

'I'm afraid that's not possible,' said the receptionist.

'Why ever not?'

'Because' – she gave me a harassed look – 'we're fully booked.'

Chapter Twenty-Six

I stared at the receptionist in horror.

'So you're basically saying that the four of us are meant to sleep together?'

That hadn't come out quite the way I'd meant.

'Ms Lucas.' She gave me a frank look. It said: *I'm-not-the-nincompoop-who-booked-a-family-room*. 'I can only repeat my suggestion. Telephone Mr Dickens. Ask him to forward the details of his emailed booking confirmation. You will then see that the error is his, not ours. Bookings are taken online to avoid any mistakes on our part.'

My shoulders drooped in defeat.

'It's fine,' I said wearily.

'No, it is *not* fine,' hissed Jen. She gave me a furious look. 'You'll have to find somewhere else to sleep, Lottie. I'm not being denied my romantic break.'

'I don't mind sharing,' Stu quavered. The receptionist's mouth twitched. Stu instantly turned the colour of a Royal Mail letterbox. 'I-I mean' – he stuttered, looking mortified – 'the bedroom. Not me. O-Obviously.'

Jen's eyes widened, and her mouth dropped open.

'For God's sake, Stu,' she hissed. 'Shut up or else people will get the wrong idea about you.'

As if on cue, we all stared at Stu. A vision in an anorak.

'Look,' I said, attempting to break the tension. 'Jen, you and Stu go on up to the room. Meanwhile, I'll try and raise Ryan. Get him to sort things out.'

'Yes, you do that,' Jen snapped.

Stu picked up their suitcases. Head bowed, he followed Jen up the staircase.

I turned back to the receptionist.

'Can you tell me when you will next have availability?'

'Of course.' She turned to the computer and tapped a few keys. 'You're in luck. Room 3 are checking out on Sunday morning.'

'But that's forty-eight hours away,' I gasped.

'Sorry,' she shrugged. 'That's the best I can offer.'

'Right,' I nodded. 'I guess there's no choice but to take a taxi and check in elsewhere.'

'You'll be lucky,' she said ominously.

I sighed. What now?

'Every November' – she continued – 'this part of Cornwall hosts a two-day annual rock festival. All hotels within a thirty-mile radius – and that includes B&Bs – will be fully booked. That's why I can't offer you anything until Sunday morning.'

'Okay, in which case I'll have to find something in a *forty*-mile radius.'

'You could,' she said doubtfully. 'Did you bring your own transport, or travel with your friends?'

Oh help. I could hardly ask Stu to drive me another

forty miles. Or even further. An eighty-mile-plus round trip would have Jen hyperventilating with fury.

'I travelled with my friends, but it's not a problem. I'll order a taxi.'

'Ah. The thing is, when the festival is on, the drivers get booked up in advance. You might have more joy securing a taxi in the morning.'

Oh for…

What a day this was turning into. Resisting the urge to bury my head in my hands, I instead raised my eyes to the ceiling, as if trying to contact God.

Can you hear me, Father? I'm starting to get a bit frustrated with Ryan. I mean, why can't I have a reliable boyfriend? Okay, he can't be here because his son isn't well. But how on earth did he manage to end up booking a family room? However, it's not just this situation. It's everything really. Like money. Yes, especially money. I'm not yet earning from my books. So, I have *another* source of income. I'm sure you don't approve. Fair enough because I don't approve either. Anyway, going back to Ryan. There is always an issue. I mean, he constantly puts his family first. And whilst that's a noble thing to do, it does leave me questioning if he will *ever*, just for once, turn to Heather or Joshua and say, "Sorry. I can't repaint the lounge/plumb the new washing machine/go to the dump/chase a wasp out the window. I'm spending the weekend with Lottie."

But God had nothing to say on the matter.

The receptionist gave a little cough. Behind her, a staff

room door opened. A man came out, holding his mobile in one hand. He paused to check its screen. The receptionist coughed again.

'So' – she prompted – 'shall I register you for check in on Sunday morning?'

'Um…'

I didn't know what to do.

As I dithered, the man put away his phone and looked my way. He had hazel-green eyes, dark hair, and skin that looked like it tanned no matter what the season. It was a striking combination. Enough to make me do a sharp intake of breath. As those mesmerising eyes held mine, I experienced a weird sensation. It was as if he'd peered right into my soul. Flustered, I looked away. Concentrated on the receptionist. I opened my mouth to speak.

'I think–'

But I got no further. My phone let out a piercing *dinggg*. A text. My heart flooded with hope. Ryan? Frantically, I scrabbled in my handbag. Yes! He'd messaged. Oh, thank God. Ryan would soon sort out this mess. But, as I read his text, any hope withered and died.

Hi, Lottie. Sorry to be so late with the update. Joshua still hasn't been seen by a doctor. The good news is that we are now fifteenth in the queue. However, I won't be down tonight, darling. Apologies. Hope you are having fun with Jen and Stu. Sending lots of love xxx

No, no, no!

I immediately tried telephoning. But Ryan had switched

141

off his phone. Instead, I was directed to voicemail and invited to leave a message.

'Er, hello,' I said into the handset. 'I hope Joshua is seen soon. You must be exhausted. The thing is… there's been a reservation error at the hotel. We're all booked into a family room and, um, Jen isn't best pleased. Currently she's refusing to let me sleep with her and Stu. I suppose it's understandable. They've both paid for a romantic break. They don't want me lousing it up. Anyway, um, the thing is… er, *the thing is…* the hotel is fully booked until Sunday morning. Also, there's some annual gig going on. A music festival. Everywhere is booked up – for miles apparently.' My voice cracked for a moment. 'So, um, right now, I'm a bit stuffed. Can you ring me. Urgently. Please.'

I ended the call. Blinked away some tears of frustration.

What a shambles.

Chapter Twenty-Seven

One tear refused to stay within the confines of my eye socket. It ran down my cheek. It was swiftly followed by another. And then another. Oh *help*.

'Are you okay?' asked the receptionist, as my lip wobbled perilously.

'Of course she's not okay,' said the stranger behind her. In a flash, the man had moved around the side of the desk. 'Come with me,' he instructed.

Oh no. Not sympathy. I couldn't bear it. That would make the whole situation so much worse. It would be far better if he could berate me for having an absent boyfriend who'd cocked up the hotel booking. That way, I'd get a handle on these blasted tears.

'You've clearly had a taxing day,' he said gently. I was now being guided over to a sofa by the fire. 'Sit down.' He turned back to the receptionist. 'Pru, get a brandy, please. Actually, make it two.'

The stranger flopped down next to me, inexplicably sending my heartrate soaring. I was horribly aware of his proximity and could feel the heat of his thigh – which was barely a millimetre from mine.

'Why don't you tell me all about it?' he said kindly.

It was too much. The dam burst. Everything that had recently gone wrong tumbled out in a garbled heap of words.

'I've lost control of my life,' I wailed. 'DI Draper has yet to pay me any money but I bought a pair of pink shoes anyway and it attracted Mr Muppet and then Mabel Plaistow caught me in a field and now everyone thinks I have a thing about seagulls and then Ryan said he'd take me to Cornwall but Jen and Stu came too and then Joshua and Heather stopped Ryan from coming and now Jen is mad because she wants sex with Stu and' – I took a great big shuddering breath – 'I CAN'T COPE ANYMORE!'

I nosedived into my lap decorating my denims with tears and snot. Oh, to hell with it. Was it such a big deal to make a spectacle of myself? One hundred years from now, it wouldn't matter, so why should I care in this moment?

Everyone, roll up, roll up! Watch Lottie Lucas make a prize prat of herself. Again. Whether in a farmer's field in Little Waterlow or a hotel in Cornwall, Lottie will never let you down in the entertainment stakes.

I was aware of the receptionist suddenly standing in front of us. Despite the tears stuffing up my nose, I caught a whiff of brandy.

'Drink,' said the man, coaxing me upright. He pressed a glass balloon into my hands just as Pru hastened back to reception to answer a ringing phone.

'Th-Thank you,' I stammered, chest still heaving.

'You're very welcome,' said the man softly. 'Cheers.' He

tapped his glass lightly against mine before taking a sip. 'One way or another, we've both had a stressful day. Mine started with the discovery that my cat had passed away in the night.'

'Oooh nooo,' I wailed, staring at him in horror.

Was it my imagination or did those hazel-green eyes suddenly look very bright? Hastily, I took a swig of my own brandy while he composed himself.

'Coco was nearly twenty-one years old,' he said eventually. 'It was time for her to go. Even so, selfishly I'd hoped she'd be around a little longer.'

'I'm s-sorry you've had such an upsetting day,' I said, swiping one hand across my eyes. The brandy was hitting its spot and I was feeling a little calmer.

'Oh, it didn't stop there.' He gave a mirthless chuckle. 'A little while later, my best mate rang. Eddie was in a terrible state. His wife had upped and left. Walked out on him.'

'How awful,' I said, while rummaging up one sleeve in search of a tissue.

'Bummer,' the man agreed. He swallowed down some more brandy. 'And you know what they say… that rubbish stuff comes in threes. The third thing was arriving at work only to discover that Alice, my receptionist, had cleared off without giving notice.'

'Your receptionist?' I frowned, just as my fingers located the tissue.

'Yup. I'm the owner of Penwern Lodge. Pru – the lady on reception – is my sister. She lives in one of the cottages on the estate with her husband. Between them, they look after the grounds, along with one or two other people. Pru is an outdoor girl and was none too pleased at having to stand in on reception after Alice unexpectedly left.'

'O-Oh dear,' I said, putting the tissue to my nose and making a sound like a baby elephant. 'So why did Alice leave without any warning?'

'Ah. Well, this is where things get interesting. It transpires Alice has run off with my mate's wife.'

'No!' I said, my bloodshot eyes widening.

'Indeed. It then fell to Yours Truly to break the news to my pal. Needless to say, he took it badly. Even worse, because I employed Alice, somehow, I feel responsible for the breakup of Eddie's marriage.'

'Well, you're not responsible,' I said firmly. 'It's nothing to do with you. It's simply an appalling coincidence.'

'You're right,' the man sighed, then drained his glass. He leant forward and set it down on the occasional table in front of us. Then he turned to me. 'My name is Fin Trewarren, by the way.'

'Charlotte,' I said, suddenly feeling shy. 'But everyone calls me Lottie.'

'That's a pretty name,' Fin smiled. 'Well, Lottie.' He took my empty glass and set it down next to his. 'Now it's your turn. Why don't you tell me again – this time slowly – about your disastrous day.'

Chapter Twenty-Eight

Fin listened to my revised, more sensible version of events. In this second version, I omitted any mention of Mr Muppet, Mabel Plaistow, and seagulls. Fin then surprised me with an unexpected proposal.

'Look,' he said. 'You're clearly in a bit of a pickle. Your partner is making sure his son is okay, and who knows when he will get here. Meanwhile, your friend is asserting herself because she wants her romantic break. Fair enough. She might well change her mind later and let you share the room–'

'Ha!' I interrupted, rolling my eyes. 'You don't know Jen.'

'Indeed. So, I have a suggestion. You're welcome to use the spare room in my flat, until a room is available at the hotel.'

'Your flat?' I repeated.

'Yes, I have an apartment here. At the hotel,' Fin explained. 'You might have noticed a turret to one side of the entrance, before coming into reception.'

'I did,' I nodded. 'I thought how gorgeous it was. It's like something out of a fairytale.'

Fin laughed, and the transformation was astonishing.

Those hazel-green eyes, previously tired and dull, suddenly lit up. His smile revealed teeth that wouldn't have looked out of place in a toothpaste ad.

I found myself wondering how old he was. At a guess, I'd have put him at around forty. Younger than me anyway. Not that I was interested. I had Ryan after all. Although, right now, that was debateable, thanks to his absence.

'I had the tower converted when' – Fin hesitated for a moment – 'I unexpectedly found myself experiencing a change of personal circumstances.'

My curiosity was instantly piqued, and I wondered what event he was referring to. Divorce? Possibly. My eyes flicked to his left hand. No wedding ring. Mind you, some men didn't like wearing jewellery. That said, if there *was* a Mrs Trewarren, he'd yet to mention her. Plus, I'd have thought he'd have cleared it with the wife before offering me the spare room.

'The turret has three levels,' Fin continued. 'The entrance opens into a kitchen-cum-lounge with cloakroom. The first floor contains the master bedroom, and the second level is a spare room for guests. Although, so far, it's only ever been used by my parents when they visit.'

'Do they live far away?' I asked.

'They retired to Devon. It's only a couple of hours away. However, these days Dad isn't keen on driving any distance. So, once a month, my parents spend a long weekend here in order to see me and Pru. However, right now the room is yours. If you want it, of course.'

'I don't want to impose,' I said, chewing my lip.

'You're not.'

'Well, if you're absolutely sure.'

'I am.'

'In that case, thank you. That's incredibly kind of you.'

'Think nothing of it. You're a damsel in distress, so a turret room is probably quite fitting,' he laughed. I found myself grinning back.

I wondered what Ryan would say about me sharing personal space with another man. Fin was a stranger, after all. And a very good-looking one, too. Might Ryan not approve? But, then again, he currently shared space with his ex-wife, so he was hardly in a position to moan – especially as he was the one who'd fluffed up the booking in the first place.

'Come on,' said Fin, standing up. 'Let's fetch your suitcase. You can have the spare key, so you can come and go as you please.'

I stood up too and followed him back to the reception area. Pru looked up from some paperwork and smiled.

'Feeling better?' she asked sympathetically.

'Much, thank you,' I said.

Fin walked around to the other side of the desk. He gave Pru's shoulder a squeeze.

'Leave that. I'll deal with it tomorrow. Meanwhile, Lottie is going to stay in my guest room until we have availability on Sunday morning.'

'That's a good idea,' said Pru, putting the paperwork to

149

one side.

'Um, there's just one thing,' I said nervously. 'My boyfriend might manage to get here tomorrow – so potentially there could be two of us in your guestroom.'

'That couldn't matter less,' Fin assured.

'Let me go and make up the spare bed for you,' said Pru.

'Oh, I can do that,' I protested.

'Nonsense,' she said firmly. 'Anyway, my work here is done for today.' She looked at her wristwatch. 'I'll route the switchboard through to your mobile, Fin.' She retrieved a plastic sign from under the reception desk and set it on the countertop. It displayed a phone number alongside a polite request for guests to call the number in the event of reception being unmanned. 'Mr and Mrs Fairweather have yet to arrive and check-in,' Pru added.

'Okay,' he said. 'Meanwhile, let's get Lottie settled.'

Pulling up the handle on my suitcase, I wheeled along behind Pru and Fin. The three of us took a short walk along a side corridor. This led to another passageway where the entrance to Fin's apartment was located.

He unlocked the door and disappeared within. As I stepped over the threshold, I let out an involuntary cry of delight.

'Oh *wow*. What a gorgeous place you have,' I sighed, looking around.

'Thanks,' said Fin. 'I refurbished the place myself. Well, with the help of a plasterer, electrician, and a plumber,' he chuckled. 'But you know what I mean.'

'My brother has an eye when it comes to interior design,' said Pru. 'He's very artistic and has great taste.'

Ah. Was she trying to tell me something? Everyone knew that gay men were awesome at transforming ordinary homes into showhouses. Did Fin swing that way? Had he busted up with a lover causing the *unexpected change of personal circumstances* that he'd mentioned earlier?

As he walked around the beautiful living area, I watched him with fresh eyes. There was a distinct lack of wiggle to those hips. Nor did he hold one hand aloft, as if an invisible handbag were dangling off his fingers. But then again, not all gay men were camp. Perhaps I could discreetly ask a nosy question.

'You've done an amazing job,' I complimented.

The ground floor reminded me of a Kent oast house. It was basically one huge round room. At the far end was a contemporary kitchen. Reclaimed polished floorboards covered the entire space. In the living area these boards were semi-covered by a brightly coloured rug, upon which the three of us were standing.

Just like the hotel's reception room, there were squashy sofas either side of an occasional table set in front of a woodburning stove. A flatscreen television adorned one wall, while abstract artwork made a vibrant statement on the other.

'Are you the artist?' I said, nodding at the canvasses.

'I am. It's how I destress.'

'They're very good.'

'Thanks.'

'And, er, does Mrs Trewarren share your hobby?'

Okay. A bit crass. And possibly a bit obvious. But at least the question was now out. However, it went unanswered due to Fin's mobile suddenly ringing. One glance at the screen had him making towards the front door.

'Sorry, Lottie. Looks like my late arrivals are waiting in reception. I'll let Pru settle you in. Dinner, by the way, is in the main dining room from six o'clock.'

And he was gone.

'Let me show you the guestroom,' said Pru cheerfully. 'Are you ready to deal with the stairs to the top floor? There's quite a few more than a standard staircase.'

'Yup,' I said, picking up my weekender.

I wondered if I could glean any information from Pru about her handsome brother, and why he lived – apparently all alone – in a beautiful turret tower.

Chapter Twenty-Nine

Fin's spare room was a delight to my inner child.

Dumping my case on the floor, I rushed over to a tall – almost floor to ceiling – window and stared, enthralled, at the view far below.

Despite the fading light, I could see, to the right and beyond a line of hedgerows, the carpark. There was Stu's faithful old bone-rattler. It was currently languishing between a snazzy Land Rover and a brand-new BMW.

To the left were rolling fields, many dotted with sheep. I could also see an area of woodland. Beyond this was a handful of estate cottages, and then, further still, one could glimpse a grey looking sea.

The previously dark purple clouds, so ominous upon arrival, were now gunmetal grey. As I stared at them, they chose that moment to empty their load. For a few seconds, the rain was torrential. There was a rumble of thunder followed by a flicker of lightning. In the distance, the ocean turned silver.

'Do you like what you see?' asked Pru, as she reversed out of a cupboard bearing an armful of linen.

'This view is stunning,' I declared, turning away from the window. 'I now know exactly how Rapunzel felt in her tower.'

Pru laughed.

'Except you're not a prisoner like Rapunzel. Which reminds me.' She dug in one pocket. 'Here's the spare key to this place.' She set the key down on the bedside table.

'Thank you,' I said.

'Come and go as you please. There's no need to rely on Fin.'

She picked up a flat sheet and shook it out.

'Here, let me help you,' I said.

'Absolutely not,' said Pru. She shooed me away with one hand. 'Tell me about your boyfriend's son. You mentioned the lad wasn't very well. Nothing serious, I hope.'

I sighed and sat down on a little stool by the dressing table.

'Joshua has suspected meningitis.'

'How awful.' Pru grimaced as she set to work making up the bed. She tucked and folded corners with swift expertise. 'Let's hope he makes a full recovery.'

'Yes,' I agreed. 'Children are always such a worry when they're unwell.'

'Indeed. I can remember when my Megan was a little girl. She had to have her appendix out. I hardly slept a wink until she'd had the op.' Pru began posting a feather duvet into a voluminous floral cover. 'So how many children do you have, Lottie?'

'Just the one. Sally is currently at university.'

'Ah,' Pru chuckled. 'That brings a different kind of worry.' She shook the quilt vigorously, then began snapping together popper-fastenings. 'I'm sure she's a sensible girl – like her mum,' she smiled, before picking up a pillowslip.

For a moment, I couldn't speak. Me, sensible? I hoped to goodness that Sally never turned out like me. One failed marriage. Currently earning money in a most dubious fashion.

'What do you do for a living?' Pru asked, as if reading my thoughts.

'I'm a writer,' I quickly answered.

'Good heavens,' said Pru, shoving a pillow into its case. 'Should I have heard of you?'

'No, but I hope one day you will. I recently signed a three-book deal with a new digital publisher. However, publication day is still a little way ahead.'

'How exciting!' She picked up a second pillowslip. 'I wish you every success. Just think, one day I'll be able to tell all my friends that I've met the famous Lottie Lucas. Fin will be most impressed to hear he has an author staying with him.'

Ah, yes, Fin. The man who'd dashed off before answering my nosy question.

'And, um, what might Fin's wife say? Hopefully, she will be impressed too,' I grinned, trying – and no doubt failing – to pull off an air of nonchalance.

A shadow passed over Pru's face.

'Fin's a widower.'

'Oh,' I gasped, the air whooshing out of me. How did one reply to *that*. 'I-I'm so sorry,' I stuttered, feeling horribly awkward. 'Was it… I mean… what happened?'

'Leah had a riding accident.' Pru paused in her pillow bashing. 'She'd worked with horses practically all her life – born in the saddle, as they say. Certainly, she was an accomplished rider. She used to back and break horses, then bring them on. She had a reputation for being one of the best trainers in the area. However, it all went very wrong when she took a three-year-old out on the road. Fin was with her at the time. He saw what happened.'

'Oh God,' I muttered.

'A discarded plastic bag had found its way into a hedgerow. The handle had caught on twigs. It was whipping about in the wind, making lots of scrunchy noises. It unnerved Leah's horse. It shied. Bolted. Tried to jump a five-bar gate. Then, at the last minute, it had second thoughts and jammed its brakes on. Leah, however, was unseated. She went straight over the gate – minus the horse – and broke her neck on landing. She died instantly.'

My hand flew up to my mouth.

'That's shocking.'

'It happened a couple of years ago. Fin went to pieces at the time. Mentally, he's in a better place now. Life goes on, etcetera etcetera. However, when such tragedies happen – especially to someone in their prime – it serves to remind how fragile life can be. Leah was only forty-one. She was here one minute and gone the next.' Pru clicked her fingers by way of demonstration. 'The suddenness left everyone reeling.'

'Has Fin managed to… move on?' I asked hesitantly. 'As in, you know, met anyone else?'

Pru finished arranging the pillows and straightened up.

'Oh, he's met several someone elses,' she chuckled. 'My brother is an attractive man. The ladies love him. His current flame is a stunningly beautiful but fiery redhead. She's an ex-model. He met Marina at Penwern Lodge's summer ball. We hold events here.' She waved a hand by way of explanation.

'That's nice,' I smiled. 'I mean, it's nice to hear that you hold special events and, er, nice that Fin has met a lady who might be another special someone.'

I flushed, aware that I was fishing. Wanting to know if the luscious Marina might be a permanent fixture. Although I had no idea why Fin's personal life should be of such interest to me. After all, I'd known him for all of five minutes.

Pru made a harrumphing noise.

'My brother could do a lot better than Marina. She's extremely high maintenance.'

'O-Oh really?' I said ultra-casually. 'In what way?'

Pru rolled her eyes.

'Super needy for starters,' she said. 'And then there's her diet. That's something else. She exists solely on edamame beans and cottage cheese. If you offered her a roast potato she'd likely go to pieces. Marina is the sort of woman who'd dial 999 for a broken fingernail.'

I giggled and Pru flushed guiltily.

'Sorry. I shouldn't say such things. That wasn't very kind of me. I don't usually gossip about people. Somehow, Marina brings out the worst in me.'

'It's fine,' I assured. Music to my ears in fact. Now why should that be?

'Fin said he was trying to extricate himself from her,' Pru confided. 'However, the woman is still around. I suspect she's like superglue. Hard to shift. Anyway, it's not my place to say anything. What my brother really needs–'

'Yes?' I said breathlessly.

I was aware that I was suddenly behaving like an eager student hanging on to Teacher's every word.

'What Fin *really* needs' – Pru repeated – 'is someone who's solid. Dependable. Supportive.' She picked up a decorative throw and placed it over the end of the bed. 'What about you?'

'Me?' I startled. For a moment I thought she was asking if I was solid, dependable, and supportive. 'Oh, er, I'm divorced,' I explained. 'And currently seeing a guy who' – my shoulders drooped – 'well, even though I know Ryan's son is unwell, the truth is that most of the time I feel like I'm dating a married man.'

'Are you sure your chap *isn't* married?' Pru raised an eyebrow.

'Ryan is definitely divorced, but… it's a strange set-up.'

'In what way?'

'He's still living in the marital home.'

'That would be a no from me.'

'It was nearly a no from me too,' I sighed. 'However, he always has a plausible explanation for everything. He's very persuasive.'

'Married men usually are,' she said knowingly. 'I speak from experience – although it was a long time ago,' she added. She adjusted the position of the throw and then smoothed a crease with one hand. She gave me a frank look. 'It seems to me that you could do with someone solid and dependable too.'

Was it my imagination, or was she dropping a hint?

Chapter Thirty

'I have to say, Lottie' – Jen aggressively shoved a potato in her mouth – 'I'm starting to go off Ryan.'

The vibes over the dinner table weren't the best. Stu was suddenly very engrossed in a slice of beef and had his head firmly down. His body language spoke volumes. *Jen's rant is nothing to do with me.*

The three of us were seated in the hotel's cosy restaurant. Our table was, mercifully, tucked away in a corner. This afforded us some privacy from other diners overhearing the conversation.

'Booking a family room was a mistake that anyone could have made,' I said calmly.

'Only if they couldn't read,' said Jen sourly.

'Look, all's well that ends well,' I said, adopting a pacifying tone. 'You and Stu have the room to yourselves, and I'm in Fin's apartment.'

Jen speared a piece of meat with her fork, then stabbed the utensil in my direction. Her eyes flashed.

'And you call this a situation that's ended well?'

'Of course,' I said.

'I'm afraid I don't agree.' The fork was now waggling about mid-air and being used to emphasise the point Jen was determined to make. 'You came here to have a romantic break too. However, your other half is nowhere to be seen. That is *not* a case of all's well that ends well.'

'There are mitigating circumstances. Joshua is ill.'

'I'd probably be more gracious about Joshua if this wasn't yet another example of Ryan letting you down. He drops everything for his ex-wife and son, Lottie. From Joshua having a meltdown over his studies and needing good old Dad to prop him up, to Heather urgently requiring a fuse for the plug to her heated hair rollers. The excuses just go on and on.'

'They're not excuses,' I said, on the defensive, even though I knew Jen was right.

'Well it seems that way,' she persisted. 'When is Ryan arriving in Cornwall?'

'As soon as he can.'

'That doesn't answer my question. I asked when. Tomorrow? The day after? Or the day after that? In which case, he'll arrive just in time to check out.'

'Jen, *please*,' I implored.

She caved in.

'Oh, why should I care?' She shrugged her shoulders and finally popped the loaded fork into her mouth. For a moment she said nothing. Then, 'It's not me having a rotten time.'

'I'm not having a rotten time,' I protested. 'I'm looking forward to us all going for a long walk tomorrow and exploring–'

'No, Lottie,' Jen interrupted. Her knife plunged into a Yorkshire pudding. 'The rambles, coffee stops, walks on windswept beaches, and candlelit dinners were only ever going to happen when there were four of us. Now we're down to three. It puts a different slant on things.'

'Does it?'

'Yes! You'll be playing gooseberry.'

'Oh.'

Stu was now hacking away at his dinner. Soon he'd dig straight through that porcelain plate and end up in Australia. But, given Jen's current mood, perhaps putting distance between me and her was what he secretly wanted.

'It's not fair on us, Lottie,' Jen implored. She gave me a beseeching look, then softened her tone. 'Don't you see?'

'Well, now that you've so kindly pointed it out to me, yes, of course I see. But if the situation had been reversed, I wouldn't have objected to you tagging along with me and Ryan.'

'But that's the difference between you and me,' she said gently. 'I wouldn't have presumed.'

Right. Well, thank goodness she'd put me straight on a few things. If my skin had had plumage, my feathers wouldn't now be so much as ruffled, as well and truly plucked and littered across the floor. A horrible thought suddenly occurred to me. I went cold.

'So… I take it you're not too chuffed about me sitting here having dinner with the pair of you this evening?'

Stu hastily shovelled so much food in his mouth, there

wasn't a chance of him commenting for the next five minutes.

Jen gave me a sympathetic look.

'I'm not that much of a cow, Lottie,' she said.

'Good to know,' I said lightly.

'Now you're offended.'

'Look, Jen. You're right. Ryan – for whatever reasons – has spoilt the weekend. I appreciate you want to salvage it as best you can. I won't get in your way. There's plenty to keep me occupied. I have no issue about doing things by myself. In fact, it will be quite nice. It will give me some much-needed headspace to do some serious thinking about everything going on in my life.'

'I agree,' said Jen. 'And top of your list should be whether to continue this so-called relationship with Ryan.'

That thought had already occurred to me.

Chapter Thirty-One

I couldn't wait to leave Jen and Stu to continue their evening together – alone.

Declining coffee with them, I stood up and, yawning ostentatiously, said I'd see them later. Whenever *later* might be.

Letting myself into Fin's apartment, I was surprised to see the man himself sprawled out on the sofa. Remote in one hand. Bottle of lager in the other. By the look of it, he was scrolling through Netflix looking for a movie to watch.

'Oh, sorry,' I apologised. I shut the door behind me. 'I didn't mean to interrupt your evening.'

'You're not,' he assured. 'I haven't found anything to watch yet.'

'Well, I won't disturb you.' After Jen's rather searing pep talk, I'd had enough of being a nuisance to other people. 'I'm going up.'

'So soon?'

'Yes, it's getting late.'

'Really?' He checked his wristwatch. 'It's two minutes past seven. Is that way past your bedtime?' The hazel-green eyes twinkled with amusement.

I opened my mouth to say something, but nothing came

out.

'What's up?' he asked, his brow furrowing. Then he rolled his eyes, as if the dawn had come up. 'Forgive me,' he groaned. 'That was such a stupid question. You've had a rubbish day, so it's hardly surprising that you want to hibernate under the duvet.'

'It's not that…' I trailed off.

'Oh Lord.' Fin inhaled sharply. 'You've not had bad news about your partner's son, have you?'

I shook my head.

'No,' I said sadly. 'I haven't heard anything further.'

'Well, you know what they say.' He gave me an encouraging smile. 'No news is good news.'

'Quite.'

'So what else is bothering you?'

'Nothing,' I shrugged.

'In woman-speak, that means *everything*,' he smiled wryly. 'You know, I haven't grown up with a sister without learning a thing or two about you girlies.'

I gave him the ghost of a smile. Being only a couple of birthdays away from the Big Five-Oh, the *girly* reference was faintly amusing.

Fin patted the sofa.

'Sit and offload.'

I flopped down on the couch, making sure I sat at the far end. I'd been all too aware of his body heat earlier, when I'd sat next to him in reception. His proximity had made me feel a bit peculiar. Was that the right word? No, not really.

More… perturbed? No, not that word either. What was the feeling I was trying to describe? Unsettled. Yes. That was it. Unnerved – and in a secretly thrilling way.

'But first' – Fin put down the remote swiftly followed by the lager – 'can I get you a drink?' He got to his feet and headed towards the kitchen area. 'A coffee? Tea? Or I can whizz up a steaming hot chocolate on this rather stormy evening. Or would you prefer a glass of wine?'

'The hot chocolate sounds very tempting.'

Just like you.

Oh God. Where had that thought come from?

'One hot chocolate coming up,' he grinned. 'Can I also tempt you with a biscuit or three?'

You can tempt me with anything you like.

'Yes, please,' I gasped, desperate to block my inner voice. It was making a most unexpected nuisance of itself.

'And when you've finished unburdening your woes' – Fin continued – 'you're welcome to watch a movie with me. The remote is on the table. I was going to watch something uplifting. I felt a need to enjoy something with the feelgood factor.' Of course. Fin had had his own sadness this morning. He'd lost Coco. His darling cat. 'Have a scroll. Pick whatever you fancy.'

I fancy you.

Noooo. This could not be happening.

'Um, okay,' I said, picking up the remote. 'That might be rather nice.'

'Sachet all right?' he asked. He raised his arm and

waggled a packet of instant powder.

'Perfect,' I smiled. 'You're my sort of guy.'

Really, Lottie?

'I mean' – I flushed – 'you're like me. Not impartial to taking short cuts.'

'Anything for an easy life,' Fin agreed as he stuck the kettle under the tap. 'I'm all for that.'

For a moment neither of us said anything. He busied himself looking for biscuits, and I scrolled through the movie options. I heard the water eventually reach boiling point, and a switch clicked. The off button. Fin now had his back to me. As he reached for the kettle, I glanced away from the television and discreetly admired him. He had such gorgeous dark hair – and plenty of it. And I liked the way his torso tapered, like an upside-down A. It showcased the broad shoulders and narrow hips. Alarmingly, I found myself wondering what he looked like naked.

'Have you found anything worth watching?' he called.

You.

'Erm, not yet.'

He turned and caught me staring at his bum. Hastily, I looked away. Concentrated hard on the television screen.

'Here you are,' he said, setting everything down. He'd placed my drink and the plate of biscuits alongside his lager. Hell. Now I'd have to wiggle along the sofa to reach them, which would mean sitting closer to him. Reluctantly, I shuffled a few inches along, then made a cartoon long-arm and grabbed the hot chocolate.

'So,' he grinned, settling down beside me. The mesmerising hazel-green eyes snagged on mine. For a moment, I had trouble breathing. 'Tell your Uncle Fin all about it.'

Chapter Thirty-Two

There is something very therapeutic in talking to a total stranger about all the things that have gone wrong in your life – both past and present.

Fin and I didn't watch a movie together. Instead, I hoovered up both the hot chocolate and biscuits in a matter of minutes, and then he went to a cabinet and removed a bottle of something plus two glasses.

Oh, hello, brandy. We meet again.

'I know it's not yet half past seven' – he plonked the bottle and balloons on the coffee table – 'but as you said you wanted an early night, have a nightcap before you go up.'

'Thanks,' I said. 'I don't usually like the stuff. However, the one I had earlier was strangely pleasant.'

'I'm not trying to lead you astray. It's not good to use alcohol as an emotional prop – but once in a while it helps,' he twinkled.

'Agreed,' I laughed. I slipped off my shoes and tucked my feet under my bottom.

Aren't you being a little over-familiar making yourself at home on this man's sofa?

'God, sorry,' I apologised, instantly removing my legs from the upholstery. 'Force of habit. Thought I was back in my cottage for a second.'

'Don't be silly,' said Fin. 'For now, my home is your home.' He poured some brandy into the first glass. There was a satisfying glug–glug as the liquid left the bottle. 'In fact, I insist you put your legs back where they were.' He passed me the glass. 'Make yourself at home.'

'No, sorry. I really can't.' I was now squirming with embarrassment from the faux-pas.

'Up to you,' Fin shrugged. He set about pouring himself a measure. 'But excuse me if I do.' He kicked off his shoes, then swung his feet on to the coffee table. 'Ah, that's better.' He wiggled his toes. 'Sorry if you catch a whiff of ripe socks.'

'Couldn't matter less,' I assured, taking a sip of brandy. On autopilot, my feet once again tucked themselves under my bottom. 'Oh,' I said, turning red.

Fin laughed.

'I'm glad you're now following my lead. So' – he crossed one ankle over the other – 'you mentioned that you live in a cottage. Tell me about it, Lottie.'

'Catkin Cottage? It's chocolate-box pretty, but sadly not mine. I rent it. That said, I wouldn't mind buying the place one day – *if* I ever have the means, and *if* the owner decides to sell. The owner is currently living in Italy with her new man.' My lip suddenly curled. 'Naturally he's the love of her life.'

'Oooh, words so cynically delivered,' Fin teased. 'You sound like a woman who has yet to find true love.'

For a moment I didn't reply and instead stared at the liquid within my glass.

'Maybe,' I said quietly. 'I'm forty-eight years old, Fin. Old enough–'

'You don't look it,' he interrupted. 'I thought you were in your late thirties.'

'You're very kind,' I said, not really believing his words. 'The point I'm making is that I'm old enough to have accrued some wisdom. However, all I've done with my life so far is monumentally fluff up.'

'Says who?'

'Me.'

And suddenly the verbal floodgates opened. I found myself unburdening about my absent boyfriend. The helpless ex-wife. The needy son. My vocal bestie. Her wishy-washy boyfriend. Even my blasted ex-husband.

If Fin was horrified by my outpouring, he didn't let on. Instead, he listened. Occasionally he refreshed our glasses. Eventually, I burbled myself to a standstill.

'Well,' he said, recrossing his ankles. 'Personally, I think you've turned around some serious life challenges. And in a most creative way. After all, Pru tells me you're on the threshold of fame and fortune. Three novels are about to be unleashed upon the world.'

'Ha!' I snorted. 'Do you know how many writers there are in my profession?'

'A few,' he acknowledged.

'The competition is horrendous. The publisher will be

monitoring the data. The ratings. The ranking. If my DI Draper flops, then I'll be back to…'

I trailed off and cradled my balloon.

'Back to what?' asked Fin gently.

'Looking at other ways of making a living,' I answered, not quite managing to meet his eye.

Chapter Thirty-Three

I'd like to say that my marriage to Rick was memorable. That he presented himself in a morning suit. That I wore a beautiful long white dress. That the air whirled with confetti. That a professional photographer captured the moment. Except none of that was the case.

Doreen and Neville, my future in-laws, had harped on endlessly about weddings being a waste of money. They'd been singularly unimpressed with the news about our brand-new detached house. Doreen had even gone so far as to tell me I was a bad influence on her son. She'd said that I had too many *airs and graces*.

The pair of them had also threatened to boycott the wedding unless it took place at their local registry office. They'd also been vocal about where the wedding breakfast should be held. Neville had made it clear that he would not eat in any restaurant with a *pretentious* menu.

I'd initially hoped that Rick and I would get married at a spa hotel. Goldhill Grange had provided a *small and intimate* package. This had been tailored for the bride and groom with a modest number of guests. It had included a five-course wedding breakfast in their gorgeous orangery restaurant. The orangery had overlooked the hotel's stunning manicured grounds complete with lake and swans!

However, Doreen had heaped disdain upon the idea.

'We're not posh people.' She'd wrinkled her nose. 'I'm not up for goin' to some swanky place full of upstarts who think they're better than the likes of me and Nev.'

I'd privately wondered how Rick and I were going to coax Neville out of his favoured attire. I wasn't a snob but had drawn the line at Neville turning up in his favoured braces over a string vest. Was it such an issue, for one day, to wear a smart pair of trousers with a shirt and tie? When I'd assured Doreen that Rick and I would meet the costs of a suit for Neville plus something elegant for her, she'd let out a squawk of horror.

'Who do yer think I am?' she'd glowered. 'The bleedin' queen? If yer want to fit in with this family, Lottie, yer need to get off yer high horse.'

Chastened, I'd backed down. Rick – very much in his mother's thrall – had said it was the right thing to do, echoing that weddings were a waste of money.

'But' – I'd rounded on him – 'at the time of me paying the deposit on our house, you'd said you'd take care of the wedding and my engagement ring.' I'd stared down at the sparkler on my third finger. A cubic zirconia from Argos. Naturally, Doreen had approved. 'So why can't we at least have a decent wedding, Rick?'

'It's not worth upsetting Mum,' he'd soothed. 'And anyway, never mind the wedding for a minute. After we're married, I have a fantastic surprise for you. I've been extravagant, and you're going to love it!'

I'd been mystified.

'Can't you tell me what it is now?' I'd asked.

'Nope. You're just going to have to be patient and wait.' He'd looked so delighted with himself that I'd found myself getting excited again. 'I haven't told a soul,' Rick had added. 'Not even Mum and Dad. I don't want a bucket of cold water poured over my plans.'

I was all for that, after *my* plans being a washout.

We were married at Dartford Registry Office. Rick wore a suit. I – still trying to gain Doreen's approval – wore a three-quarter length cream dress. Neville arrived in a tracksuit. Doreen was attired in a floral pinny-dress. She could have passed for Alf Garnett's wife. Kevin turned up in jeans and a white polo accessorised with a black eye. He'd received a pasting, the previous evening, from his pregnant ex-girlfriend's father.

'Sorry, Lottie,' Kevin had shrugged. 'Shannon's dad has been itching to deck me. He finally got his wish.'

In that moment I'd been glad about foregoing a photographer. Indeed, there had been only one photograph to mark the special day. It had been taken by the registrar. A snap of Rick and I, heads together, showing off our new rings. Yes, they'd been from Argos too.

Afterwards, the newly married Mr and Mrs Lucas had headed off with Doreen, Neville and Kevin to a pie and mash shop on the high street.

I'd often wondered if my parents had looked down from

Heaven that day. Watched my wedding from the sidelines. Raised their eyebrows.

Mum and Dad hadn't been snobs. Nor had they been posh. Far from it. As far as I was concerned, they'd been ordinary folks. Down to earth. Hard working. Polite. They wouldn't have dreamt of putting Rick down the way Doreen did me. Nor would they have bullied with barbed comments, or non-stop criticisms. They wouldn't have chipped away at another person's self-confidence. Nor made that person repeatedly apologise – whether over a preference for *Coronation Street* instead of *EastEnders*, or a traditional Christmas dinner instead of fish and chips out of newspaper.

In Doreen's eyes, I was hoity-toity. A madam. Someone who had grand ideas above her station.

As time went by, I ended up knowing my place with her and behaved accordingly. I turned into a quiet little mouse who dared not speak lest she offend.

Chapter Thirty-Four

Rick's secret surprise turned out to be a honeymoon.

'Wow,' I'd said, trying to sound excited. 'The Bahamas. Amazing.'

'What do you think?' he'd beamed.

'Well,' I'd said, playing for time. 'When is it?'

'Not for another couple of months. They didn't have availability until then. Also, the travel agent said something about waiting until after the hurricane season had passed.'

'Right,' I'd nodded.

By that point, my pregnancy bump would have been very visible. Also, I hadn't felt entirely comfortable about showing my belly by the pool in a bikini, not to mention dealing with a nine-hour flight.

'You don't seem very enthusiastic,' Rick had said, his smile fading.

'Oh, I am, I am,' I'd said hastily. 'But' – I'd reached for a handy excuse – 'whatever will your parents say?'

'We won't tell them,' he'd declared.

'Don't be daft,' I'd laughed. 'After all, we'll be coming home with a tan.'

'I mean it, Lots.' Rick had been adamant. 'We'll tell them we went to Bognor for a fortnight and made use of a local salon's sunbeds.'

He'd been deadly serious.

'Right,' I'd said, blowing out my cheeks.

'After all' – Rick had pointed out – 'if Mum found out, we'd never hear the end of it.'

'Well, quite,' I'd agreed. 'And, er, how much *did* the honeymoon cost?'

'Five grand.'

'Five thousand pounds?' I'd squeaked.

In my book, that had been a hideous amount of money to blow on a jaunt to the Caribbean. For a moment, I'd found myself having a *touch of the Doreens.* I'd have much preferred it if Rick had paid for a week in Spain with the rest of the money going on a lovely engagement ring. I'd then immediately felt shallow for wanting a diamond instead of an enormous cubic zirconia.

'This is a once-in-a-lifetime trip, babe,' Rick had pointed out. 'Let's enjoy ourselves. Why have money if you can't spend it?'

Rick had made it sound as though we were millionaires.

Our new house had cost considerably less than the selling price of the apartment in Greenwich. Consequently, there was a nice little nest egg sitting in my bank account. Yes, *my* account. I'd been twitchy about putting the money into a joint account.

Initially Rick had moaned about not having direct access. He'd pointed out that what was mine was his, and vice versa. However, some inner instinct had told me not to put all my eggs in one basket.

In fact, there'd been a bit of a row about it. However, I'd been adamant. The money had been set aside for any emergencies. Also, for our baby's future. Like… if he or she one day wanted to go to university.

Rick had rolled his eyes. He'd said I should learn to live for today and let tomorrow look after itself. To my relief, he'd eventually dropped the subject. I'd also been relieved that he'd paid for the honeymoon out of his own pocket, thus leaving the nest egg untouched.

'I've always wanted to go to the Bahamas,' he'd happily prattled on. 'Apparently, the Lucayan National Park has one of the largest underwater cave systems in the world. It will be incredible to explore.'

I'd felt claustrophobic just thinking about it.

'They've also got this huge Aquaventure attraction at Atlantic Paradise Island,' he'd added. 'There are loads of high-speed water slides.'

'Sounds fun,' I'd said carefully. 'However, I'm not so sure it's a good idea for a pregnant woman.'

'That's okay, babe,' he'd assured. 'You sunbathe on the amazing pink sand beaches. I don't mind going off and doing that on my own.'

'Sure,' I'd said, forcing a smile.

It was no good being negative about the trip. The deed had been done. Rick had booked it. Paid the money. And if Neville and Doreen didn't find out, then actually, why not try and enjoy it? I might not have been able to leap the waves on a jet ski, or drink something boozy at the *Daq Shack*, but while Rick explored ecological treasures and had an adrenalin rush down waterslides, I'd have a massage on Cabbage Beach or order some fried conch in Nassau.

As Rick had said, it was a once-in-a-lifetime trip – even if he had been horribly extravagant. We'd not be going to flashy places once the baby had arrived. The following year it might well be Bognor Regis.

'Happy?' he'd asked, peering at me anxiously.

'Of course,' I'd said, and flung my arms around him.

In that moment I'd told myself not to be a killjoy. To embrace the break. That, one way or another, it would be a honeymoon to remember.

And it was. However, as I later discovered, there are some memories one does not wish to keep.

Chapter Thirty-Five

Doreen and Neville pursed their lips while telling us to have a good time in Bognor. We politely said thank you, then set off to Heathrow.

The Bahamas was beautiful. However, as I've already said, there are some memories that are best forgotten. As a result, mine are now a little fuzzy around the edges.

I do remember perching self-consciously on a sunbed. Alone. I was wearing my newly purchased maternity swimsuit. Rick had befriended an American woman with a deep tan and huge breast implants. Her name was Kay. Rick and she were inseparable.

My husband arranged several excursions. A waterpark. A visit to underwater caves. A speedboat trip. Paragliding. Water skiing. None of these activities were suitable for a pregnant woman. I'd stayed on my sunbed, reading. Occasionally I'd taken a dip in the pool. I'd been aware that Kay had booked the same excursions as Rick.

I'd told myself not to be jealous. After all, what could they possibly get up to in public? However, the evenings were different. Rick and I would have dinner together. Afterwards, he'd make his excuses. Go into town. Visit a casino.

'It's no place for a lady,' he'd said, when I'd asked if I could go to.

'I see,' I'd said lightly. 'Is it a place for whores?'

He'd looked startled, then laughed.

'What are you inferring? I'm going with some of the guys I met earlier at the bar.'

'What bar?' I'd frowned.

'The swim-up bar at the pool,' he'd said with exaggerated patience. 'What is this, Lottie? The ninth degree? What's the matter?'

'I'm lonely,' I'd said. What I'd really wanted to do was let rip with accusations. The *Kay* factor. 'There is something else.' I'd taken a deep breath. Spat out the crux of the matter – something that had bothered me since we'd arrived. 'You've not made love to me once since getting here. We're meant to be on honeymoon.'

Rick had taken my hands. Held them in his.

'Don't take this personally, Lots…'

'Yes?' I'd prompted.

'I love you. You're gorgeous…'

'But?' My voice had sounded harsh.

'But… right now… well, I mean, look at you.'

'What do you mean?' I'd cried.

But I'd known what he'd meant. What he hadn't wanted to say out loud. Physically, he'd gone off me. He didn't find my baby bump sexy. I'd read about it, of course. How some men thought their wives looked even more attractive. Couldn't keep their hands to themselves. Pleased

182

as punch that it was *their* seed that had widened their woman's hips. Filled her belly.

And then there were the men that fell into the opposite category. Men like Rick. Men who couldn't get their heads around the fact that there was a *baby* in there. Men who found it a huge mental barrier.

In the second week of our honeymoon, Rick had stayed out later and later. He would creep into bed in the early hours of the morning. He'd try not to disturb me. He never knew that I'd been laying there, wide awake. Eyes open in the dark. Waiting for his return. And then, one night, he didn't return at all.

The following morning, I'd gone down to the pool. Chosen my usual lounger. However, instead of settling down upon it, I'd placed two rolled-up towels under a larger beach towel. I'd then arranged a straw hat at one end, sunglasses perched askance on the hat's rim. A passing American woman had given me a strange look.

'I haven't been to breakfast yet,' I'd explained. Catching her sidelong look, I'd felt obliged to offer an explanation. 'I don't want the pool staff thinking I'm reserving a bed. It's against the rules. Hopefully they'll take one look at this and think it's a person having a snooze instead.'

'Oh really?' she'd drawled. 'Can't say I've ever seen anyone sunbathing with a heap of towels over them,' she'd snorted.

'Us Brits do,' I'd retorted, ignoring her sarcasm. I'd opened a paperback. Rested the book over the towel's *abdomen.* I'd then tucked a pair of flip-flops in at the other end. Et voila. Feet! The American woman had been unimpressed.

'It's official. The British are bonkers.'

Mission accomplished I'd returned to my room. I'd then gone out to the balcony and gazed down at the pool area. More specifically, my sunbed. From such distance, the mound had resembled a person having a kip.

And then I'd waited. Bided my time.

I'd jumped at the sound of a key in the lock. But it hadn't been Rick. Instead, one of the housekeepers had come into the room. Her arms had been full of clean linen and bath towels.

'Sorry, ma'am,' she'd apologised. 'Shall I come back?'

'No, it's fine,' I'd said. 'Please, carry on.'

Upon seeing my bump she'd beamed widely. As she'd whisked about the room, she'd enquired after my health. Asked if I knew the sex of the baby. I'd answered her questions with a serene smile. A calm air. Inside I'd been seething. Where was my husband?

After the housekeeper had left, I'd settled down in an easy chair. Tried to read. I'd done plenty of that on this so-called honeymoon. I'd also read how a pregnant woman's hormones could go a little out of whack. Make her… let's just say, a little *psycho.*

When Rick had finally returned, I'd been in the bathroom. I hadn't shut the door because I'd been listening out for him. Therefore, I'd heard, rather than seen, his return to the room. The sound of footsteps and a door opening had told me he'd gone straight out to the balcony.

I'd cracked open the bathroom door. Silently observed him looking down at the pool area. He'd then turned and I'd caught the huge grin on his face. It was one of derring-do.

'The coast is clear,' he'd called out.

Seconds later, Kay had sashayed into the room.

'I don't know why we can't do it in my room, like usual,' she'd drawled in her transatlantic accent.

'Because it's more thrilling doing it here,' Rick had said. 'It's more dangerous.'

'In what way?' I'd said, stepping out from the bathroom.

Rick had instantly paled. He'd looked like he might have a coronary. Unlikely in one so young. For one vicious moment I'd wished it upon him.

Kay had clutched her breast implants as if her life had depended upon it.

'Marry in haste,' I'd said and smiled sweetly at her. 'Repent at leisure.' I'd then turned to Rick. 'So, you fancy some danger, eh?' In a flash, I'd grabbed an ornament from a nearby console table. 'Have this on me.' I'd then hurled it in his direction.

The ornament had only narrowly missed his head. Instead, it had smashed against the wall. A complimentary bowl of fruit had followed next. As I said... a little psycho. I'd then turned to the mini fridge. A bottle of champagne had been directed at Kay. It had exploded at her feet. It was at that point she'd come to her senses, screamed, and fled.

'Oh, dear,' I'd said to my shellshocked husband. 'It looks like your bit of sexy excitement has done a bunk. You'll have to give yourself a hand job instead. Appropriate. Because you're a wanker.'

And then I'd turned on my heel. Stalked from the room. Left my slack-jawed husband staring after the madwoman who'd once been his docile wife.

Chapter Thirty-Six

The rest of the honeymoon had passed in a blur.

There'd been lots of tears. On both sides. Rick had kept saying that I was the love of his life. That his behaviour had been an aberration. Never to be repeated.

'It's only because you're pregnant, Lottie,' he'd said, as if that explained everything.

'I'm not a leper,' I'd growled.

He'd raised his arms in the air, then dropped them back by his sides.

'I'm sorry. What more can I say?'

'*I* say that you can apologise until you're hoarse,' I'd retorted. 'It won't change how I feel, so you might as well bugger off.'

'Are we finished?' he'd demanded. 'Is that what you're telling me?'

I'd looked away. Not replied.

The truth of the matter had been that I'd not known what to do. I'd felt stuck. Trapped, as they say, between this surprise devil and the deep blue Bahamian sea.

However, if I'd walked away from Rick, then I'd deprive our unborn baby of a father. *That* was what had made me dither. My inner voice hadn't wasted any time in piping up.

But, in the beginning, you were prepared to go it alone. You were up for being a single parent.

True. However, that was when I'd not known how Rick was going to react to the news that he'd impregnated a virtual stranger. The goalposts had changed considerably since then. First, he'd been elated at hearing the news. Second, we were now married.

Can't you give him another chance?

Could I? Should I? These thoughts nagged constantly at the corners of my mind.

'Lottie?' Rick had prompted. 'I love you.' His voice had cracked. 'Please don't leave me. I can't bear it. I don't know what I'd do without you.'

'Probably have endless rampant sex with a silicon-breasted tart,' I'd snarled, raising my hands above my head, and balling my fists.

It was a gesture of frustration, but Rick had mistakenly thought I'd been about to punch him. He'd grabbed my wrists. For a moment, I'd fought him. However, he'd been too strong for me. Like a damp firework, all the fight in me had sputtered out. I'd collapsed against his chest, sobbing profusely.

'Don't, Lots,' he'd implored. 'All this upset isn't good for our baby.'

Our baby.

Tentatively, he'd released my wrists. Put his arms around me. Held me tight. He'd whispered how much he loved me.

Over and over. Stroked my hair. Cupped my face. Kissed away the tears flowing so copiously down my cheeks. He'd promised it would never happen again. And then he'd played his ace card.

He'd said he wanted us to be a family. That he couldn't wait to welcome our son or daughter into the world. That he wanted to be the best dad ever.

It was listening to those words, so earnestly delivered, that had been pivotal in making my decision. I'd stay with him. We'd put this behind us. Move on.

And so that was what we did.

Chapter Thirty-Seven

Once back in England, life continued as if we'd never been away.

Doreen and Neville had made no comment about our tanned faces. That said, they'd given Rick a funny look when he'd said he missed eating fried conch.

My husband had been super-attentive, although there'd been no sex. It had been an unspoken agreement between us that intimate relations wouldn't resume until after the birth. That aside, Rick had been caring and affectionate. Enough to provoke Doreen into doing an eye roll. She'd asked Neville to pass her a sick bag.

Our daughter Sally had arrived two days after her due date. Rick had been over the moon. He'd rushed out and bought cigars for all the hospital staff. The midwife had looked astonished when Rick had presented her with a Hamlet.

'Oh!' Rick had slapped his forehead. 'How stupid of me. Give me a mo. Back in a bit.'

And off he'd charged, this time to buy chocolates.

'Keep the cigar for your hubby,' he'd later told the midwife. 'This is for you.' He'd plonked a kiss on her cheek, then thrust a purple box into her hands. 'Here's one for you, too, Lots,' he'd grinned. 'You need to keep up your strength after all that pushing.'

Euphoric, Rick had then disappeared out of the delivery room. He'd handed out choccy gifts to every female he'd come across, including a lady in Delivery Room 2. He'd accidentally barged in on a woman who'd been sucking up gas and air like it was going out of fashion.

'Who the bleedin' hell are you?' the expectant father had spluttered. 'The friggin' Milk Tray man?'

Rick had hastily reversed out. He'd then crouched down and pushed one of the boxes around the delivery suite's swing door.

And so the three of us, a brand-new family, had returned to our brand-new home. I'd like to say we'd lived happily ever after, but you know that wasn't the case.

I don't think Rick ever cheated on me again. Not as far as I was aware, anyway. That said, I'd already made up my mind to never have another child. I hadn't wanted to risk going through that awful rejection ever again.

Mind you, in hindsight, cheating might have been easier to deal with. There was a new boulder that was about to smash into our marriage. That of financial crisis. Both infidelity and hardship carry their own stresses. Both have the capacity to make or break a relationship. However, the fallout is very different.

Twelve months later, not long after Sally's first birthday, Rick took me to one side. His face had been pale. He'd looked both angry and frightened.

'I need to talk to you,' he'd whispered.

Our daughter had chosen that moment to scream loudly. A new tooth had been troubling her, and she was fed up with sore gums and pain. I'd jiggled Sally on my shoulder.

'What's up?' I'd asked over her cries.

'I can't tell you with that racket going on,' Rick had winced. 'Go and sort her out. Then come and sit down. I've had some bad news.'

There'd been something about his tone that had put a chill around my heart.

I'd taken Sally upstairs, all the while rubbing her little back and making shush-shush noises. As I'd rooted around in the bathroom cabinet looking for Calpol – ever the practical mother – another part of me had mentally scampered off to my brain's very own *Panic Room*. I'd started to play the *What If* game.

What if Rick had recently visited the doctor without telling me?

What if the doctor had examined a lump?

What if Rick had already had a secret biopsy?

What if the results were back and the prognosis was dire?

I'd extracted the Calpol along with a dosage syringe, then squirted pink syrup into Sally's mouth.

'There, there, poppet,' I'd soothed. 'What naughty toothypegs. They're a nuisance when they come, and a nuisance when they go.'

She'd regarded me for a moment with her big, beautiful

eyes. Even now, all these years later, I can recall her eyelashes spiky from tears. They'd looked like little black starfish. Then her head had flopped down. She'd nestled into my neck.

'Are you a tired little girl?' I'd crooned. 'Perhaps my darling babe needs a nap, hmm?'

I'd walked into our daughter's nursery, decorated just as I'd previously envisioned. It had been a Beatrix Potter haven of framed prints and soft furnishings.

Laying Sally on the cot's mattress, I'd reached for her quilt. Gently, I'd placed it over her. The cover had displayed multiple images of a mischievous Peter Rabbit. He'd been carrying armfuls of stolen carrots while his sisters – Flopsy, Mopsy and Cotton-tail – had looked on with delight.

Straightening up, I'd gazed down at Sally. Sleep had already claimed her. For a few moments I'd simply stood and marvelled at how utterly exquisite she was. It had always amazed me that Rick and I had created this tiny miracle. We had a gorgeous baby. A beautiful house. I'd stood there and thought *yes, this is nice. I'm so lucky. Life is good.*

In that moment, I'd not known that it would be years before I'd ever have that feeling again.

I'd switched on the baby alarm and tiptoed from the nursery, shutting the door quietly behind me.

Chapter Thirty-Eight

I'd returned to the lounge to find Rick slumped in an armchair. He'd been holding his head in his hands.

I'd perched on the edge of the sofa. Looked at him with wide, fearful eyes.

'What's happened?'

Rick had rubbed his face with the heels of his hands.

'I didn't want to tell you.' He'd heaved a sigh. 'For a long time now, I've hidden a truth from you.'

I'd gone cold. Hugged the tops of my arms. Prepared myself to hear the worst. How long had he got left? A couple of years? A few months? Maybe just a handful of weeks?

'Just tell me,' I'd said quietly, my body tense.

'You're not going to like this.'

Rick had held my gaze. Stared at me bleakly. Instinct had told me not to rush him into speaking. Not to get hysterical at demanding he spit out the truth of his condition. Calmness had been paramount. If my husband was about to announce he was terminally ill, then he wouldn't have wanted his wife going to pieces. He'd need supporting. The silence had stretched on. I'd been the first to cave in.

'Are you trying to tell me you're sick?' I'd gently

prompted.

Rick's expression had changed in a flash. From despair to bafflement.

'Sick?' he'd repeated. 'No, I'm not sick. Not at all.'

'Then… what is it?' My brow had knitted in confusion.

Oh, God. What now? *Another* woman? And was this one pregnant? Was Sally about to have a half-brother or half-sister? Would maintenance be required? Would I have to go back to work to help out with finances? And, if so, no way were Doreen and Neville looking after Sally.

It's amazing how many thoughts can whirl through the brain in a matter of seconds. But nothing could have prepared me for what Rick had said next.

'I'm in debt,' he'd mumbled.

'Debt?' I'd repeated stupidly. 'You mean… you're in debt to someone as in… as in owing a favour, right?'

'No, Lottie,' he'd grimaced, then leapt to his feet. He'd paced the living room. Back and forth. Back and forth. 'I owe money.'

I'd struggled to get my head around this revelation. After all, we had no mortgage. How many newlyweds were lucky enough to be in *that* situation? Almost none.

When we'd married, the deal had been that if I bought the house, Rick would support me and Sally. He'd promised to take care of the utility bills. To put food on the table. To clothe us. It wasn't a big ask. Nor was there any reason why his earnings shouldn't cover this – and some.

I hadn't been an extravagant wife. Doreen had instilled

that in me. A Lucas woman didn't go to the hairdresser for fancy highlights. Make-up was a no-no. As was nail polish. From time to time, I'd defied my mother-in-law and worn the palest of nude lipsticks, a flick of mascara and a clear coat of polish on my nails. But nothing obvious. And anyway, I'd never bought expensive brands.

Likewise, Sally's clothing had been cheaply sourced. Usually from either Primark or the local supermarket. Ditto for me. Rick, however, had always worn *brands*. Under his overalls there had always been a pair of Armani jeans teamed with a Boss shirt. Even his boxers had been Calvin Klein. No undies from Asda for my husband.

I'd sat there. Dazed. Not quite able to comprehend Rick's confession. As he'd paced the room, I'd tried to fathom how he'd gotten into debt. Yes, he'd been self-employed. And no doubt his earnings had fluctuated. But he'd always been busy. Always had work. Well, so he'd said. I'd never had reason to doubt him.

'How can you possibly owe anyone money?' I'd asked, baffled.

'Er, it's not actually me that owes the money.' He'd raked one hand through his hair in agitation. 'It's you.'

'What?' I'd said, poleaxed.

'You,' he'd repeated, and stopped pacing. Rick's eyes had locked on mine. '*You* are in debt.'

I'd shaken my head.

'That's not possible. I don't owe anyone anything.'

'Let me explain.'

And then the whole sorry story had tumbled out.

When I'd met Rick, he'd told me he'd had substantial savings. Cheap wedding and engagement ring aside, he'd led me to believe these savings had paid for our honeymoon.

The trip to the Bahamas had cost five thousand pounds. However, Rick hadn't paid for it with any savings. He'd lied. There were no funds. Instead, he'd taken out a loan.

His passion for expensive clothes and shoes had meant he'd only made the minimum repayments. Consequently, the exorbitant interest had quickly mounted up. The original sum of five thousand had become ten. Then twenty. Even worse, he'd taken out the loan in my name and forged my signature.

'What?' I'd shrieked.

But there was more to come.

This finance hadn't come from a bank. Rick had taken out a high-cost short-term loan with an unscrupulous lending company. In later years, this company would come to the attention of the Financial Conduct Authority who would launch an investigation. The result would be a crackdown on irresponsible lending with the insistence that such companies adhere to a rate cap. However, this was long before the FCA got involved in such matters.

'I'm sorry, Lottie,' Rick had whispered. He'd collapsed back down in the armchair.

Horrified, I'd leapt to my feet. It had then been my turn to pace. I'd nearly worn a hole in the carpet striding up and down. My arms had waved like windmills as I'd tried and failed to understand Rick's thought processes. That he could *do* such a thing. And, moreover, that he'd done it in my name!

'I don't believe I'm hearing this,' I'd cried, over and over.

'I'm sorry,' he'd repeated.

And then I'd stopped pacing. Put my hands on my hips.

'How the *hell* am I meant to pay off a debt that has nothing to do with me?'

'But it does,' he'd countered indignantly. 'After all, you went to the Bahamas.'

'What point are you making? I didn't *ask* you to buy the holiday. You did it without so much as a mention. You said it was a surprise.'

'And it was, wasn't it? After all, you enjoyed yourself.'

'That's debatable,' I'd hissed. My eyes had narrowed as a sudden memory of Kay had sprung to mind. Her fake breasts entering the room a second before the rest of her.

'The point I'm making' – Rick had scowled – 'is that I did something nice for the two of us. Primarily, however, *I did it for you.*'

'Sorry, Rick' – I'd glowered back – 'but I'd have been just as happy with a weekend in Bognor. How *dare* you say you only did it for me. I didn't ask you to blow five grand on a holiday. I didn't ask you to borrow money. And more importantly' – I'd shrieked – 'I DIDN'T ASK YOU TO TAKE OUT A LOAN IN MY NAME.'

The baby alarm had crackled into life. My rant had

awoken Sally. I'd made to go to her, but Rick had caught my arm.

'Leave her for a moment,' he'd growled. 'Like it or not, Lottie, you're going to have to pay this debt.'

'What with?' I'd roared. 'Chocolate buttons?'

He'd given me a look.

'You know what with.'

Ah, yes. The nest egg. The money I'd put aside for Sally's future.

'I've a fucking good mind to report you to the police,' I'd raged, although I'd known in my heart that I'd never do that.

'But you won't,' he'd said with certainty. 'Because you love me.'

'Don't bank on it,' I'd snarled.

Sally's cries had revved up. Turning on my heel, I'd stalked from the room.

Chapter Thirty-Nine

The embers from the wood burner were glowing redly. The colour reflected the warmth in my belly, likely from the four brandies I'd now consumed while chatting with Fin. I felt very mellow. Also, slightly squiffy.

'So' – Fin prompted – 'I'm assuming you paid off your husband's surprise debt by using the money you'd set aside for Sally's future.'

'Yes,' I sighed. I stared into the dying fire. 'Repaying it wiped out all of my savings.'

'And afterwards, were things okay between you and Rick?'

I shook my head.

'I kidded myself that they were. I now realise things were never *right* between the two of us. How could they be?' I shifted on my bottom. Re-tucked my legs the opposite way. 'I'd started a relationship with a virtual stranger. We got to know each other as the days, weeks and months went by. After a year together, it dawned on me that I'd married a man who knew how to deploy charm with a total lack of responsibility. Rick promised he'd never get into debt again and that he'd be honest about finances. However, truth was never one of his strengths. I belatedly realised that my husband had delusions of grandeur. He'd lived way beyond his means. Also – and I'm ashamed to admit this – he likely saw me as a cash cow. Simply someone to fund his lifestyle.'

For a moment the two of us were silent. The remains of a log crackled and popped, then turned to ash. Outside, the rain continued to lash against the window.

'What happened next?' asked Fin gently.

I blew out my cheeks.

'The years passed. When Sally started school, I found employment locally. An office job. It didn't pay much but it worked well with school hours. Meanwhile, Rick and I lurched from one financial crisis to the next. He repeatedly reneged on his promise to stay out of debt. For example, he bought a Mercedes. He claimed business was good, and that the cost could be offset against his tax bill. In fact, Rick used to change his car every year. He insisted that appearances were everything. He skipped days off work to go to the races and generally carried on like a member of High Society. Without telling me, he took out credit cards. He'd use them to make payments on other credit cards. Eventually they were all declined. Likewise with bank loans.'

Fin shook his head. For a moment he looked confused.

'But how did you get out of fresh debt, Lottie, when your nest egg had been used?'

'Ha!' I gave a mirthless laugh. 'Well, the first thing to go was the house. We moved. The detached became a semi. The released equity was then used to clear all monies owing. This pattern repeated over the years. From a semi, to a terraced. Then into a one-bedroomed flat. Sally had the bedroom while Rick and I shared a pull-out sofa in the lounge. Finally, we ended up living in caravan in my in-laws' back garden.'

Fin shook his head. From the expression on his face, I could almost read his thoughts. I knew what he was going to ask next and didn't have long to wait.

'Why didn't you leave him sooner, before you ended up in a caravan?'

'Good question,' I nodded.

Yes, why hadn't I left? Because I'd believed – *wanted* to believe – that each time I'd bailed Rick out, he wouldn't do it again.

'Those who aren't in such a situation' – I answered, picking my words carefully – 'never understand why you stick with someone who drags you down. It's a bit like asking a battered woman why she won't leave her violent husband. It's a complicated answer. I could say that I didn't know how to get out of the situation. Also, that I wanted Sally to have her father in her life. I could also say that a part of me still loved Rick. That I wanted to believe his endless promises that he'd change. My in-laws were very vocal on the subject. They used to tell me to put up and shut up.'

I shook my head, as if to remove a sudden image of Doreen. Lips pursed. Eyes narrowed. She'd stood over me as I'd opened a brown envelope. It had been yet another stomach-churning demand for payment. I'd dissolved into tears. She'd told me to man up and sort it out.

'That said' – I continued – 'I also suspect that it's our own traumatic histories that make us stay put. I'd lost my parents at a relatively young age. There were no other close relatives. Deep down I'd told myself that my in-laws, despite being charmless, were family. Also, each time I'd paid a debt off, and we were financially square again, a period of peace would ensue. I used to revel in those moments. You see, it was during such weeks or months that life would seem good again. However, I now recognise that such a period was when I'd been at my most gullible. For it was *then* that I'd told myself that Rick had finally seen the error of his ways. Even when we moved into that caravan, he used to cheerfully tell me that the situation was temporary. He'd give me a hug and, like Del Boy, say, "This time next year, Lottie, we'll be millionaires.'

The brandy had loosened my tongue. Without meaning to, I'd ended up confiding in Fin. I'd revealed a lot about myself. My life. However, not everything. Nor was I going to. *Fifi Footsy* had helped shrink my debts faster than putting a bundle of woollies in a boil wash. But that was classified information.

Fin regarded our empty glasses.

'Another one?'

'Why not? I might as well get totally smashed and obliterate all these memories. Sorry if I'm boring you.'

Fin shook his head and laughed.

'You're not boring me at all. Anyway, you haven't heard my life story yet,' he teased.

'I'd like to hear it,' I said, and meant it.

I watched him as he refreshed our glasses. Oh, but he was attractive.

I had a sudden overwhelming urge to lean over and run my fingers through that dark hair... caress those chiselled cheekbones... touch the curve of his lips... and then glue my mouth to his.

As Fin lifted the bottle to pour the brandy, I wondered what it would be like to have him lift *me* – right off this sofa and up to his bedroom.

What the heck, Lottie? What's with the sexual thoughts?

I don't know, I mentally shrugged. Maybe it's the brandy.

Either that or you're sexually frustrated.

Probably the latter.

Fin handed me my glass.

'Cheers, again,' he said, clinking his glass against mine. 'So, where we were we? Oh, yes. You were living in a caravan. I take it, though, that this was the last straw? That this time you *did* leave Rick?'

I gave Fin a sheepish look.

'I'm embarrassed to say... no.' I shook my head. 'I didn't leave him. Rather, Rick left me. I didn't even know he'd gone until my mother-in-law told me. He'd telephoned her, you see. Left a message with her, for me. Said he'd needed some headspace. Rick had also refused to tell his mum and me where he was. In short, he'd left me to face the music on his behalf. Doreen was beside herself. She was upset that her precious son had gone off the radar. Also, she blamed me for everything. Unlike before, when I had a property to sell, this time I was in real trouble. There was precious little left of any real worth. Certainly not enough to pay off Rick's latest debts and make the nasty letters go away. Later that day, there was a knock on the caravan door. Two bailiffs were standing there. They apologised and were pleasant enough. However, they told me to leave the caravan forthwith. This included everything within it. I handed over the keys and they told me I wasn't liable for Rick's debt. That said, I later discovered there were outstanding loans once again in my name. They totalled the best part of fifty thousand pounds. Rick had managed to borrow without my consent via online companies. I took legal advice and was told it was fraud and forgery. A solicitor told me I could open both a civil and a criminal action. However, despite everything, I just couldn't bring myself to do that to Rick. Instead, I contacted the various companies. Contested the loans. Told them that Rick had not been authorised to act as he had. Long story short, a good proportion was written off. I was left with approximately twenty thousand pounds to clear.' I shrugged. 'And I've been paying it off ever since.'

'Lottie, that's outrageous,' Fin declared. 'But – hang on – you mentioned earlier that you've been writing.' He gestured with one hand. 'However, you also said that your crime series isn't yet live. So far there have been no royalties. How on earth have you been making ends meet?'

'Oh, you know,' I said vaguely. 'A bit of bar work here.

Some cleaning work there.'

That much was true. It just wasn't the whole truth.

Fin put his head on one side. His eyes snagged on mine.

'I sense there's more to this story than you're letting on.'

'Maybe,' I said, but didn't enlarge.

I couldn't. Just couldn't. It was one thing to unburden about Rick and the mess he'd left me in. It was quite another to divest a secret about how I'd *really* been paying off this final debt. If I told Fin about my online alter ego, he'd be shocked. Repulsed even.

'We've all been there, Lottie,' he assured.

I regarded him. Silently wondered what bad decisions he'd ever made. He was the owner of a thriving business. A gorgeous hotel set in considerable acreage with tenanted cottages. He lived in a beautiful apartment. There was a ravishing girlfriend. Okay, Pru had confided that Fin was a widow. He'd known tragedy. But he wasn't hugging a shameful secret. He now regarded me kindly.

'You look like you're mentally beating yourself up, Lottie. Please don't. Tell yourself that everything you've done in your life has been for the greater good.'

'Really?' I said wryly.

'Absolutely! Like… making sure Sally had a dad … and supporting Rick. You gave him every chance to change. And sometimes people *do* change. Remember that. It's not your fault you ended up with nothing. Anyway, you've nearly turned that financial battleship around.' He gave me an encouraging smile. 'That tells me that you're a very enterprising lady.'

My head was starting to feel heavy. I'd given away too much about myself. I needed to pull back. Before my mouth failed to consult my brain and revealed my deepest, darkest secret.

'I'm not enterprising, Fin.' I shook my head. 'Also, if you knew how I've made the bulk of my income, you'd be unimpressed.'

'Don't tell me,' he teased. 'You've been mugging little old ladies after they've collected their pensions. Am I getting warm?'

'It's worse than that.'

'Nonsense,' he tutted.

Fin leant across the space between us and patted my knee. It was meant as a reassuring gesture. However, the effect upon me was electrifying, as if he'd pushed a seat-ejector button.

I shot upright as his touch sent zinger after zinger whizzing up my spine. How many could I handle before slumping forward in a heap of lustfulness?

However, such thoughts dispersed like the coloured patterns of a kaleidoscope when Fin's mobile began to ring. The interruption, on my part, was unwelcome. How dare someone disturb my lovely evening with this gorgeous man!

The phone was resting on the coffee table. I caught a glimpse of the background picture. A glamorous redhead with pouting lips. The caller display revealed her name. *Marina.*

Chapter Forty

'Excuse me,' Fin apologised.

Leaning forward, he picked up the handset and answered the call.

'Hello?' There was a pause as he listened to Marina. 'You're only around the corner? No, I'd rather you didn't. Not tonight. Why? Because in the morning I'm up with the sparrows. You know how you don't like being disturbed. Oh, well. It's up to you.'

I took this as my cue to take myself off. It was late now. Definitely time for bed. I drained my glass, then set it down on the table. Stood up. It was only then that I realised how drunk I was.

Fin glanced up at me. I mimed that I was going upstairs. He gave me a thumbs up, then covered the microphone with one hand.

'Sleep well, Lottie,' he said warmly.

Once again I noticed how mesmerising those hazel-green eyes were. How that blowtorch smile made me light up.

Phwoar, said my inner voice.

Indeed, I silently replied.

What a hunk. Oh, wait. Did people still use that word?

Wasn't it a bit, you know, naff? I remembered Sally once referring to a boy she liked as *buff.* Jen would say *fit.* Fin was both those words and any others you cared to add.

'Goodnight,' I replied. 'And, er, fanksh. I mean, thanksh.' Hell. My mouth wasn't working properly. I gestured expansively with one hand. 'For ever'shing.'

I stumbled. Recovered myself. Stumbled again. The room briefly spun. Then, half crouching, half leaning, I slowly negotiated the path around the coffee table and away from the sofa. Flipping heck. That would teach me to guzzle my host's brandy.

I tottered off towards the staircase, one arm extended like a Dalek, in case I needed to steady myself.

Behind me, Fin carried on talking to Marina. She must have heard me saying goodnight to him and then asked who he was talking to.

'I have a houseguest,' I heard him say.

I stood at the bottom of the staircase. Contemplated it. Rather how a rock climber might consider a cliff. I wondered if Marina would ask any further questions about me. My ears pricked up, keen to catch anything else Fin might add. I didn't have long to wait.

'Yes, my guest is female. No, I'm not sleeping with her.'

More's the pity, my inner voice leered.

Clearly, Marina was the possessive type.

Tentatively, I put one foot on the first step.

'Oh, for heaven's sake, Marina. Why are you interrogating me?' Fin gave a gusty sigh. 'Okay, okay. Her name is Lottie. There was a bookings mix-up. She's sleeping in my parents' room. Happy? No, she's not as young as you. Yes, she is pretty.'

If I'd have been a cat, I'd have started purring.

Fin's voice dropped and I struggled to catch what he said next.

'No, she's not as pretty as you.'

If I'd have been a dog, I'd have started growling.

I lifted my other foot. Aimed for the second step. Missed, and promptly nose-dived onto the stair tread.

'Just a moment,' I heard Fin say. Then, 'Are you okay, Lottie?'

'Never better,' I trilled, hauling myself upright. I had a nasty feeling I'd said *bever netter.* 'Night,' I repeated.

I grabbed hold of the safety rail with two hands. The staircase seemed to be moving. Well, fancy that. At some point during the evening, an escalator had been fitted. Unfortunately, I was having difficulty balancing upon it. Might a handy elevator have been installed too? I stared around wildly. Sadly not. How annoying.

I dropped down on all fours. Steadied myself. Then paused. I was still within earshot of Fin. Might there be any further snippets of juicy conversation? Silence reigned. I risked a quick look over my shoulder. Fin was staring at me. No doubt wondering why his guest was attempting to climb the stairs like a squirrel clinging to a tree.

A pep talk was required.

'You can do this, Lottie,' I told myself. 'Attagirl. You've

got this.'

'Do you want a hand?' Fin called.

'No,' I yodelled back. That would mean standing up. Right now, that wasn't an option. 'All good.' I tried to focus on the staircase. 'Just taking a moment. Admiring the, er, carpet.'

'Sorry, Marina' – I heard Fin say – 'but I'll have to call you back.'

Suddenly a pair of strong arms were lifting me upright.

'*Eeep*,' I squeaked. A thousand zingers shot through my torso and exited via the crown of my head. It was tantamount to being tasered. 'I'm fine,' I gasped, desperately trying to gather my wits.

'I'm not convinced that's the case,' said Fin. 'If you don't mind, Lottie, I'll escort you to your room.'

Oh, how masterful.

'After all' – he added – 'I don't want you taking a tumble. These stairs are steep.'

Okay, he's not being masterful. Just thoughtful. Even so, he hung up on his girlfriend to help me. Ha! Bet that annoyed you, Sabrina... Melina... oh, whatever.

'S'okay,' I slurred, straightening my spine as – oh! – we were off. Sailing up the stairs at quite a speed too. 'This escalator is amazing,' I marvelled.

Fin shook his head.

'I'm sorry, Lottie.'

'Wha' for?' I blinked at him owlishly as we bowled on upwards.

'I shouldn't have given you so much brandy. You're going to have a hangover in the morning.'

'Nonsense.' I waved one hand and nearly fell backwards.

'Careful,' warned Fin. He wound one arm tightly around my waist.

'*Nnggg*,' I squealed. More zingers scorched up my spine, through my head and threatened to fry my eyeballs. Suddenly we were on the top landing.

'I suggest you have a big drink,' he advised. 'Stay hydrated.'

'Hydrated?' I sniggered. 'Are you suggesting I have another brandy, you naughty boy!'

Mayday, Lottie. You're seriously drunk. Zip the gob.

Fin's arm was still around my waist. I looked up at him. Delivered a sizzling come-hither look – although it might have been a pissed leer. I tried to lean back against the bedroom door, all set to deliver a few smoulders. Unfortunately, the door wasn't shut. I fell backwards into the room, taking him with me. We landed in a heap on the floor.

'*Ooof*,' I grunted.

For a moment we both lay there, too winded to say anything. My head was really starting to ache now. My vision had gone fuzzy. However, there was nothing wrong with my hearing.

Down below, a door slammed. This was swiftly followed by the thumpity-thump of footsteps hastening up two flights of stairs.

I sensed rather than saw what looked like a two-headed avenging angel standing in the doorway. Narrowing my eyes, I struggled to focus. The two heads blended. Became one.

A staggeringly beautiful woman with flowing red hair glared down at us. I didn't need a pair of binoculars to see that she was livid.

'What the *hell* is going on?' Marina demanded.

Chapter Forty-One

I awoke the following morning with a thumping headache. My throat was so dry I momentarily wondered if an evil gremlin had visited in the night and filled my mouth with sawdust.

I lay there for a bit, alternatively staring at the ceiling and wincing at the light streaming through a gap in the curtains.

What had happened last night? I had no recall of getting undressed and putting myself to bed. I frowned. Lifted the cover. Good heavens, how strange. I was still wearing yesterday's clothes. And then, just like that feeling of dread one has when visiting the dentist, nasty memories nudged at the corner of my mind.

Hazy recollections. Me on the floor. Fin on top of me. Fin getting to his feet. Crouching over me. Trying to help me up. A machine-gun round of zingers. My arms shooting out. The big double bed dominating the room…

I gulped. Hot on the heels of that last memory, another unfurled. The bed had pulsed in and out of my vision. Almost like a cartoon graphic. At one point I could've sworn there was a caption taped to the headboard: *The Action Starts Here.*

And then I remembered flopping down on the mattress. Dissolving into giggles. And – oh *noooo* – something truly awful. Marina. I'd declared that there was only room for two people in the bed and please could the cross-looking female standing in the doorway leave the room forthwith.

Hell's bells. It was tantamount to telling Marina to bog off while I had sex with her man. I groaned. What had happened after that? Everything had gone black. Presumably, I'd passed out.

How dreadful. And humiliating. My toes curled at the thought of making a prat of myself in front of Marina. But, even worse, I'd embarrassed myself in front of Fin. I'd probably made him squirm too. Fancy insinuating that his girlfriend should sling her hook before he climbed into bed with me.

Oh God. I'd have to leave. I couldn't possibly stay in Fin's apartment now. I'd insulted his partner and abused his hospitality.

I'd have to tell Jen that enough was enough. Tonight, I would be sleeping in the family room with her and Stu, whether they liked it or not. The room had an ensuite. If they wanted to get fruity with each other, they could flipping well go in the bathroom. What was wrong with having a bonk in the bath? Or Jen climbing on Stu while he straddled the loo? Nothing! They just needed to use their imagination, for heaven's sake. Where there was a will there was a shower room, and that was that.

Why hadn't I put my foot down from the start? And

where *was* Jen? Why hadn't she messaged me to ask how I was? Or if I'd like to join her and Stu for breakfast?

And where was Ryan? It was high time I put him straight too. Enough of this pussyfooting around his ex-wife and son. I wanted my boyfriend. And I wanted him now! If he'd been here in the first place, I'd never have propositioned another man.

Oh, Lord. *Had* I propositioned Fin? I simply couldn't remember.

Never mind. I'd be gone by Monday. And then I'd never have to see him or the snotty Marina again. Thank goodness for small mercies. Only another forty-eight hours to go. Then I was out of here. I'd never visit Cornwall again.

And where was my phone? I needed it. It was time to send a few texts. Time to metaphorically put my boot up a few backsides. Oh, yes. Lottie was about to become bossy. It was time to jackboot about. Make a few of my own demands.

I made a long arm. Located the bedside table. Pat-patted with one hand. My fingers curled around my mobile.

As I peered blearily at the screen, I was surprised to note the time. It was almost eleven o'clock. Seemingly, I'd slept through the *dings* of several text messages. The first was from Jen.

Morning, Lottie. I hope you slept well. Sorry I was grumpy at dinner last night. It's not your fault that Ryan mucked up the booking. I just want to say that Stu and I are so grateful that you've let us have the family room to ourselves. You're a wonderful friend letting us have this fabulous romantic break. Me and Stu are going for an all-day hike along the coastline. We look forward to catching up with you over dinner this evening. Hopefully Ryan will have arrived in time to join us. Lots of love, Jen xxxx

After reading her gushing text, some of my gung-ho melted away. Ah, well. Maybe I'd tone down my planned verbal assault. Ask her nicely, instead, if she and Stu could retire to the ensuite for sex. If it wasn't too much bother. Please. Thank you very much.

The second text was from Ryan.

Hello, darling. Heather and I are home after an all-nighter at the hospital. I'm exhausted. Good news. Joshua is much better. It was one of those twenty-four-hour things. Isn't that marvellous? The doctor has suggested Joshua goes to a sauna to clear his nasal passages. I'm going to take him to my gym. There's a steam room. But first, I need sleep. Meanwhile, Heather is applying copious amounts of Vicks Vapour Rub to Joshua's chest. I will drive down to Cornwall early on Sunday morning. We will have Sunday night to finally ravish each other. See you tomorrow. Toot toot! Xxxxx

I stared at Ryan's message in disbelief. So basically, his son had been whisked off to hospital over a cold. Heather had panicked over a blocked nose. Really? *Really?* And was I meant to be thrilled that my boyfriend was finally coming to Cornwall to spend less than twenty-four hours with me?

The third and final text was from an unknown number.

Curious, I clicked on the message.

Morning, Lottie.

I hope you don't mind me messaging you. I took your number from the guest check-in data. With a bit of luck, you've now slept off any hangover. I saw your friend and her boyfriend earlier. They said they were going out for the whole day. Pru is covering Reception. She's also organised a temp and overseen a few other matters for me. Consequently, I have a few hours free. I wondered if you'd like me to show you some of Cornwall. Call me if you're up for it.

Fin

Was I up for being taken out by a handsome man with spare time on his hands? What sort of a daft question was that? I didn't even need to think about it. The answer was yes.

Fin hadn't mentioned anything about the luscious Marina coming too. Jolly good. Things were perking up.

Suddenly, Jen, Stu and Ryan were irrelevant. I'd message them later. For now, the only text I was responding to was this one – the gorgeous proprietor of Penwern Lodge.

With a delicious sense of anticipation, I saved Fin's number to my phone, then pressed the call button.

Chapter Forty-Two

Fin answered on the second ring.

'Hello, Lottie.' I could tell from his voice that he was smiling. 'Do you have a banging headache? Or have you escaped unscathed, like I did?'

'I'm feeling okay,' I assured. Well, I would be when I'd jumped in the shower, and guzzled water from the showerhead at the same time as washing myself.

'I'm just helping Pru with a query, and then I'm free. Do you fancy some fresh air?'

'Absolutely.' I beamed into the handset. 'However, I missed breakfast. Is there any chance we could grab a sandwich while out?'

'We can do better than that,' he said. 'Let's have a proper Cornish cream tea.'

'Oooh,' I squealed. 'That sounds like heaven.'

Just like you.

'I'll be done in ten minutes. Meet me in reception.'

Ten minutes? Blimey, I'd have to get a wiggle on.

'Make it fifteen,' I said. 'See you soon.'

I threw back the quilt, pulled the bed together, and had the quickest shower in history. I dressed hurriedly, added some warm layers, then grabbed my lippy.

As I stood in front of the mirror, I was surprised to see that my skin was glowing, and my eyes sparkling. There was no trace of yesterday's boozy night. Even my mouth seemed to be smiling away, all by itself. How peculiar.

I hastily brushed my hair, then scooped it up into a ponytail. Outside it was windy. I didn't want strands whipping about my face and sticking to my lipstick.

I bounced down the two flights of stairs. In one hand I had my walking boots. In the other, a waterproof. My ponytail swung jauntily, and I started to whistle. For the last couple of minutes, a tune had been playing in my head. *Oh, what a beautiful morning!* And it was. Okay, outside the sky was the colour of bruised plums. But inside my heart, the sun was shining. All was well in my world.

As I approached the bottom of the final staircase, my inner child rushed to the surface. I had a juvenile urge to leap the last three steps. Launching myself into the air, I shrieked in delight.

'*Wheeeee*!' I squealed, a huge grin covering my face.

'Ah, so you're up at last,' drawled a female voice.

Aghast, my head snapped up. Marina was perched on the edge of the sofa. She was seated in the exact spot Fin had occupied last night when we'd been sharing his brandy and my confidences. Her unexpected presence had caught me off guard.

'O-Oh,' I stammered. Somehow, I felt guilty. Even though I'd done nothing wrong. I could feel my cheeks turning pink. 'Good morning. Sorry, I didn't see you sitting there.'

'Evidently.' She arched one eyebrow. 'If you don't mind my asking, what are you doing here?'

Wow. This was a woman who didn't bandy her words. My cheeks further reddened. Suddenly I felt like a schoolchild standing before a headmistress.

'I'm Fin's houseguest,' I replied, raising my chin defiantly.

'Yes, he did say something of the sort,' she conceded. 'I gather there was a bookings mix-up. However, that doesn't explain the absence of your partner – assuming there really *is* a partner?' Now both her eyebrows were raised.

Ah, yes. Memory was flooding back. Fin had taken a phone call from Marina before I'd gone up to bed. She'd given him the third degree. Demanded to know who was keeping him company. Then she'd rushed over and hotfooted up to my bedroom. I could feel my face heating up even further, but this time with annoyance.

'Yes, I have a partner. Unfortunately, he's been delayed due to a family emergency.' I gave her a level look. 'Why?' I asked – rather bravely, I thought.

She cocked her head to one side. Made a show of considering my words before replying.

'Let's just say that *my* partner' – I noticed the possessive emphasis – 'is often pursued by preying women.'

My eyes widened. Was she bracketing me into that description? I didn't have long to wait for the answer.

'You seem to have conveniently forgotten that I

witnessed your behaviour last night. Behaviour that left me in no doubt that you're wildly attracted to Fin.'

'W-What?' I stuttered. 'I-I'd had too much to drink and fell–'

'Therefore' – she swept on – 'I thought it prudent to give you some friendly advice.' She gave me a spiteful look and for one moment I was reminded of Lady Tremaine, Cinderella's wicked stepmother. 'Don't embarrass yourself further, eh? Stop mooning after Fin. He's taken. Do you understand?'

I stared at her, my mouth hanging open. For a moment I was too gobsmacked to reply.

'Thank you for the speech,' I said eventually, desperately gathering my wits – what was left of them anyway. 'However, I have my own boyfriend, thank you very much. I certainly don't want yours.'

That's not entirely true, piped up my inner voice. *Last night I thought you were going to snog–*

Shut it, I mentally retorted.

Now was not the time to have an argument with myself about last night – which, let's face it, had been down to too much booze on an empty tummy. Thanks to Jen's little homily previously, I hadn't eaten much when I'd been in the dining room with her and Stu.

I inwardly sighed. One way or another, I was receiving rather a lot of lecturing right now. And anyway, so what if I thought Fin was attractive? There was nothing wrong in admiring a good-looking guy. I had a soft spot for several men. Patrick Dempsey. Robert Downey Jr. It didn't mean I wanted to wrestle them to the ground and rip off their trousers.

But where Fin's concerned, you'd like to, taunted the inner voice.

Sod off, I silently snarled.

Oooh, you've gone all hot.

I'm peri menopausal. Now leave me alone.

'Was there anything else?' I said crossly.

'I think we've covered all bases,' said Marina smugly. 'Anyway, I'm now off to Falmouth. I'm getting my hair done. Having some me time. I'm absolutely *exhausted* after last night. Fin and I had a total sexual marathon. He can be so demanding.' She gave me another smile. It didn't reach her eyes. 'We're always so vocal. I hope we didn't disturb you. I'm afraid noise can be a by-product of an energetic sex life.'

She bared her teeth again, this time looking like a Doberman about to lose the plot. I peeled back my own lips and grimaced. I wasn't in the mood for hearing about this woman's sexy thrills.

'It really couldn't matter less,' I said sweetly. 'My boyfriend and I are exactly the same. In fact, the last time we did it, the neighbours wrote to the local council. They lodged a noise complaint. Has that ever happened to you, Marian?'

She dropped the fake smile.

'My name is Marina,' she hissed. She gathered up her

keys along with a flashy handbag that had been languishing on the coffee table. 'I'm going. I don't want to be late for my appointment.' She flicked her shiny mane as she attempted some cordiality. 'Have a nice day.'

'Thanks, I will,' I said.

As she made to leave, I automatically shrank back from her. Best not mention who I was spending my day with.

Chapter Forty-Three

'Look, um, I don't want to, er, tread on anyone's toes,' I said tentatively to Fin.

We were standing in reception. Fin was standing over a printer and Pru was hovering nearby. Fin's sister might appear to be busy with paperwork, but I knew she was earwigging.

'You're not treading on my toes,' said Fin, looking perplexed.

'Not yours,' I said, feeling more uncomfortable by the moment. 'I'm referring to Marina's. She's not thrilled about me staying in your guest room.'

'It's none of her business who stays in my guest room.'

'She seems to think it is.' I took a deep breath. 'Listen, I will understand if you would like to change your mind about showing me around today. It's not an issue for me. I don't want you getting into trouble with Marina.'

'I'm not changing my mind.'

'Fin' – my toes curled at the point I was trying to make – 'I don't want to feel awkward when I see Marina back at yours. It doesn't sit right with me that I'm spending a few hours with you after…well, after she basically warned me off. Not that I need warning off,' I hastily added.

I was getting a bit hot under the collar. I didn't want to refer to the moment Marina had seen Fin and I sprawled on the bedroom floor. Especially in front of Pru. Marina had misconstrued the situation. I hoped that Fin was alive to what I *wasn't* saying, as well as what I *was* saying.

'Lottie,' he said, as the printer spat out sheets of paper. 'I know we've only known each other for twenty-four hours.' He gathered up the printouts of this evening's menu. 'But I might as well tell you this. Marina and I are no longer an item.'

Pru looked up from her paperwork in amazement. She then pretended she'd not overheard and quickly reshuffled some documents.

'Erm' – I frowned – 'have you told Marina that? Only that's not the impression she gave me.' No way was I alluding to the energetic sex romp that Marina had mentioned.

Fin sighed.

'You're obviously not aware that, last night, Marina and I exchanged a few heated words.'

No, I wasn't aware. Probably on account of passing out. I'd been dead to the world for hours.

'After Marina accused me' – now it was Fin's turn to colour up – 'of starting something with you, I ended up being rather brutal. I've been trying to extricate myself from her for weeks. However, she's steadfastly refused to take no for an answer. Last night, when everything came to a head, I ended up being bluntly honest. I told her that I didn't want to be with her anymore. I haven't felt the same way as her for some time. Anyway, she refused to leave my apartment. So I left her in my room and slept downstairs on the sofa. I also took back my housekey from her. Rest assured, she won't be unexpectedly barging in on you and your partner – when he eventually gets here.'

'Oh,' I said. I blinked rapidly, digesting everything Fin was saying.

'So now you know, Lottie. Ending my relationship with Marina is nothing to do with you. Instead, it's everything to do with Marina being–'

'A basket case,' Pru muttered under her breath. Fin gave his sister a sidelong look. She gave him an apologetic grin. 'Sorry,' she said, sounding anything but. 'I couldn't help overhearing what you were saying to Lottie.'

Fin shook his head and gave Pru a mock look of exasperation.

'I was aware that you and Marina didn't get along,' he said. 'However, I didn't think you thought her a basket case.'

'She's definitely a few eyeshadows short of a makeup box.' Pru clicked her tongue. 'And let's face it. Marina doesn't get on with anyone. The only person she loves is herself. I believe the word is *narcissist.*'

'Indeed,' Fin conceded. 'My big sis' – he turned to me – 'is very overprotective. She's always tried to fight my battles. Ever since we were at school together. What she fails to understand is that I'm now forty-five years old. A big boy.'

Forty-five? Fin was older than I'd thought. I also felt

wildly heartened to know he was only three years younger than me.

Why should that matter to you? interrupted my inner voice.

It doesn't, I silently retorted.

That's fifteen years younger than Ryan.

Great maths, but what's that got to do with anything?

Everything! Less mileage on the clock for starters.

You are bizarre.

Not really. Ryan will soon be drawing his pension whereas Fin is years away from retirement.

Sorry, you've lost me.

I'm pointing out that Fin is young(ish) and now single. Get in there, Lottie!

Hang on a minute. I'm not single. I'm with someone.

Really? So where is he?

Stop it. Just… stop.

'Someone has to look out for you,' said Pru sternly. However, she was looking at her brother with affection.

Fin gave Pru a look of exasperation.

'I'm perfectly able to look after myself. Anyway' – he turned to me – 'now that we've cleared up that little matter, I trust you're still up for going out?'

'Yes,' I said quickly. Now I knew Marina was off the scene, wild horses wouldn't stop me.

'See you both later and have a fabulous time,' Pru beamed. Was I mistaken, or had she just given me the ghost of a wink? 'And don't hurry back,' she said to her brother. 'I have everything under control.'

I followed Fin out of reception and across the carpark and, as I did so, there was a spring in my step.

Chapter Forty-Four

We crunched our way across the gravel carpark.

Fin stopped next to Stu's old banger. For one crazy moment, I thought we were getting in Stu's car. Instead, Fin popped the locks on another vehicle parked alongside – a snazzy looking Land Rover. He slid behind the steering wheel.

'Hop in,' he said.

I settled down in the passenger seat. Oooh, very nice. Loads of leg room and sumptuously comfortable.

'If you're cold, there's the button for the seat warmer,' Fin pointed.

'Thanks, but I'm good.'

The last thing I wanted was a warm backside. It might cause me to have a hot flush. They didn't happen often. Nonetheless, I was aware of subtle changes going on in my body. I could still remember how my ex-mother-in-law used to voraciously fan herself with magazines. Doreen had often told me that women *of a certain age* had nothing to look forward to. That, from fifty onwards, it was downhill all the way. However, Doreen had been a woman who'd thrived on negativity.

Fin shunted the gear into first, and we set off. I observed

the road signs along the way. It didn't take me long to realise we were heading towards Falmouth. Oh, crikey. Hadn't Marina said she was going there too? Yes, she had a hair appointment.

As we crossed a roundabout near Falmouth University Campus, a knot of anxiety landed in my stomach.

At a second roundabout, Fin took a left turn. We were still heading towards Falmouth. The tummy knot did a few clenches, causing me to squirm with discomfort.

'What's up?' Fin glanced across the space between us.

'Nothing,' I said miserably.

Me and the *Law of Sod* were sworn enemies. It would be just my luck to bump into Marina while out with Fin. It was one thing to be on the receiving end of her having a pop at me in his apartment, but it would be quite another if there was a public showdown. I could imagine her now. Ranting that I had no business to be with a man she deemed exclusively hers. Onlookers nudging each other as they watched the floorshow.

'Earth to Lottie,' Fin prompted. 'Come on, tell me. What's up?'

'Um, I can't help noticing that we're heading towards town. That's where Marina is. She's getting her hair done.'

'Good for Marina,' said Fin neutrally. 'Don't fret, Lottie. I'm not taking you to the hairdresser.' He gave me a wink. The car was now cruising through a village called Mawnan Smith. The Land Rover braked slightly as we took a right fork in the road. We accelerated past a pub and continued onwards. 'We're going to Trebah Gardens. I can guarantee that we won't bump into Marina. It's not her sort of place.'

'Ah,' I said, trying not to visibly sigh with relief. 'Trebah Gardens sounds nice. Is it a park?'

'It's a little bit more than that,' he chuckled. 'The are four miles of footpaths which wind prettily through some dazzlingly exotic planting. In the summer months it's a sight to behold. Everything is in bloom with all the colours of the rainbow. However, the season of autumn brings its own glory. Reds. Golds. Lots of burnt orange. Therefore, even at this time of year, visitors are still enthralled by this little patch of England with its secret corners and private beach.'

'You make it sound beautiful.'

'That's because it is,' Fin smiled.

We were now following brown-and-white tourism signs. The Land Rover braked, and Fin spun the steering wheel sharply to the right. We'd reached our destination and were bouncing through the entrance.

'Wow,' I said, as my head swivelled this way and that.

'You ain't seen nothing yet,' he grinned, as the Land Rover came to a standstill.

Despite the time of year and the colder weather, the carpark was over fifty per cent full. To my left, a couple of tots were hanging on to their mother's hands. Their father was wrestling with an expensive looking double buggy. His expression was one of bewilderment. The mother threw back her head and laughed. She then said something to her partner. He gave a shrug of defeat, and they swapped places.

As he took their kiddies' hands, the woman effortlessly shook the pushchair into an upright position. I could almost hear her singing *ta-dah*. The man grinned, ruffled her hair, then lifted one of the tinies into a seat. Seconds later he was looking bewildered again, stumped by the safety harness. I smiled as the woman gave him a playful thump. She then shooed him out of the way and hunkered down to deal with the strap.

Suddenly, a memory of doing the same thing with Sally flooded my mind. There she was, a mere sprog, waiting to be lifted into her pushchair. However, Sally's buggy had been bought from eBay for ninety-nine pence. Thanks to a broken harness, I'd utilised one of Rick's belts. A second memory instantly followed. That of Rick snatching back the belt. Apparently, it had been Gucci. Instead, I'd borrowed a belt from Doreen, who'd always shopped at Primark.

I mentally shook the images away. Why had I stayed with Rick for so long? It was a question I still repeatedly asked myself, even though I knew all the answers. Hindsight was a marvellous thing.

My eyes swept over the carpark, now resting on the far side. A Rottweiler and Corgi were off lead. The two dogs were barking excitedly. No doubt they were looking forward to exploring such a lush place. All those tree roots to sniff – and lift legs against.

Fin moved around the side of the Land Rover. He followed my gaze.

'There will be a few dogs along the way. You're not

scared of them, are you?'

'Some of the bigger breeds make me a little nervous,' I confessed. 'That Rottweiler, for example.'

'One of my friends has a Rottie. His name's Albert – that's the dog, not my mate,' Fin chuckled. 'Ron swears the breed are great family dogs because of their pack mentality. They have a strong loyalty, sweet-nature, but guard-dog instincts. Ron insists that Albert is a very people-oriented dog. That said, Albert has had plenty of obedience and social training.'

We stood for a moment and watched. The two dogs were now waiting patiently at the rear of a hatchback. Their owner appeared and shut the tailgate. Suddenly a side door flew open. Two small kids jumped out – a girl and a boy.

The little girl was holding a doll which, a moment later, she'd dropped in a puddle. A wail went up. The Corgi ignored the child's cries. However, the Rottweiler carefully picked up the doll, gave it a little shake, then nudged the child's hand. She immediately stopped crying and took it from the dog.

'Look at that,' said Fin. 'A four-legged gentleman. I don't think you need have any worries if we come across that lad a little later.'

'You're right,' I smiled, reassured.

We set off towards the entrance, walking together companionably.

'Now then,' said Fin. 'Back at the hotel, you mentioned the small matter of hunger pangs. So, before we embark on our trip around the gardens, how about we visit the onsite café first? They have some excellent scones. They're served with Cornish clotted cream and locally sourced strawberry jam. Both taste amazing. If you like, we can have a hot meal first. The café also does a mean fish and chips.'

My stomach chose that moment to groan with hunger. It had been a long time since I'd eaten properly.

'Both sound delicious,' I replied.

We walked into a large refectory-type restaurant full of tables and chairs. To the right, beyond floor-to-ceiling windows, I could see an outdoor terrace. The raised platform was full of rustic trestle tables. The whole place was surrounded by abundant, towering trees including evergreens, palms, and an explosion of shrubs. It looked like a slice of Heaven.

'Go and find us a seat and I'll order the grub,' said Fin. 'Fancy a pot of tea with it?'

'Now you're talking,' I said, rubbing my hands together. 'Oh, wait a mo.' I rummaged inside my handbag, looking for my purse.

'Put that away,' he said firmly. 'I invited you out, so I'm picking up the tab.'

'But—'

'No buts.' Fin put up a hand to halt my protests. 'I insist. However, if you want to buy me a gin and tonic at a pub later, that will be most acceptable.'

'You're on,' I grinned.

I shoved my purse back inside the bag and resisted the

urge to skip over to an available table. Goody-goody. A lovely lunch with Fin. A tipple afterwards. And no chance of bumping into Marina either. This was turning into a perfect day. Bring it on!

As I sat down, I thought about Jen and Stu. I wondered what they were up to right now. My mind then wandered to Ryan. Had he caught up on his sleep? Or, maybe, he and Heather were currently administering Calpol to their strapping teenaged son. With a jolt, I realised I didn't care.

Chapter Forty-Five

'Tuck in,' said Fin. He set upon the table a tray loaded with food.

A tantalising smell shot up my nostrils. Flaky cod in a hot, crispy golden batter. Mmm. I had to stifle a moan of greed. And look at those scones! They were just waiting to be devoured. I didn't need telling twice and picked up my knife and fork.

'I like a woman who enjoys her food,' said Fin. He reached for the salt and pepper.

I smiled but didn't reply. This was on account of my mouth being full of food. However, his comment sent my brain whirring. So, Fin liked a woman who enjoyed her food, eh? Was he possibly trying to say… that he liked *me*? Oh, don't be so ridiculous, Lottie. He's just dumped a beautiful – and much younger – woman. After Marina, he'd hardly be interested in the likes of you. Even so…

I swallowed down the delicious fish and smiled at Fin. Gave my ponytail a jaunty flick at the same time.

'And I adore a man who loves his grub,' I said.

Are you flirting? gasped my inner voice.

No, but I'd like to.

You cannot be serious.

It's only banter. Loosen up!

Fin is out of your league.

I know, and you don't need to remind me.

And what about Ryan?

Ryan, Ryan, Ryan. The man isn't here. And you know as well as I do, the guy has never been there. Not properly. I don't believe for one moment he'll show up on Sunday. It's all talk. Always has been. In fact, when I go home to Catkin Cottage, I'm going to end the relationship.

Omigod. I can't believe you just said that.

Neither can I, but I mean it.

The worm is turning.

About bloody time, I silently retorted. I stabbed my fork into a fat potato fry. Fin watched me. Eyebrows raised.

'Whoa, what did that poor chip do to you?' he laughed.

'Sorry,' I apologised. 'I just had a fleeting thought about… stuff.'

'Personal stuff?'

'Yeah,' I sighed.

'Want to share the details?'

'Crikey, I've shared so much with you already. I don't want to bore you.'

Fin picked up the bottle of mayonnaise. Squirted it over the golden batter.

'That's never going to happen,' he assured.

'Okay, well' – I took a deep breath – 'I don't think things are working out between me and Ryan.'

'I'm sorry to hear that,' he said carefully. 'What's

prompted that thought?'

'This weekend. Yet another example of us making plans which have turned to ashes. It's taken this latest situation to enforce that realisation. He's a nice enough guy, don't get me wrong. He's just not *my* guy.' I picked up the ketchup bottle and gave my chips a few liberal squirts. 'He's still living with his ex-wife. It's like dating a married man.'

Fin put his head to one side, as if considering.

'Don't do anything you might regret. Why not talk to him about how you feel?'

'I have. Many times. It's always the same. He gives me loads of reasons why I should be patient. Peppers his words with lots of reassurance. However, ultimately, it's all empty promises. I mean, this trip was meant to be…' – I trailed off awkwardly – 'about, er, getting to *know* each other.' I widened my eyes meaningfully. 'But where is he?'

'I thought his son was seriously ill?' Fin frowned.

'It turned out to be a cold. I don't want to come across as heartless, Fin. After all, I'm a parent myself. I'm fully aware of the worries and concerns that go hand in hand with raising a child. Of being a protective mother. But Ryan's ex is… well, she's either the biggest panicker on Planet Earth or else she wraps their son in cotton wool. Anyway, even if Joshua hadn't put the kybosh on this weekend, it would have been something else. I realise that now. And the thing is, Fin, enough is enough. I now realise that I've been too much of a people pleaser. I used to let the ex-in-laws boss me about. Ditto my ex-husband. I stayed to give my daughter a father and *stability*. Ha!' I gave a mirthless laugh. 'Stability,' I repeated sadly. 'What a joke. Moving from house to house. Ending up in a caravan, for God's sake.' I could feel myself getting upset. But not with tears. Rather, anger. It was starting to pulse through my veins. 'And here I am. In Cornwall. Still being a people pleaser. Allowing Jen and Stu to take over the family room that Ryan mistakenly booked. Inadvertently foisting myself on you. I mean' – I swallowed down the resentment – 'it's not on. I'm forty-eight years old, Fin. It's taken almost every one of those years to finally understand that there are times in one's life where you have to say *no*. No, Rick, I will not subsidise you. No, Doreen, I will not let you put me down. No, Neville, I will not let you destroy my confidence. No, Jen, I will not be sleeping in Fin's turret bedroom just so you can get your leg over with Stu.'

I realised my voice had risen. Heads were turning our way. Blimey, it was all coming out now, wasn't it? However, this wasn't the time or the place.

I picked up a chip. Dipped it slowly in some sauce. My eyes were on the plate, but my mind was still entangled with the past. 'Sorry,' I mumbled. 'Rant over.'

'There's no need to apologise for anything, Lottie,' said Fin gently. 'And no way have you *foisted* yourself on me. It has been my absolute pleasure to have you stay. I mean that. You're great company. Easy to talk too. And, well, because of the stuff you shared with me the other night, I feel at ease with you. In fact, that was why I brought you here today.

240

To, er, help me. If that makes sense.'

My head shot up. I gave him a puzzled look.

'What do you mean?'

'I'm a widower, Lottie.'

'I know. Pru told me.'

Fin rolled his eyes.

'Good old Pru. Miss Blabbermouth.'

'She wasn't gossiping,' I said quickly. 'It just came up in conversation.'

'Right. Well, Pru might not have told you that I visited Trebah Gardens with Leah on the day she died.'

'What?' I said slowly. 'Pru said your wife died in a riding accident.'

'She did. However, Leah and I came to Trebah in the morning before the accident happened. We spent about five hours here. Just ambling about. Exclaiming over the beauty of the place. We got home late afternoon. That was when Leah decided to take Cracker out for a quick hack. He was a novice, so I said I'd join her. I was there when the accident happened. Perversely, I've driven past the spot where it happened many times. However, for some reason I've never been able to bring myself to come back here, to Trebah.'

'Memory substitution,' I breathed. 'Perhaps your brain recognised that you'd have to cope with regularly driving past where the accident happened – that you'd *have* to cope with it. So, instead, your brain swapped that memory with coming here, to Trebah.'

'Who knows,' said Fin slowly. He gave me a haunted

look. 'But coming here with you today just somehow felt right.'

For a moment we just gazed at each other. Was something going on here? I was aware that a huge shift had taken place between us. Was it empathy? Or something else? I didn't dare want to presume the latter.

Chapter Forty-Six

Fin told me more about Leah as we walked through the twenty-six acres of Cornish valley garden.

'She was my life,' he said simply. We were now strolling through vibrant tunnels of colour, under canopies bursting with exotic blooms. 'It's shocking to have someone here one minute and gone the next. There wasn't even a chance to say goodbye.'

'I can't begin to imagine what you went through,' I murmured.

His story sent chills down my spine. I suppressed a shiver. Since starting out, the temperature had dropped a couple of degrees. I stuffed my hands in my pockets. Wiggled my fingers within the silky lining. Tried to infuse some warmth into them.

'Leah loved this place,' Fin continued. 'In spring, the whole area comes alive with colour. Can you believe that some of these plants – camellias, rhododendrons, and magnolias – are over fifty years old? She particularly liked *Hydrangea Valley*. It contains over two acres of the plants. You can see them, over there.' He pointed to an ornamental bridge. 'We'll cross that later. It goes over *Mallard Pond*. However, it's beautiful in autumn too, as you can see.' He nodded at a haze of china-blue and soft white flowers.

'It's stunning,' I agreed.

'They were Leah's favourite flowers. She said they reminded her of mop heads.'

'I can see what she means… meant,' I quickly corrected.

My eyes drank in the surroundings. Currently we were heading into a maze of paths known as *The Bamboozle*. Appropriately named, because it contained nothing but bamboo. The canes were a mix of black, golden brown, yellow, and green. Some soared upwards and had to be thirty feet tall.

A loud woof made me startle. A second later, a huge Rottweiler lumbered past, tongue hanging out. It was the same dog that we'd seen earlier in the carpark.

'See?' Fin smiled. 'He's not concerned about us. He's more interested in chasing after Trebah's moths and birds.'

'Rick didn't care for dogs,' I said. 'Did Leah like them?'

'Yes, she did. That said, horses were her passion.'

'I gather you didn't have any children.'

Fin kicked a stone with the toe of his boot.

'No. The year before she died, she'd had a miscarriage. It mentally knocked the stuffing out of her. She was forty at the time. An older mum-to-be. Personally, I don't believe the lost pregnancy was age-related. After all, she always glowed with good health. However, the Big-Four-Oh birthday had bothered her. She'd cited it as a likely cause for the miscarriage. Consequently, she didn't want to try and get pregnant again.'

'That's a shame. If she'd had a baby… well, you'd still have a part of her. If that makes sense.'

'Hmm.' Fin shook his head. 'I can't say I share that sentiment. Sure, a child would have had Leah's DNA. Also, there would have been some physical likeness. Hair. Colouring. Eyes, maybe. But ultimately that child would have been a unique human being. Yes, I'd have looked at our kid and always been reminded of Leah, but it wouldn't have *been* Leah. Whatever her essence was… her soul, her spirit, whatever you want to call it… that had gone. And nothing was ever going to bring it back. Not even a whole army of kids.'

'I see what you mean,' I conceded. 'Certainly, I don't look at my daughter and think of Rick. Sally is her own person. However, I haven't been bereaved. I was left bereft in an entirely different way.'

'Do you know where Rick is?'

'Not as such,' I shook my head. 'He moves around. I haven't seen him since the day the bailiff called at the caravan.'

'What about Sally? Doesn't she want to keep in touch with her father?'

'She's seen him a couple of times, but not particularly bothered. I haven't influenced her,' I added hastily. 'She's a young woman and able to make up her own mind.'

We walked on. We were now heading towards Trebah's *Water Garden*. Fin told me that it had been built around a natural spring, flowing downhill through a series of pools.

These, in turn, were criss-crossed by a meandering path. It was covered in leaves and bordered with a plethora of plants. Some I recognised, like the *Candelabra Primula*. This would be a riot of colour when in flower. But I also spotted plenty of yellow-speared *Skunk Cabbage*.

'What's that?' I asked, pointing. Ahead was an open-fronted summerhouse. It had cob walls and a thatched roof.

'Leah loved that place,' Fin smiled. 'It's a re-creation of the original structure which was built by Charles Hext for his wife, Alice. They bought Trebah in 1907. All the materials – the green oak timbers, the cob, and even the cobbles, all come from here. Alice and Charles together chose plants that would give the best fragrance in summer. Leah used to say she could almost see Alice sitting outside, the sun on her face as she breathed in the scents of *Osmanthus*, *Myrtus* and *Christmas Box*.'

We walked on, this time in a companionable silence, each with our own thoughts. Occasionally a twig would snap underfoot. Now and again, we'd hear a child's shout of delight, or the distant bark of a dog. But other than that, nothing disturbed the peace and tranquillity.

And still we strolled on. Past ancient tree stumps and great fronds of ferns. Our shoes sank into the soft earth when we reached an area known as *Cascade*. Fin told me that it was here the waters poured over a natural rock face. I followed him down several steps to a place known as *Koi Pool*. It was set against a huge backdrop of granite boulders and leafy foliage.

'What stunning fish,' I said. Leaning forward, I trailed my fingers in the crystal-clear waters.

'The pool is full of Koi Carp and Sturgeon,' said Fin.

'Look at the size of them,' I marvelled. 'They've got to be at least eighteen inches long.'

For a moment we simply admired their vibrant bodies and graceful movements as they swam about.

'Has it got any easier?' I asked abruptly. 'I mean, since Leah passed away.'

'Of course,' said Fin. 'That first aching sense of loss... well, eventually it becomes an acceptance of the situation. The passing of time gives gentle healing. The grief is no longer raw. But there's still sadness. There probably always will be.'

'And I take it you've not since met anyone special?' I asked gently.

'I've filled the void with a number of women.' He gave a deprecating shrug. 'To be honest, I've behaved like a bit of a tart. I'm not proud of myself.'

'We all have our coping mechanisms,' I pointed out.

'Is that what you did then, Lottie?' He raised his dark eyebrows. 'Healed your split from Rick by taking a string of men to your boudoir?' There was a teasing tone in his voice.

'Er, no.' I shook my head. 'When Rick did a runner, I had some serious financial problems. He left me, as the saying goes, *to face the music*. I was like a conductor without a baton trying to pacify an angry orchestra. The last thing I wanted was another man in my life. I had so much anger at Rick. I ended up transferring it to all men. So, if a man smiled at me, instead of doing the same, I'd scowl instead. If a guy walked past and happened to say, "Good morning," I'd stop and snarl, "Is it?" I'm sorry to say that I held all men in contempt.'

Which attitude had helped enormously when taking their cash for pics of my feet.

'So, you had to have a big rethink about making a living,' said Fin. 'Hence writing your books.'

'Um, yes,' I said vaguely. 'Where there's a will there's always a way. I've dabbled in everything to put food on the table and clear the debt Rick left me with.'

'Do you have a pseudonym?' Fin asked.

For a moment I wondered what he was talking about.

'Oh, you mean a pen name. No.' I shook my head. 'I write as Lottie Lucas.'

It was elsewhere that I worked under a different name.

Chapter Forty-Seven

'I really enjoyed that,' I said. I hopped into Fin's Land Rover. We both buckled up and he put the car into reverse. The vehicle began to roll backwards. 'Thank you so much for showing me around Trebah.'

Fin braked sharply. For a moment the car hovered, half in the parking bay, half out. He looked at me.

'On the contrary, Lottie. It should be me thanking you.' His voice was grave. 'Today, you helped me face my demons. By revisiting Trebah, I now know the place isn't a precursor to doom. Instead, it's a place full of joy. Happy memories. And I've just made one more.' His expression was both earnest and sincere.

'I'm glad,' I murmured.

'I'll go to Trebah again,' he said determinedly. 'Maybe next time I'll take Pru. And then, instead of walking around the gardens reminiscing about only Leah, I'll then be reminded of both you and my sister too.'

'That's it,' I said encouragingly.

His face relaxed and he gave me a grin that instantly made my stomach flip.

'So, are you still up for buying me that G and T?' he asked.

'You bet,' I nodded. 'Where shall we go? Back to Penwern Lodge?'

'Good heavens, no.' Fin looked aghast. 'That would be coals to Newcastle, as they say. I know the perfect place. It's called The Pandora Inn.' He released the brake and changed gear. The Land Rover moved forwards. 'To be honest, it's a shame we're travelling there by car because the pub has its own mooring pontoon. It's directly outside the building. As a consequence, many patrons visit the inn via the Falmouth water taxi. It makes getting there a bit more of a treat. The pub is located right on the edge of Restronguet Creek, which is home to several slipways, including Loe Beach. You can imagine how popular it is in the summer. We'll take our drinks outside. It's chilly, but we're dressed appropriately and can enjoy sitting on the pontoon. There's something rather uplifting in watching all the boats bobbing about on the water and the fisherman returning with their day's catch. It's also very peaceful. We should just about catch half an hour before the light fades.'

'Sounds brilliant,' I smiled.

Minutes later, we were parking up again.

'Oh!' I exclaimed in delight. 'This pub is so pretty.'

The Pandora Inn was cottage-like in appearance. Its exterior was painted in a pale gold and overlaid with a chocolate-brown thatched roof. It reminded me of a freshly baked golden loaf of bread. Inside it was all low beams and flagstone floors. A cheerful barmaid came over to serve us.

'What can I get you guys?' she asked.

'Two gin and tonics, please,' I said. I turned to Fin. 'Fancy some crisps?'

'Go on, you've twisted my arm,' he said. 'Cheese and onion are my favourite.'

'Mine too,' I said.

I paid the barmaid and Fin then led the way outside. We followed a path around the side of the inn, and walked to the end of the pontoon. Fin stopped at the last table by the safety rails. I sighed with pleasure and sat down.

'You have such beauty here,' I said. 'It's everywhere.'

For a few minutes we sat in a companionable silence, simply admiring the view and listening to the squawk of the gulls as they weaved through the sky. Every now and again, one would break off from the flock to soar low and dip its beak in the water.

Several swans were majestically paddling around the pontoon. Their beady eyes were on the lookout for offerings from patrons. I watched, fascinated, as they effortlessly glided about. Such handsome birds.

'What's your village like?' asked Fin.

'Pretty enough,' I said, crossing one leg. 'Little Waterlow is a small blob on the North Downs. It's surrounded by fields and trees. There's a lot of grazing sheep and cattle. There's a woodland country park with its own café, which is popular with both dog walkers and ramblers. On the outskirts are a couple of characteristically ancient pubs that date back a few hundred years. But the village isn't like this' – I waved a hand at the surrounding area – 'and we don't have anything like Trebah Gardens. Well, unless you count Ightham Mote. That's a manor house that dates to the fourteenth century. However, the surrounding gardens are on a far smaller scale. It's beautiful, but not as magnificent as Trebah.'

'Do you like living there?' Fin asked.

'It's okay. I'm relatively new to the place. It's one of those locations where you must have a family tree dating back three hundred years to properly be accepted. Otherwise, you'll always be thought of as a newcomer,' I laughed.

'It sounds lovely,' said Fin loyally.

'It would be better if it didn't have a smalltown mentality,' I sighed. 'Everyone knows everyone else's business.'

'That can be annoying,' Fin chuckled. 'Does that mean that everyone has discovered your deepest, darkest secret, Lottie?' he teased.

'Almost,' I said lightly. If only he knew. I was suddenly reminded of the moment Mabel Plaistow had stepped into that field. It had been a close call. 'But a secret it shall remain,' I bantered. 'That said, Little Waterlow's biggest gossip is doing her best to catch me out.'

'This place isn't much different,' Fin confided. 'Everyone knows everyone and–'

He abruptly broke off. Stared ahead. My head whipped round and I followed his gaze. A woman was striding along the pontoon. A sudden breeze lifted her newly highlighted hair which flew around her head like Medusa's writhing snakes.

'Marina,' I breathed.

For one crazy moment I had an urge to dive into the creek and sharply swim off. The desire to be elsewhere – anywhere – was overwhelming.

Don't be ridiculous, Lottie. Stand your ground. You've done nothing wrong.

'Hello, Fin,' said Marina. Her voice was cooler than a North Pole icefloe. 'How peculiar. I could've sworn you said you weren't dating this woman. And yet, here you both are. Inseparable. This time enjoying a drink together.'

'We're not–' I protested.

However, I got no further on account of Marina snatching up my glass and chucking gin in my face. A slice of lemon slid off my nose. I was too stunned to react. Marina glared at me.

'I told you this morning,' she snarled. 'Keep your paws off.'

'Marina–' warned Fin, jumping to his feet.

Seconds later his own drink was dripping down his cheeks.

'You'd better take me off *Locator*, darling,' Marina hissed. 'Otherwise, I will continue to track you down and make your life the same hell as what you're currently putting me through.'

And with that she burst into tears, collapsed against Fin's chest, and flung her arms around his neck.

Chapter Forty-Eight

'Erm…'

I stood up, anxious to distance myself from any further drama. A little further up the pontoon, a married couple were watching with interest. Their eyes were on stalks.

Oh no. Please don't let them believe I'm *the other woman*. Too late. The pair of them were now whispering behind their hands. The wife tossed some contemptuous looks my way. I gathered up my bag.

'I'll make my own way back to Penwern Lodge,' I muttered.

'Lottie, wait a min–'

'Oh, Fin,' Marina howled. 'Finny-Win-Win, don't leave me.'

She pushed him back into his chair and upped her wailing. My eardrums momentarily reverberated. Marina was now prostrate on Fin's lap and keening like a wounded animal. Fin attempted shifting her. However, Marina held on tightly. She'd prised herself to him like a barnacle to a Cornish fishing boat.

I hastened along the pontoon. As I passed the married couple, the woman shot me a filthy look.

'Females who come between spouses deserve everything

they get,' she loudly declared.

Face flaming, I ducked inside. Locating the barmaid, I asked if she had the telephone number of a local taxi firm.

'Where do you want to go, love?' she said.

'Penwern Lodge.'

'I'll take you,' said a man. He drained his glass of cola.

Oh God. This was all I needed. From *scarlet woman* to *picked up woman* to possibly *murdered woman*. The last thing I wanted was a lift from a stranger.

'Thanks, but–'

'You're all right, love,' the barmaid interrupted. 'Brian is a local taxi driver. I can personally vouch for him because he's my hubby,' she grinned.

'Ah, right,' I said. My shoulders sagged with relief. 'In that case, thank you very much, Brian.'

The journey back didn't take long. Darkness descended enroute. As the taxi pulled up outside the hotel, I thought how welcoming it looked. All its lights were twinkling and glowing against the inky black backdrop. I thanked Brian, paid the fare, and went inside.

When I walked into reception, Pru was there and on the phone. She looked up and smiled, then frowned when she realised Fin was absent.

I wasn't in the mood for explanations. Instead, I gave Pru a quick wave and hastened off towards Fin's apartment.

Before letting myself into the apartment, I left my walking boots outside the front door. They were still a little muddy. I then hurried up the two flights of stairs to my turret bedroom.

Moodily, I peeled off my coat. The collar was still soggy from melted ice cubes. I dumped the garment on the floor. I wasn't normally an untidy person but, for some reason, this act of defiance felt rather good. In fact, I could see exactly why my daughter did it. Sally was still partial to leaving a trail of garments across the carpet.

I wasn't a teenager, but right now I was feeling horribly rebellious.

Stuff Marina for spoiling my lovely day. Stuff Ryan for not being here. And stuff Jen for excluding me. If it hadn't been for Fin, I'd have rattled around Falmouth like a spare part. Oh, and stuff Rick too. I might as well include him in my rant. After all, he'd landed me in debt, hence *Fifi Footsy* and a secret nearly being revealed by Mabel Plaistow. Actually, stuff Mabel too. Stuff everyone!

Stop cursing, Lottie.

Mind your own business, I mentally snarled. I'm done with people telling me what to do. Their judgments. Their opinions. Like that stupid woman on the pontoon. The silly cow. Bitch. Prat. Twat.

Stop it. Go and wash your mouth out with soap.

No, why don't you instead?

I'm not the one ranting.

Oh, fuck off.

I peeled off my jeans and left them, inside out, on the floor. My damp fleece and wet shirt followed. Wow. How liberating.

I whipped my hands behind my back and unhooked my bra. I then flung it across the room. It landed on the flatscreen; the strap hooked over one corner. To hell with it. It could stay there.

Stripped down to my pants and socks, I flopped backwards on the bed. Stared up at the ceiling. A fake candelabra hung directly over the bed. The light fitting had imitation candles. A second later, I'd removed my pants, scrunched them into a ball and lobbed them upwards. They landed on part of the light fitting, disturbing a tiny spider. He scuttled up a faux candle in terror.

I was just about to take off my sweaty socks when I paused. After being encased in hiking boots, the socks looked grim. Ah. Perfect. I'd take a quick pic. Upload it to *Fifi Footsy's* platform.

Getting off the bed, I went to the wardrobe and retrieved my suitcase. Within the zipped lining was my other mobile. *Fifi's* phone.

Switching it on, I was surprised to see that Mr Muppet had messaged. There were three texts. The last one had been sent just five minutes ago. I checked the phone's battery. It was still at forty-six percent. Okay. No time like the present.

I raised my eyebrows at the first text.

Fifi. Please tell me honestly. What's your opinion of me liking dirty, smelly, cheesy feet? You can be as obtuse as you like. Usual fee.

I sighed. Honestly? I reckoned the guy was nuttier than a pack of peanuts.

257

Me again. Can I have a video? I'd really like to see some of you in it.

Yeah, bet you would, sunshine. You might faint if you saw what I really looked like.

Fifi, are you there? It's not like you to take so long to reply. Look, I have an outrageous suggestion. I'd like to meet you – and your feet, of course. I know this would mean revealing your identity but, financially, I'd make it worth your while. I'm not dangerous. Promise. And I don't want to sleep with you. I just want to… do things… with your feet.

For one crazy moment, I considered it. I then recoiled in horror.

Was this how low I'd sunk? A peri–menopausal woman seriously considering taking money from a man who wanted to… you know.

However, I was still in a rebellious mood. I'd already made up my mind to blow out Ryan. He wasn't coming to Cornwall. I knew that. He knew that. We were kidding each other. I was done listening to all his excuses. I'd phone him on Monday. When I was home.

However, along with my discarded clothes, Ryan wasn't the only thing to dump. It was time to say goodbye to *Fifi Footsy* too. I'd had enough of her. She wasn't me. I didn't like her. However, she was an extension of me, the *real* me, and I didn't want to dislike the real me. After all, the real me was a decent person. Except, lately, I'd been feeling tarnished. Stained. Like a white shirt with a ketchup mark that, no matter how many times washed, wouldn't go away. I wanted to put this sordid little chapter behind me. Wipe the slate clean. Get rid of that last bit of debt.

Soon, my books would go live. I'd be able to manage financially when the royalties came in. I was sure of it. My brain started to whirr.

I picked up my regular mobile, clicked on the banking app and logged in. How much was left to pay off? I scrolled down. Eight hundred and thirty-one pounds, twenty-three pence. Chucking down the phone, I picked up Fifi's mobile and began to type.

Okay, Mr Muppet. I have a proposition for you.

Chapter Forty-Nine

I had no guilt about my proposal to Mr Muppet. He was using my feet for thrills, and I was using his money for bills. It was a two-way thing.

However, enough was enough. Also, if I was going to kill off *Fifi Footsy*, then I should do it in a way that gave absolute resolution.

My fingers flew across *Fifi's* phone:

I am prepared to do everything you ask, with the exception of meeting you. This will also be the last time. Fifi is retiring. This final service will include a five-minute video – yes, a whole five minutes – which will feature me, naked, apart from my socks and footwear. I will give you a shoe-and-sock-tease… complete with voiceover. I will tell you what I REALLY think of you. My fee is eight hundred and thirty-one pounds and twenty-three pence precisely. This is non-negotiable.

I wasn't really expecting a reply. If the guy did respond, it might be along the lines of taking a running jump – socks included.

The phone dinged.

Fifi. That's a lot of money. Too much.

I didn't waver.

Take it or leave it.

The phone dinged again.

Not five minutes. Ten minutes. If so, you have a deal.

I didn't hesitate.

Deal.

Bloody hell. I boggled at the phone's screen. Bloody *bloody* hell. In another thirty seconds, I was going to be financially liberated.

I felt a rush of something. Whatever it was, it was whooshing upwards. Towards my head. Had my circulation gone haywire? No. It was the feeling of relief. Sweet, *sweet* relief.

Tears sprang to my eyes. For the first time in years… decades… I was going to be free. Truly free. I could be me again. The *real* me. Born again. A brand-new shiny person. Bye-bye, Fifi. Hello, Lottie.

It was time to live my life. Fearlessly. Shamelessly. Nobody knew about my alter ego. And nobody ever would. I realised, with a jolt, that the only person who had been judging me… was me.

Feeling almost giddy with newfound optimism, I inhaled deeply, then slowly released the breath. It seemed that, as I exhaled, all my secret shame, all my private despair, all my personal demons, exited my body on that one, long, slow out-take of breath.

Another ding of the phone.

Money transferred. I await in anticipation.

Chapter Fifty

I would like to say that my video was tasteful. But it wasn't.

I nipped downstairs and retrieved my grubby hiking boots. Back in my room, I slipped them on, then removed a baseball cap from the bottom of my suitcase. Ramming it on my head, I tucked my ponytail in at the back, then pulled the peak down hard over my face. So far, so good.

Propping the mobile on a console table, I pressed the button and started filming. I mentally kept my fingers crossed that Mr Muppet would be deluded enough to think I was a woman in my thirties, rather than a perimenopausal female lurching towards the Big Five-Oh.

Keeping my face well away from camera, I strutted around Fin's turret bedroom. There was no need to worry about being identified from these surroundings. The room wasn't mine and soon I'd be checking out, never to come here again. I set to work – a wobbly-bottomed vision in hiking boots with socks at half-mast.

I found myself silently thanking God for Marina's earlier appearance on the pontoon. If she hadn't buttonholed Fin, I wouldn't now be available to Mr Muppet and joyfully debt free. It was also reassuring to know that Fin wasn't around to hear me rant to a stranger who spent stupid sums of money on an even more stupid fetish.

I stridently ridiculed Mr Muppet. Told him he was certifiable for liking smelly feet. That he had a screw loose. Needed counselling. Was a prat of the highest order. That he should seriously get a life.

In short, I gave it to him with both barrels. Simultaneously, a part of me acknowledged that this rant was cathartic for me too. Here I was, releasing years of pent-up misery on a total stranger. Bizarrely, that stranger was paying a fortune to be on the receiving end of my outburst.

I continued to prance around the bedroom. As I wiggled past the television, I grabbed my bra. Standing under the light fitting – from which my M&S undies continued to dangle – I waved the bra above my head like a football rattle. Throughout, I ensured my face was hidden. As a result, Mr Muppet wasn't getting much of a full frontal. No matter. If he felt short-changed by just my bare backside and cellulite, then tough. As far as I was concerned, I'd been shortchanged all my life. Mr Muppet, deal with it!

I draped my bra around my shoulders, then retrieved my phone from the console table. Taking care not to accidentally touch the *pause* button, I then sank down on the dressing table's stool.

I pointed the camera lens at the floor – and immediately flinched at the state of the carpet. Flipping heck. There was mud everywhere. But never mind that for now. I zoomed in on my feet. Steadying the camera, I started to use the tip of each boot to rub at the shoelaces. First the left foot. Then the right.

After plenty of shoelace foreplay, I slowly eased out one foot. My sweaty socks were revealed in all their manky glory. I wiggled my toes within their unattractive eighty-denier confines. Then I rubbed the balls of my feet against one shin. Then the other. It was important to string it out for a bit. Nice and slow. The guy wanted his ten minutes, so I'd give him his money's worth. No worries.

Gradually, I used my left big toe to slide down the top of the right sock. Little by little. Second by second. Half a minute later, one sock was puddled around an ankle. I then did this all over again with the other foot. Throughout, I told Mr Muppet that the smell was putrid. That he was a weirdo to get any thrill from what I was doing.

Finally, *finally*, the socks were off. I wiggled and waggled my feet about, this way and that. I displayed the underside. The soles. The fleshy ball joints. I also included a closeup of my cracked heels that were in dire need of repair cream.

I then zoomed in on the mole under the big toe, pausing to run my other toe over it. All the while I kept up a stream of verbal nonsense, while my heart sang with joy. For make no mistake, I was revelling in the knowledge that – once the pause button had been pressed – I'd never, ever, do this again.

Chapter Fifty-One

I'd just finished vacuuming the turret room – clothes back on again and pants retrieved from the light fitting – when there was a tentative knock on the door. I looped the flex around the machine's upright handle.

'Come in,' I yodelled.

'Oh, Lottie,' Fin protested. 'You didn't need to clean your room. I pay staff to do that.'

'Er, I wanted to,' I said quickly. 'I forgot to take my boots off. It made a bit of a mess.' I straightened up. 'Is everything all right?' I wondered if Marina was downstairs again. Whether there had been a grand reunion. Fin dodged the question.

'Here, let me take that.' He grabbed the vacuum and stowed it away in the cupboard on the landing, where I'd found it. 'Come downstairs. It's been a few hours since our fish and chip lunch. I don't know about you, but I'm feeling peckish again. I was going to make a cheese and tomato sandwich and wondered if you'd like one too. Unless, of course, you're joining your friends in the dining room. I saw them both earlier. They came in at the same time as me.'

'A sandwich would be great,' I said. 'Anyway, I haven't heard from Jen. Therefore, I'd rather not presume to eat with them. If that's okay with you,' I added quickly.

Best to double check. After all, he still hadn't confirmed if *madam* was downstairs. I wasn't sure I fancied having a snack at the same table as her. After Marina making free with my drink earlier, I might be tempted to retaliate. Maybe use my fork as a catapult. Lob some sliced tomato at her.

'Fancy a G and T?' Fin asked. 'I seem to recall we didn't get to finish our drinks.' He gave me a meaningful look.

'Um…' I hesitated for a second. 'Sorry, Fin, but I must ask you. Is Marina downstairs?'

'Good Lord no,' he said. 'There will no repeats of flying ice and lemon.' He rubbed his face with the heel of one hand. I suddenly noticed how tired he looked.

'That's reassuring,' I grinned. 'In which case, lead the way.'

I followed him down the stairs, privately admiring his pert backside. What I'd give for a derriere shaped like his.

My mood was buoyant to say the least. Prior to vacuuming the bedroom, I'd transferred the money from *Fifi's* account, then deleted everything.

It had been such a liberating experience. I no longer felt guilty about using *Fifi* to make money. I could forgive her customers their foibles and weaknesses. There hadn't been that many of them, in all truth. And only one had gone above and beyond the average spend.

In fact, I was in such a forgiving mood, I could even excuse Rick for what he'd put me through. I now realised that I'd played a part in his financial dramas too. You see, I'd enabled him. I'd given him permission to take advantage of me. Oh, not in words. No. Rather, by my actions. The constant bailing out. Believing his empty promises. Then the whole repeat of this emotionally draining cycle. If I'd said no from the get-go, we'd never have ended up in a caravan.

Somewhere along the way, I'd lost myself. But now, Lottie Lucas was back! Goodbye *Fifi Footsy*. I wished my alter ego all the best. It was time to tell myself that I *did* have a proper job. I was a writer. And I was also respectable, thank you very much.

'Let me help you,' I said, following Fin into the kitchen area.

He waved me away with one hand.

'I'm not one of those helpless males, Lottie. I do know how to find my way around a kitchen. Go and sit down. Put the telly on. I'll bring the food over in a mo.'

'I'm not bothered about watching the telly,' I said. 'I'm quite happy chatting. Anyway, I really would like to help you.'

'Okay,' he conceded. 'You make the drinks. There's a bottle of tonic water in the fridge. I think there's some fresh lemons in there, too. The gin is in the cabinet in the lounge – same one that the brandy is kept in.'

Brandy last night. Gin tonight. What will it be tomorrow? asked my inner voice.

I ignored the dig.

Moments later, I was swizzing ice cubes around my gin glass while Fin made a small pile of sandwiches. He'd bought a fresh crusty loaf from the local bakery. There was no cheap flannel-like bread in this kitchen.

As he buttered and sliced, we made small talk. Apparently Pru had been on *LinkedIn* earlier. She'd already interviewed a potential new receptionist. Business was good. Blah blah. Marina wasn't mentioned. I was dying to know what had happened earlier, and where she was now.

I tried not to dribble as Fin transferred the sandwiches to prettily patterned porcelain plates. He handed one to me.

'Thanks,' I said. I made my way over to the far end of Fin's squashy sofa.

He followed but didn't opt to sit at the other end. Instead, Fin sat himself down next to me. Close enough to put an arm around me – should he so wish.

Is that what you want? said my inner voice.

Wouldn't say no, I mentally shrugged. After all, I'm a free agent.

Ahem. Reminder alert. There is a man in your life. His name begins with R.

You know fully well that he's not here. Also, that he's unlikely to turn up. You also know that I will be ending this relationship–that–never–was when I'm back at Catkin Cottage on Monday.

I see. So once you've finished that sarnie, are you hoping that Fin is going to turn to you and stick his tongue down your throat.

I wasn't, but now that you've mentioned it, that sounds most agreeable.

You don't stand a chance.

How dare you! For all you know, Fin might have his gin goggles on. He might think me utterly ravishing.

He'd need double measures to ever think that.

Why do you always put me down?

You're forgetting that I am you. Therefore, you put yourself down.

Suddenly, my previous euphoria did a bunk. What was I doing sitting next to this man – a virtual stranger – with my heart banging away? Even now, my breath was periodically catching in my throat. I knew I'd blush if our hands unexpectedly touched. It was the behaviour of an overgrown schoolgirl.

Did I really dare to hope that Fin would make a move on me? Declare that he fancied me rotten? Push me back on the sofa as our sandwiches slid off our plates? That he'd kiss the life out of me as our bodies squashed bits of cheese and tomato into the sofa?

Well, yes, maybe. I was aware that he was newly single – even though barely two hours had passed since he'd gained that status. However, I was single too. Or at least I would be come Monday.

But the reality was that nothing was going to happen between us. Fin wasn't interested in me. My conscience had already pointed out that he was out of my league.

I stared at the bubbles in my drink. Perhaps I should logon to *YouTube*. Watch one of those tutorials about feeling worthy. Stand in front of a mirror. Ignore the bags under my eyes. The crepe to my neck. Instead, repeat over and over, *I lurve you.* Yeah, and pigs might fly.

'You look a million miles away,' said Fin. He'd already eaten half his sandwiches. He leant forward and picked up his gin. 'What are you thinking about?' He took a long sip, eyeing me curiously.

'Oh, something and nothing,' I shrugged. 'Anyway' – it was no good, I had to ask – 'how did you get on with Marina?'

He put his glass down and made a tutting sound.

'I eventually managed to prise her off my lap. I then firmly told her that she needed to move on. To be honest, Marina knows that. I think it's her pride that's hurt more than anything. She's never had someone end a relationship with her before. It's a whole new experience. One that she doesn't like. As far as Marina is concerned, *she's* the one who does the dumping.'

'I'm not sure I wholeheartedly agree with you, Fin. I mean, earlier, she did seem genuinely distressed.'

'Lottie, you don't know her the way I do. Also, I don't wish to be unkind, but she's extremely manipulative. Very good at emotional blackmail. She's also a total fantasist,' he added. 'I won't bore you with the details—'

'Nooo, it's fine,' I assured. Give me the details. The more, the better. For some reason, I wanted to know everything about Marina.

'Just take it from me,' he said. 'The moment she's met some other poor sod and set out to bleed him dry—'

'What?' I interrupted.

'She's a gold digger, Lottie,' Fin sighed. 'I might not drive a Ferrari, and I might be mortgaged up to the hilt with this place, but women like Marina go on first impressions. She thinks I'm loaded. And while I'm not scraping the barrel, I still have bills and overheads to deal with. Take it from me' – he waggled a finger to emphasise his point – 'the minute Marina meets someone else, preferably Lord Many Acres from the next county, she'll be off like a fox after a rabbit.'

'Good,' I said. 'I mean' – I reddened – 'that will be good for you. You know, not to have to keep looking over your shoulder. As it were.'

'Quite,' Fin nodded.

My phone suddenly dinged with a message.

'Excuse me,' I said.

'Perhaps that will be your boyfriend with some good news,' said Fin warmly.

My heart did a few erratic beats as I digested Fin's tone of voice. Right. So, in other words, Fin wanted Ryan to turn up. It was only me who didn't.

'I doubt it will be Ryan,' I muttered, reaching for my phone from where I'd left it on the coffee table. I peered at the screen. 'It's a text from Jen.'

Hi Lottie! Hope you've had a fab day. Stu and I had a great time exploring the coastal footpath. We're going to have dinner in bed – as you do when you're on a romantic break! Xxx

'Is she wanting you to join her for dinner?' asked Fin. 'In which case, give her my apologies for plying you with sandwiches before having your evening meal.'

'On the contrary,' I sighed. 'Right now, Jen would not appreciate me turning up. If you catch my drift.'

'Ah,' said Fin. His tone conveyed that he understood. 'Meanwhile, what about Ryan?'

'What about him?' I said gloomily.

Fin gave me a curious look.

'Have you heard from him?'

'Yeah. He said he'll see me tomorrow.'

'That's nice.'

'Is it?'

Fin put his head on one side. Gave me a quizzical look.

'Well, surely the answer to that is yes. Tomorrow will be your grand romantic reunion.'

You should tell Fin about the zingers he gives you. Now that's romantic!

Oh, do be quiet, I silently replied. Fin doesn't have a clue about how I feel.

Omigod, serious crush alert.

Please go away. Now is not the time to be whispering in my ear.

'Fin, I might as well be honest. As I said earlier, I'm not expecting Ryan to turn up. I've learnt the hard way that the guy is full of hot air. Ryan says one thing but then does something else. It happens all the time, and I simply can't be bothered with it anymore. When Jen and Stu take me home

272

on Monday, I'll be having a heart to heart with Ryan. Basically, I'm going to tell him that we're finished.'

'I'm sorry to hear that, Lottie,' said Fin quietly.

I shrugged and sighed.

'It's fine. *I'm* fine.'

'In which case, as you seem to think you'll be on your Jack Jones again tomorrow, would you like me to keep you company?'

Yes, yes, yes!

'That's very kind of you,' I said carefully. 'However, I feel bad that I'm taking you away from your work.'

'Nonsense,' he said. 'I can easily juggle things about. I want you to leave Cornwall with a little piece of this place firmly lodged in your heart.'

'Thanks,' I smiled.

Little did he know that that had already happened. However, it wasn't Cornwall my heart was holding. It was him.

Chapter Fifty-Two

When I awoke the following morning, daylight was streaming in through the cracks between the drapes.

Jumping out of bed, I flung the curtains wide. The breath caught in my throat. Little Waterlow had some amazing views, but right now they were being trumped by the vista before me.

Friday night's storm and Saturday's rain had given way to a Sunday sky the colour of forget-me-nots.

Puffy white clouds seemingly chugged across a blue background. It was as if someone had opened a bag of cotton wool balls, then glued them to the heavens.

The fields seemed brighter. The grass was a dazzling emerald, still glittering with raindrops that had yet to dry up. Even the sheep appeared to be whiter. In the distance, a cobalt sea shifted and sparkled.

The estate cottages looked as if they'd fallen from the lid of a fancy box of chocolates. A door to one of them now opened. Pru stepped out. I watched as she made her way along the gravel path and headed this way.

Behind Pru was an area of woodland. It currently looked like something out of an Enid Blyton creation. *The Enchanted Forest* came to mind. I half expected Moon-Face and Silky the Fairy to step out, wave, and urge me to join them for an adventure.

With a shiver of delight, I thought about the day ahead. I was going on my own adventure – with Fin. He'd promised to take me to a surprise destination.

I hugged myself. At the same time, I made some strange squeaking noises. It was hard to contain my excitement.

Yesterday evening, we'd settled down on the sofa again, armed with our gin and tonics. We'd chatted away until Pru had knocked on the apartment's door. She'd apologised for interrupting but asked if Fin could spare five minutes for a guest who had a list of complaints.

'There's always one,' she said with an eyeroll. 'Mr Archibald would probably like his loo seat warmed if we offered such a service.'

I'd taken it as my cue to go upstairs. The time had been getting on anyway. Sally had also messaged from her digs at uni. She'd been after a FaceTime session and catch up.

Fin had told me to make myself at home. To help myself to whatever I wanted. I'd thanked him, but said I was going to have a catch up with my daughter, and then enjoy a hot soak in the bath.

Once alone, I'd also texted Ryan.

Hi. Hope all's well. Listen, I've had a think. It's ludicrous to drive all the way to Cornwall tomorrow. By the time you get here, it will almost be time to go home. Apart from anything else, we need to have a serious chat. While here, I've had time to reflect on our relationship. Anyway,

I'm not going to say anything else by text. Such a conversation needs to be had face to face.

He hadn't replied. To be honest, I hadn't expected him to. The undertone to the message was clear. As the saying goes, *the writing was on the wall.*

Nor did I think Ryan would be upset. I barely featured on his radar at the best of times. After all, there was always so much going on in his life at home. What with Heather making one demand. Joshua making another.

Last night, I'd gone to bed with a huge sense of relief. Now I could enjoy Sunday with a clear head and heart. When Monday morning rolled around, I'd never see Fin again. But right now, he was here. And I was too. I wanted to make the most of being with him, even though he had no idea how I felt.

I continued watching from the turret tower's window. Pru was now crossing the carpark area. Perhaps she sensed someone was watching because she glanced up. Catching sight of me, she waved. I grinned and waved back, then turned away. Jen had texted a few minutes ago. She'd invited me to join her and Stu for breakfast. Perhaps she had a guilty conscience having so thoroughly excluded me.

I'd texted back, accepting her invitation. After all, I wanted her and Stu to drive me back to Little Waterlow tomorrow morning.

I quickly dressed and gave my hair a good brush. No ponytail today. I left it loose and let it waterfall over my shoulders and down my back. Rick had once said that my hair was my crowning glory. Today I wanted as much glory as I could muster. Fin might be out of my league, but there was no reason not to try and look my best.

'You're looking very sparkly-eyed,' was Jen's opening gambit as I sat down at the breakfast table with her and Stu.

'So are you,' I said, smiling at the two of them.

This wasn't strictly true. Jen was nursing a pair of spectacular putty-coloured eyebags while Stu's eyeballs were the colour of red roadmaps. Evidently very little sleep had been taking place. Stu was almost slumped over his cornflakes. Jen, however, was tucking into her Full English.

'I took the liberty of ordering you the same as me,' she chirped, popping half a sausage in her mouth.

'Thanks,' I said. I reached for the coffee percolator stationed centrepiece on the crisp white linen.

'Until the waitress comes, have one of these to be going on with.' Jen pushed a toast rack towards me. 'Stu says he hasn't the energy to eat a large breakfast. It's a shame to let the toast and marmalade go to waste.'

'Oh dear,' I said to Stu innocently. 'Did yesterday's coastal walk take it out of you?'

He nodded mutely while Jen shot me a furtive look.

'That and a three-hour session in bed,' she said under her breath.

Three *hours*? Good grief. No wonder the poor chap looked all in. Jen was one of those friends who loved to tell you exactly what she got up to with a guy. From her past tales, I immediately knew vast amounts of energy had been expended. I wouldn't be surprised if this had included launching herself off a wardrobe, swinging like Tarzan from the light-fitting, then impaling herself onto Stu. The guy wouldn't have stood a chance.

'So how have you been entertaining yourself,' asked Jen. 'I hear the handsome hotel owner hasn't left your side.'

'Says who?' I replied, playing it cool.

'The lady on reception. I gather she is his sister.'

'Yes, her name's Pru. She's lovely.'

'Like her brother,' said Jen, waggling her eyebrows. 'Come on, then. Spill the beans. Is something going on between you and Mr Dishy?'

'Don't be daft,' I tutted. 'However, I agree that he's very attractive.'

If Stu was listening to this girly chit-chat, he didn't respond. From my peripheral vision, he appeared to be fixated on his cornflakes. A part of me wondered if he'd fallen asleep at the table – too exhausted to even shut his eyes.

'Fin has been very kind,' I continued. 'In fact, he's taking me out today. He won't tell me where. It's a surprise.'

'Ryan had better watch out.' Jen raised her eyebrows. 'It sounds to me like he might have some competition.'

I busied myself unwrapping a pat of butter. I kept my eyes firmly on the task. I didn't dare look at Jen in case I gave anything away about my crush on Fin.

'I might as well tell you' – I picked up a knife to spread the butter – 'once home, I'm ending it with Ryan. For one reason or another, he's always letting me down. I can't be doing with it anymore.'

'Aye aye,' said Jen. Her tone suggested she'd sussed another story behind my words. 'Could it be that you're clearing the path, so to speak?'

'What do you mean?' I said, feigning ignorance.

'You know perfectly well what I mean,' she harrumphed. 'I think you want to give yourself a fighting chance with a certain hotel owner.'

'Absurd,' I muttered, letting my hair fall across my face. I reached for the marmalade and dug in.

'In which case, Stu and I will join you and Fin today. I'm quite up for a mystery tour somewhere.'

Stu suddenly came to life. His head snapped up at the same time as mine.

'O-Oh, Jen,' he stuttered. 'I–I really d–don't think I'm up for–'

I cut him off mid-sentence.

'Jen, I love you very much,' I said. 'But this is payback time. I'm going without you. And I mean that in the nicest possible way,' I added. 'There's nothing going on between me and Fin. However, I'd be a liar to say that I didn't wish otherwise. So, thanks for the offer of your company, but it's a no.'

She gave me a sly, knowing look.

'Thought so,' she smirked. She then took my hand and gave it an affectionate squeeze. 'You deserve some fun, Lottie. Go for it.'

Chapter Fifty-Three

An hour later and I was with Fin at a very unexpected location.

'A castle!' I exclaimed as Fin parked up.

The fairy-like structure was a good five-minute walk away from the carpark, and I was glad my hiking boots were back on my feet.

'Welcome to Pendennis Castle,' said Fin. 'This once belonged to that famous, much-married royal, King Henry VIII. Anyway' – he grabbed a rucksack from the backseat – 'let's take in the view before we head over to explore.'

The surrounding area – like most places in Cornwall – was staggeringly beautiful. We were on high ground overlooking the Fal Estuary and Carrick roads. There were sweeping views over both sea and river. I gazed down at a brilliantly blue estuary. Numerous boats bobbed about on the water. Inhaling the bracing air, I suppressed a shiver as a sudden breeze lifted my hair.

'Look over there,' Fin pointed. I followed his finger and squinted into the distance. 'That's Mawes Castle, which is Pendennis Castle's twin. It was built about the same time as this one.'

'Exactly how old are these castles?'

I inwardly cringed, aware that I was showing my ignorance about history. It had never been my favourite subject. All that bloodshed. All those decapitated heads impaled on spiked railings. Or was I muddling King Henry with Oliver Cromwell? Although hadn't Henry been rather partial to decapitated heads too? I seemed to remember he'd sent two of his wives to the guillotine.

'Henry VIII had it built around 1540, predominantly as an artillery fort,' Fin explained.

'I've never seen a circular castle before,' I marvelled, while shielding my eyes against a low winter sun.

'There was a reason for the shape,' said Fin. I got the impression that he was enjoying giving this impromptu history lesson. 'There was some cunning to the castle's design. It meant Henry could be sure of all-round fire from the guns.'

We walked on, heading towards the castle itself. Fin chatted about planned Spanish invasions and how the Spanish fleet had intended to land troops at Pendennis. Surreally, I felt as if there were two of me by his side. One part was listening to him. Another part had detached and was bobbing along over the two of us.

This separate part of me floated and quietly observed. I watched as the dark-haired man walked alongside the blonde woman. The man's face was alight with joy. His happiness was evident as he talked and gestured with his hands, illustrating the finer points of Tudor history. The woman, despite being in her late forties, was currently looking a decade younger. In fact, everything about her was positively glowing. There was a sparkle to her eyes that had been missing for years. The Cornish air had put roses in her cheeks. It was easy to deduce from the way she bowled along, that it was this man's company that had put a spring in her step. Let's put it this way. If she'd been a dog, her tail would have been a waggy blur. She was also giving the man discreet sideways glances. It was a wonder her tongue wasn't hanging out too.

Panting for him, are you, Lottie?

The separate part of me instantly pinged back into my body. I mentally rolled my eyes before answering the inner voice.

Ha! I was wondering when you'd pipe up.

Why don't you drop a few hints about how you feel?

No flipping way.

Fin paused, and I automatically stopped too.

'Shall we have a coffee before we go into the castle?' he asked.

'Where?' I frowned. There was no handy little café on this flat area of ground.

Fin swung the rucksack off his back.

'I brought some provisions,' he smiled.

'Blimey, you little star,' I marvelled.

Little star, Lottie? Isn't that a bit personal? A bit flattering?

You're the one that suggested I drop some hints, I silently retorted.

I cleared my throat. A regrouping gesture.

'I wondered what you had in that huge bag.'

'Some surprises,' he said, with a wink.

Oooh. Was he being a tiny bit flirty? I didn't know on account of being terrible at reading the signals.

Fin dug inside the rucksack. He produced a small blanket which he then spread across the damp ground. A thermos followed along with two plastic cups.

'Et voila,' he said. Like a magician, he then produced two slabs of chocolate cake.

'Wow, you really do think of everything,' I said. The admiration was evident in my voice.

'I try my best, madam,' he bantered. 'Please' – he indicated the ground sheet – 'do sit down.'

I lowered my derriere to the ground. The picnic rug wasn't very big. We were going to have to squash up together. It was going to be snug to say the least.

As Fin settled down beside me, the side of his thigh pressed against mine. An involuntary thrill rippled down my spine as, at the same time, a zinger shot up my leg and exploded in my privates. I let out a tiny yelp. H-e-l-p.

'Sorry,' Fin apologised. He shuffled about a millimetre away from me.

'It's fine,' I squeaked. Another zinger hurtled up my arm and catapulted against my chest. Suddenly my nipples were standing to attention.

Breathe, Lottie. Breathe.

I inhaled sharply and caught a subtle whiff of aftershave.

Oh, that gorgeous smell. So divine. I could breathe that scent for ever. I wondered if Fin would mind if I leant in and sniffed his neck. Nibbled his ear at the same time.

Focus on the view. The last thing you want is to make a fool of yourself.

'Before you pour my coffee' – I gasped – 'let me take some quick pics of the bay. It's breathtaking.'

Like you, I silently added.

'Sure,' said Fin easily. He paused; the unopened flask lodged between his knees. 'Take one of us too,' he said casually. 'I'd also like one for the album, as they say.'

'Y-Yes,' I said, trying to relax. 'I'd like to capture this moment also.'

I wasn't sure how he'd interpret that reply. Hopefully as nothing more than a throwaway comment. A hotel guest making a memory with a man she'd spent a platonic weekend with.

However, my emotions were all over the place. Totally chaotic and raging. I knew that, once home and alone at Catkin Cottage, this moment would be revisited. The digital picture captured on my mobile would be studied again and again. No doubt with an added ingredient. Like… a big dollop of fantasy. Like… pretending that this moment had been the precursor to dynamite chemistry passing between the two of us. That, seconds later, Fin had leant in, turned his face to mine, kissed my cheek… the corner of my mouth… then full on the lips… the tip of his tongue greeting mine as we went in for a full-blown snog… the phone slipping from my hand as his arms enfolded my body… the perfect choreography as he gently tipped me backwards… my hair billowing out as–

'Do you want me to take it?' Fin asked, scattering my thoughts.

I'd been miles away. Wondering whether to rewrite the last part of that scene. So that, instead of Fin pushing me back, he'd instead pulled me to my feet. Naturally he would have then scooped me up… before striding into the castle… taking me to a handy tucked-away room where King Henry had once deflowered a winsome wench and–

Lottie, you're daydreaming again! Get a grip on the rampant imagination.

'Okay,' I said. I was in such turmoil I didn't know if I was replying to my inner voice or Fin. I handed him my phone.

'Smile,' he instructed, flipping the lens so that the two of us were immediately visible on screen.

We both grinned away. I was very aware of how the sides of our bodies had practically melted into one other. Our heads were touching, for all the world like a couple in love.

But whoever coined the phrase *the camera never lies* wasn't telling the truth.

Chapter Fifty-Four

'Here,' said Fin. He passed the phone back to me.

'It's a nice one of you,' I said, staring at the digital image. 'You're very photogenic.'

'Thanks. It's a lovely shot of you too,' he said politely.

It really wasn't. I'd been about to blink, so looked bleary eyed and half-pissed.

'You know' – Fin looked reflective for a moment – 'I used to come to this place as a child and play here.'

'Really?' I said in astonishment.

'Back then, you could freely roam the grounds. I never had any problems with safety either.'

'Wasn't it creepy?'

'Yes,' he laughed. 'Very. I might as well tell you that there are loads of spooky stories about this castle. I guess that was the lure when I was a kid. Me and my mates used to hope we'd have a hair-raising, supernatural experience. That we'd belt home with our hearts pounding, secretly terrified, but giggling wildly. Of course, it never happened. That said, my mate Mikey was good at winding us all up. He was brilliant at ventriloquism and could *throw* his voice.' Fin frowned for a moment. 'There was one occasion where he swore blind that he hadn't tried to trick us, but we didn't believe him.'

'Don't,' I shivered. 'You've made me break out in goosebumps.'

Fin laughed.

'I'll tell you the myths when we're exploring inside.'

'Did Pru come here as a child too?'

'Sometimes,' he nodded. 'However, when she got to about fifteen, she deemed it uncool to hang out with a bunch of spotty lads. Especially one who was her kid brother. Me and my mates would come here on our bicycles and pretend we were ghostbusters.' Fin chuckled quietly as he remembered childish things. A ten-year-old boy in a world free from adult complexities, financial responsibilities, not forgetting health and safety regulations.

'Didn't your parents worry about you having an accident?' I frowned. I'd have gone bonkers if Sally had come to a place like this without adult supervision. 'After all, it must be very dark here come nightfall.'

'Yes, back then it was indeed pitch black. There was only an occasional moon to guide you. We used to come armed with bright camping torches. And no, we didn't tell the parents what we were up to. We used to make out we were going to each other's houses. My mum and dad never thought to check up on my whereabouts. Boys will be boys,' he shrugged.

We finished our chocolate cake and coffee, and watched the gulls ride the wind. Far below, a few brave souls in wetsuits had ventured into the swell on paddleboards.

At length, the blanket was refolded, and the flask and cups packed away. Fin slung the rucksack over his shoulder. Together, we made our way over to the castle, our elbows occasionally touching.

I longed to slip my hand into Fin's. A part of me hoped he might companionably link his arm through mine. Obviously neither happened.

Inside the castle there were several visitor information boards. The notices more or less said what Fin had already told me regarding King Henry VIII's invasion concerns.

'What it *doesn't* tell you' – Fin paused in front of a noticeboard – 'was that my mum was friends with a lady called Jean. Jean was once the property supervisor of Pendennis Castle. She was, so to speak, the keeper of the keys to this place.'

I eyed him speculatively.

'I sense a story coming up.'

Fin smiled mysteriously.

'Maybe.'

We moved away from the board and began to slowly wander. We checked out the guardhouse and then the interactive exhibition. The latter traced the history of the castle, its people, and the trade routes of the British Empire. Fin cleared his throat.

'I think it's because of my mother's stories – relayed from her friendship with Jean – that caused me and my mates to be so curious about this place. Jean told Mum that the castle had several spooky secrets. This included eight resident ghosts. There were even rumours of haunted hidden tunnels, although me and my friends never found any evidence of this.'

'Did you go looking for these tunnels?' I said, wide-eyed and not a little horrified. My vivid imagination was already conjuring up collapsed ceilings, injured kids, even one or two being buried alive. I wasn't a mother for nothing.

'Of course we looked for them,' Fin laughed. 'We were boys, not cissy girls.'

'Less of the cissy girls,' I said, prodding him playfully. 'You and your mates sound like you were a right bunch of mischievous Herberts.'

I instantly had a mental picture of the young Fin. Full of derring-do. Mud on the knees of his trousers. Shirttails hanging out as he and his gang wriggled along the ground on their stomachs. Searching the undergrowth. Shining their torches into bushes as they looked for concealed entrances and trap doors to dungeons. Such innocence.

These days an onlooker would regard such a group of boys as either intimidating or up to no good. There would be the assumption that they were either glue-sniffers or getting high on experimental joints.

'We had a blast here,' said Fin. His voice had taken on a wistful tone as his mind revisited happy memories. 'Mum said that Jean had confided in her. Apparently, the minute she'd got her hands on those keys, she'd unlocked every door marked *Private*.'

'Brave,' I murmured. I could imagine Jean. Curious.

Quaking slightly as she tiptoed about. Wondering what secrets might be revealed on the other side of these sturdy wooden doors.

'Jean claimed to have discovered several hidden rooms. She also came across a supposedly haunted kitchen, an underground prison, and an old explosives store.'

'Curiosity killed the cat,' I murmured.

If I'd have been Jean, at that point I might have telephoned Hogwarts and asked Professor Dumbledore to come to the castle, preferably armed with a fully working wand.

Fin went on to tell me about an old Tudor kitchen complete with a fireplace and bread oven. It hadn't been open to the public for safety reasons, predominantly because of a steep, winding staircase. This had led to what had once been the governors' quarters – naturally also haunted.

'Jean said that many paranormal organisations had asked if their investigation teams could explore the castle.' Fin looked deadly serious, so I had no doubt he was telling the truth. 'All were given permission to do research, and apparently all were very focused on the stairs. They claimed they'd made contact with a maid called Maud. Her main role would have been serving upstairs. Consequently, she would have gone up and down those winding stairs many times over. She was reported to be very loud.'

'Creepy,' I shivered. 'However, if I were a ghost, I wouldn't limit my haunting to a staircase. That would be awfully boring.'

'Ah' – Fin raised a finger to emphasise the point he was about to make – 'according to the paranormal team, Maud told them that she'd fallen to her death on that staircase.'

'Oh don't,' I shuddered. Fin's tales were starting to get to me.

We were now on the first floor. This was the Royal Artillery Barracks. There was an exhibition of letters, weapons, and memorabilia. This showed how life would have been for a soldier who'd trained and worked at the castle.

'It's hardly surprising that there's so many reports of ghostly activity,' Fin mused. 'After all, men, women and sadly children too, died here during the civil war. Another paranormal team reported hearing children's laughter. Also, soldiers walking about the place.'

'I think you're making a lot of this up.' I thumped him lightly on the arm.

'Cross my heart,' he said, with a wide-eyed look of innocence – although I could have sworn his mouth twitched. 'You must remember, Lottie, this castle dates back four hundred and sixty years – riotous years that encompass many battles. It's hardly surprising to hear that it's also home to several ghosts. Come on.' He unexpectedly grabbed my hand. His touch sent a scorching zinger whizzing through my entire body. For a moment, my hair stood on end for a very different reason. 'Let's go up to the rooftop.'

A minute later and we were taking in another epic view of the Fal Estuary.

'You surely can't get any higher than this,' I wheezed, experiencing a moment of vertigo.

'Wrong,' said Fin. 'Most days a member of staff scrambles up the ladder to the clocktower. Evidently, the clock itself has a habit of running ten minutes fast. It's quite a climb. You can also go up to the steeple. Apparently, that's terrifying, although I've heard the view is out of this world.'

'It seems there are several things here that are out of this world,' I said nervously.

'*Woooooooo.*' Fin startled me by playfully grabbing my shoulders and giving a theatrical moan. I instantly clutched my heart. 'Oops, sorry,' he apologised. He held onto the sides of my arms to steady me. 'I had a sudden impulsive urge to muck about,' he explained. 'I didn't mean to frighten you.' He held on to me for a moment longer, not realising that it was his touch that had caused me to stagger sideways. 'Are you okay?'

'Y–Yes,' I gasped, trying not to collapse on the floor at his feet.

'I've got you,' he assured, still holding me tight. Oh, the bliss. But, oh, how mortifying. 'My goodness, Lottie.' Fin looked surprised as he propped me up. 'I had no idea you were so easy to frighten.'

Chapter Fifty-Five

'Enough of castles and ghostly residents,' said Fin. He took my hand and led me towards the exit. 'I have somewhere else I'd like to show you. Somewhere less creepy. Also, there's a lovely coffee shop on site. They do the best cappuccinos.'

'Terrific,' I muttered.

Fin was still holding my hand when we stepped out into the bracing afternoon air. A part of me once again detached and observed. Wow. We looked just like a couple. Even more incredible, we looked so right together.

Fin was such a cliché. Tall, dark, and impossibly handsome. And me, well, I was just your average blonde. However, right now, in this moment, an onlooker might describe me as pretty. That said, my expression was a bit odd. Somewhere between thrilled to bits and utterly gobsmacked.

However, the handholding couldn't continue without it becoming indicative of something else. Something more intimate. Fin was the first to let go. We headed towards the car with our respective hands stuffed deeply into our pockets. On the way, he promised that the next venue held the *ahh* – rather than the *argh* – factor.

'Spill the beans,' I said, once we were inside the car.

'Nope.' He shook his head. 'You'll have to be patient.'

Minutes later, we were on the A39 heading towards Penryn. I knew that Jen and Stu had enjoyed a long walk around here. They'd followed the banks of the River Fal, and passed grand houses once owned by packet ship captains.

Minutes later, we arrived at a very different destination.

'A donkey sanctuary,' I said in delight.

'This is a such a special place,' said Fin. He cut the engine. 'Let me introduce you to Penny.'

'Penny?' I queried, as the passenger door swung open. I hopped out of the car wondering – admittedly a tad jealously – who Penny was. An ex-girlfriend? Perhaps any moment now a Marina lookalike would stride across those green paddocks. She'd be dressed like a cowgirl and chewing on a piece of straw. Perhaps she'd stop, stare in disbelief at Fin, grin from ear to ear, then throw her hat in the air and whoop *yeehaw!*

I rearranged my features. Best to look pleasant, and not impersonate a possessive German Shepherd. With a bit of luck, it would be Penny who looked like a dog.

'So, er, is Penny the owner of this place?' I asked. My head swivelled from left to right as we crossed a grassy area. We were heading towards a long row of barns.

A woman came out of a side office area. She immediately waved at Fin. Her face was wreathed in smiles. Okay, this must be Penny. She looked to be in her late thirties. She had laughing brown eyes, long dark hair, and the high complexion of someone who spends most of her time outdoors.

'Fin!' she exclaimed, coming over. Seconds later they were hugging each other hard. My lip curled slightly.

'Patsy,' said Fin, finally letting the woman go. 'It's so good to see you.'

Patsy?

'Always a pleasure,' she said. 'And who is this?' The dancing brown eyes landed on me.

'Patsy, meet Lottie,' said Fin.

'Hello,' I said, offering her my hand. She ignored it. Instead, I found myself enveloped in a big squashy bear hug.

'It's so bloody wonderful to meet you!' she exclaimed. Letting me go, she gave me an appraising look. 'Evidently Fin has come to his senses and got shot of Marina. How wonderful. I'm delighted for you both!'

'Oh, but I'm not—' I protested.

'Hideous woman,' Patsy interrupted. She gave an elaborate eye roll. 'Sorry, Fin' – she didn't sound remotely apologetic – 'but ever since Marina accidentally trod in a tiny bit of manure, I went off her. She screeched about the state of her designer boots, then told me my donkeys were so ugly she didn't see the point of them. After that, I had no time for her.'

'Yes, I was aware that you weren't keen,' said Fin, looking amused.

Patsy gave me a frank look.

'I tend to say things how they are.' She gave a little shrug. 'Anyway, after witnessing Marina's diva tantrum – and that was just *one* incident – it's nice to see Fin with someone more sensible.' Patsy pointed to my footwear. 'I can't see you having a meltdown about those getting mucky.' She looked at Fin again. 'I expect you've come to see Penny, right?'

'If it's okay,' said Fin.

'Of *course* it's okay,' said Patsy. 'Follow me.' We set off towards the barns. 'Thankfully, at this time of year we're a lot quieter. The place shuts in an hour or so, but I hope you'll stay for a cuppa before you go. Madge is in the coffee shop, and she's made some spectacular fudge cake. You must both have a slice.'

'We'd love to,' said Fin

Patsy led us into one of the outbuildings.

'Here's our Penny,' she beamed.

Oh! My eyes widened. Penny was a donkey. Thank God. I gave a huge sigh of relief. Patsy gave me an odd look.

'You look surprised,' she said. 'Who did you think Penny was? One of the grooms? Or perhaps an old flame?' She guffawed and slapped her thigh.

'Ha ha,' I chortled, evading the question.

A dear little brown donkey stood in an open area, which was a bit like a vast stable. She was in the company of several other big-eared friends. Penny looked our way. Her ears twitched forward. Upon seeing Fin, she plodded over.

'She always recognises you,' said Patsy. 'No doubt the darling girl is eternally grateful for you rescuing her.'

I turned to Fin in surprise.

'You *rescued* Penny?'

'Yup,' he nodded. 'She was dumped at Penwern Lodge. We never did find out by whom. The poor girl was emaciated and in a terrible way. I called her Penny as it was a little like the name of my hotel. Anyway, Penny was terrified of me, but too weak to run away. Pru and I have known Patsy for years, so we knew who to reach out to. And the rest, as they say, is history. Penny was rescued by the sanctuary–'

'With an enormous donation by you,' said Patsy gratefully.

Fin inclined his head.

'I have a soft spot for her,' he confessed.

'Oh, Fin's a regular visitor here,' Patsy confided. 'You don't ever need to worry about him taking a mistress,' she chortled. 'He's too busy having a love affair with this little lady.' She laughed riotously while I inwardly cringed. I noticed that Fin didn't correct Patsy about our relationship. Maybe that was because he was too busy tweaking Penny's ears and rubbing her nose.

'How many rescues do you now have?' he asked. Penny nudged Fin's palm, hopeful for a bit of carrot.

'We're up to fifty-eight,' said Patsy. 'Most of them have been rescued off the continent. The neglect and abuse is staggering.' She shook her head and blew out her cheeks. 'I will never understand cruelty. Anyway, this girl is here now. She's safe.'

'What do you do with all these donkeys?' I asked. 'It

must be a lot of upkeep.'

'It is, but we're open to the public. We also work closely with several charities including one for children. Therapeutic interaction. Our four-legged residents help improve a person's well-being. Both physically and mentally. The donkeys are particularly good for the kids. They help them develop transferable life skills. Like confidence. Empathy. You might be surprised to know that donkeys are emotionally intelligent, sensitive creatures. Their affection is boundless. It's particularly astonishing to witness their effect on children. And it's so rewarding to watch both the donkeys and kids interacting with each other. The sanctuary is a safe space for both sides. Anyway' – she leant forward and gave Penny an affectionate rub on the cheek – 'I'll leave you three together. Meanwhile, I need to head over to the feed shed. There's a delivery to sort out. Don't forget to pop in and see Madge for that fudge cake.' Patsy gave us both another bear hug. 'And I think you both look great together,' she whispered in my ear.

Chapter Fifty-Six

'Patsy is a lovely lady,' I said, after she'd departed.

'She's a great girl,' Fin agreed.

'That was a bit awkward for you though,' I tinkled.

'What?' His brows knitted together.

'You know,' I shrugged. 'Patsy believing we are a couple.'

Fin didn't say anything. Instead, he busied himself stroking Penny's velvety nose.

'Come on,' he said at length. 'Let's check out Madge's fudge cake.'

In the café, Madge greeted Fin as effusively as Patsy had. More hugs and hearty back-clapping followed.

'*Sooo* good to see you, Fin,' said Madge. 'And *delighted* to meet you,' she said, smiling at me.

'And you,' I replied. Oh help. Had Madge also got the wrong end of the stick about me and Fin? But she didn't make any reference to Marina. Nor was she as direct as Patsy. After a bit, I settled down and simply enjoyed being in Madge's company. It was clear she adored Fin and that any mate of his was a pal of hers.

We sat down at one of the café's tables with our cappuccinos and fudge cake. Madge lingered for a while. She made small talk about Penny the donkey, then asked for an update on what was happening at Penwern Lodge, and whether there would be a winter ball.

The conversation was interrupted when a couple of harassed young mums staggered through the door. Between them they were holding several reins and leashes. The leads were attached to four overweight beagles. The straps were keeping three tots secure. At the sight of cake, the beagles' eyes lit up like pinball machines.

'Excuse me,' said Madge. 'I'd better get back to serving.'

'Sit, Dilly!' commanded one of the women. 'Not you,' she said to one of the beagles. 'I mean YOU!' A fractious toddler was refusing to comply. 'You'll only have cake when you do as you're told.'

I stirred my cappuccino.

'They've got their hands full,' I murmured to Fin.

'Indeed,' he nodded.

For a moment, his face held a look of wistfulness. I wondered if he was remembering his deceased wife's brief pregnancy. Thinking about *what might have been.*

I sighed and set the spoon down on the saucer. One way or another, life never failed to deliver occasional dollops of sadness. It didn't matter who you were. Or where you were born. Disappointments, disasters, and devastation always found you. No one escaped Fate when it wanted to deal a dark card.

For Fin it had been the loss of a baby and then his wife. For me, the loss of a roof over my head. Also, parking my dignity to one side and taking dubious digital content to get out of debt.

Personal challenges occurred for everyone, everywhere. From losing one's crops… or suffering disease… or experiencing devastation through wildfires, earthquakes, or floods… at some point *something* knocked a person off their feet.

I wondered why life was like that. Just like I sometimes wondered what the point of life was. I mean, you went through all the crap, all the highs, the lows, and then what? Well, then you bloomin' died, that's what!

'That's a lot of sighing, Lottie,' said Fin.

'Sorry, I was miles away. Thinking about life and its lessons.'

'Now there's a subject,' Fin acknowledged. He smiled, then cleared his throat. A regrouping gesture. 'I hope you weren't embarrassed about Patsy getting it wrong. About us,' he added.

'Oh, that,' I said, reddening slightly.

'Ah. You were.'

Damn. He'd noticed the blush.

'N-No, not at all,' I blustered, turning even pinker. 'It was you I felt sorry for.'

'Me? Why?'

'Well, because… because…' – I laughed nervously – 'ha ha ha… it's just so unthinkable.'

'Is it?'

'Of course, ah ha ha *ha*!'

'Why's that then?' He wasn't laughing, but a smile was playing around his lips.

'Well, obviously… *obviously* I'm not your type.'

'Aren't you?' he said softly.

I stared at him. Was something going on here?

Suddenly, it seemed as if all sound receded. Dilly had stopped bawling. The beagles were sitting politely. The harassed mothers had eased their bottoms down on chairs. Madge was taking their orders. All around me, the world was turning but without background noise.

I continued to stare at Fin. My mouth was now half open. Hopefully I wasn't looking too gormless as I contemplated his handsome face. Those amazing hazel-green eyes were now locked on mine. Under his intense gaze, I could feel myself starting to squirm.

When I next spoke, my voice was little more than a whisper.

'A–Am I?' I stuttered. 'Your type?'

His reply was immediate.

'Yes,' he said quietly. 'You're absolutely my type.'

Chapter Fifty-Seven

'O-Oh,' I stammered.

Omigod. Fin had just told me I was his type. Did that mean… could it be… was it that…?

Yes! said my inner voice. *He likes you.*

'Sorry, Lottie,' Fin apologised. 'You look horrified.'

'N-No,' I stuttered. 'Not at all. On the contrary.'

'I like you,' said Fin simply.

See? Told you!

'I like you too,' I whispered.

'No, I mean, I *like* you.'

I nodded dumbly.

'That's what I meant too.'

'Good,' he grinned. On impulse, he leant across the table. Enfolded my hands within his. I had a fleeting concern about my fingers being sticky from fudge cake, but then realised I didn't care. Wonderful zingers were pinging up and down my arms.

'I had to tell you sooner rather than later, because tomorrow you go home. I didn't want you leaving without me saying how I felt. I've spent the whole of today wondering if you might feel the same way too. Please tell me you won't bang on Jen's door tonight in order to avoid me.'

'No,' I murmured. 'I won't be knocking on Jen's door.'

'Look' – he squeezed my hands – 'I know you live in Kent and I'm down here in Cornwall, but how do you feel about… about… I mean… oh dear, what I'm trying to say… in a most cackhanded way… how do you feel about trying a long distance relationship?'

'I'm up for it if you are,' I breathed, giddy with happiness.

Fin momentarily closed his eyes. It was then that I realised how nervous he'd been discussing his feelings for me.

'In which case' – he said tentatively – 'how do you feel about staying on for a bit?'

'You mean… not going back with Jen and Stu?'

'That's exactly what I mean,' he said.

Suddenly my face was wreathed in smiles.

'I'd really like that.'

Crikey, why had I thought Fate only dealt dark cards? I'd *completely* forgotten about Fortune coming along to balance things out. And what a fabulous card I'd just been dealt. It was like a giant painting full of golden sunshine, fluffy clouds, and silver linings. But wait. I'd forgotten something. What was it?

'Oh.' My face fell. 'What about Audrey?'

'Audrey?' said Fin, looking startled. 'I thought your daughter was called Sally.'

I laughed.

'Audrey is my cat. She won't take kindly to me

abandoning her.'

'Who has been looking after her while you've been away?'

'My neighbour. I'm sure she can manage for another couple of days.'

Ahem. Aren't you forgetting something?

Not now.

Yes. Now. You messaged Ryan, remember? You were quite adamant about seeing him tomorrow. You told him you wanted a face-to-face. That what you wished to say couldn't be done over the phone.

I gulped. Ah, yes. Ryan.

'Am I going too quickly for you?' asked Fin.

I took a breath. Momentarily closed my eyes.

'There's something I must do at home. I'm sorry, Fin, but I must go back tomorrow. You see, I messaged Ryan earlier. I told him that I wanted to discuss our relationship. Well, our *non*-relationship. Essentially, I want to do the decent thing and speak to him directly, rather than do a cowardly dump text.'

'Of course,' said Fin. He squeezed my hands again. He opened his mouth to say something, then hesitated. 'I must ask, Lottie. You're not ending things with Ryan because of me, are you?'

'Absolutely not.' I shook my head emphatically. 'You have my word. My mind was made up before you mentioned anything about… us.'

Upon saying that last word, I smiled shyly. *Us*. How

thrilling. How wonderful. How absolutely flipping fant*abu*lous. We were on the cusp of something here. Something shiny and new. And I was feeling so warm and happy and fuzzy inside – which made me totally unprepared for what happened next.

'Lottie,' said a man's voice.

Not Fin's.

I glanced about, and my eyes widened with horror. For there, standing in the doorway to Madge's coffee shop, was Ryan.

Chapter Fifty-Eight

Fin immediately let go of my hands. Had Ryan seen?

Flustered, I leapt to my feet, accidentally knocking the chair backwards in the process. It crashed to the ground, startling the beagles. They responded with a cacophony of barking.

'Whatever are you doing here?' I gasped, while wrestling the chair upright.

Ryan was all smiles as he strode over. Seemingly, he hadn't clocked the handholding between Fin and myself.

'Isn't it obvious?' he beamed. 'I'm here to spend the weekend with you – well, what's left of it.'

'W-Why didn't you go to the hotel?' I stuttered, desperately trying to regain my composure.

'I did, but you weren't there. The woman on reception said you were out. So I looked up your whereabouts on the *Locator* app.'

I inwardly groaned. Sometimes *Locator* was fabulous. Other times – like now – not so much. First Marina barging in on Fin and me. Now Ryan.

'But' – I spluttered – 'I messaged you. I said not to bother coming. That I'd see you tomorrow for a chat.'

'A chat?' he laughed. 'After a hellishly long drive, I want

a bit more than a chat.' He winked lasciviously and I inwardly cringed. 'And who are you?' he asked Fin, finally acknowledging him. 'Presumably the owner of this donkey sanctuary.'

'Er, this is Fin Trewarren,' I said awkwardly. Fin put his hand up by way of greeting but said nothing. His face was devoid of emotion, and I wondered what he was thinking right now. 'Fin is the owner of Penwern Lodge,' I explained. 'I've been staying in his guest bedroom after the booking mix-up.'

'Oh, right. Good of you to do that for us, mate.'

I cringed again, this time at the reference to *us*. So very different to the previous *us* where my heart had sung several hallelujahs.

'Well, if you don't mind, Fin, Lottie and I will now head back,' said Ryan. 'We have a lot of catching up to do,' he said meaningfully. He clapped Fin on the back in a matey way, then reached for my hand and pulled me after him.

'I'll see you back at the hotel,' I called over my shoulder to Fin.

Not surprisingly, he didn't reply.

Ryan still had hold of my hand when we crossed the yard to the carpark. Patsy just happened to be outside talking to some visitors. Out of my peripheral vision, I saw her look my way. I pretended not to see her but could tell she was puzzled.

'In you get, my pet,' said Ryan.

My pet? That was a different term to his previous

endearments. I then realised he'd said those two words through gritted teeth.

He held the passenger door open for me. I hopped in, looking up at him briefly before the door shut. Via the wingmirror, I watched him walk around the back of the vehicle. A moment later, the driver's door opened.

'Why did you come?' I repeated, as he slid behind the steering wheel. 'I sent you a–'

'Yes, yes' – he waved a dismissive hand as he started the engine – 'I saw the message. However, I didn't bother replying because I immediately knew what you wanted to talk about.' He put the gear into reverse and the car shot backwards. My head momentarily whipped backwards, and I instinctively grabbed hold of the door handle. 'You wanted to have a one-to-one. About us. Or rather, not us. In other words, ending us.'

I didn't answer. What was there to say? He'd read between the lines of my text. Got the gist of it. So why had he then driven hundreds of miles to Cornwall?

'I've behaved like a plank, Lottie,' he explained. 'As soon as I got your message, I knew I was on the slippery slope. Knew that I needed to do lots of back-peddling. Make up lost ground. So, I told Heather and Joshua that I had to go. No more delays. No more interruptions.'

'Ryan, are you really divorced?'

My question was like a pistol shot. It seemed to hang in the car's interior, hovering somewhere by the rearview mirror. The air quivered with an unpleasant energy. I was surprised my mouth had even spat out such a question. Certainly, my brain hadn't been thinking such a thought.

'I'm *almost* divorced,' he said, his voice suddenly small.

My mouth dropped open. I gazed at him across the space between us.

'Define *almost*?' I gasped.

Ryan sighed. It seemed to me as if he was exhaling from the bottom of his boots.

'Heather has consulted a divorce lawyer,' he said quietly.

'So you're really a married man!' I said indignantly. 'You *lied* to me.'

'Look, Lottie. I've more or less been honest with you–'

'More or less?' I hissed. 'I don't do *more or less*. I do *truth*.' How DARE you, Ryan. We had this conversation before, and you promised you were a single man. That you were still living in the marital home because of... oh, I don't know what the last excuse was. Something about an estate agent and getting the best agent's fee. Or was that a cock and bull story too? And slow down, please.' The light was rapidly fading, and we were whipping along singletrack lanes faster than was surely safe.

'Look,' Ryan cajoled. 'Let's talk properly when we're back at Penwern Lodge. Cards on the table time.'

'You've seen my hand,' I said tersely. 'You know everything there is to know about me.'

'Really?' said Ryan softly. His voice might have been gentle, but he was gripping the steering wheel very hard. So hard his knuckles had turned white.

'What's that question supposed to mean?' I said belligerently.

'I saw, Lottie.' His voice was barely audible.

'Saw what?' I frowned.

'That man you were with. You were both gazing into each other's eyes, like you'd hung the moon for each other.'

He gave me a sideways glance, just in time to catch the look of horror on my face.

Chapter Fifty-Nine

'There's something going on between the two of you, isn't there?' Ryan demanded.

I clung to the sides of my seat. Ryan was slinging the car around a country lane's sharp S bend. I hadn't a clue where we were. This wasn't the way Fin had driven to the donkey sanctuary. But, then again, we'd initially travelled from another direction. That of Pendennis Castle.

'Watch out!' I shrieked.

As we came out of the bend, a huge tractor was thundering towards us.

Ryan hit the brakes. For a moment there was the awful sound of rubber being left on tarmac. The car skidded to an abrupt stop.

'Bloody lunatic driver,' Ryan growled.

I didn't say anything. My focus was on the lunatic driver whose car I was sitting in. The farmer reversed his tractor back. He manoeuvred the vehicle into a small layby. This permitted us to squeeze – and it really was a squeeze – past the tractor. I found myself automatically breathing in as a thorny hedge scraped the paintwork of Ryan's car. He swore under his breath.

I was relieved when Penwern Lodge eventually came

into view. As we bounced over a cattle grid and into the carpark, Ryan aggressively cut the engine. I got out of the car with a sigh of relief. That hadn't been a pleasant drive.

There was no one on reception as we walked through the foyer. Wordlessly, Ryan followed me along the corridor to Fin's apartment. I removed the spare key from the back pocket of my jeans.

'Got your own key, have you?' Ryan sneered.

I pushed open the door. Ryan followed me in. I turned and glared at him.

'If you'd been available on Friday, then it would be you holding this key. Not me.'

'I'm not sure I believe you, Lottie,' he answered. 'Are you sure it's not a secret love nest? It seems most peculiar that Jen and Stu are nowhere to be found.'

I rolled my eyes, trying not to get annoyed at Ryan's attitude.

'You know full well, Ryan, that it was you who fluffed up the booking. I had an unbearable lecture from Jen. She made it quite clear she didn't want me third wheeling and spoiling her romantic break. It was Fin who kindly came to the rescue, although he didn't have to let me stay here. And, anyway, he knew that the booking included a fourth person – you. It just happened that you didn't show up.'

Ryan made a harrumphing noise.

'So you're telling me that Lover Boy won't object to me staying in his guest room's double bed?'

'Look, Ryan–'

'Yeah. Thought so. He's going to object, all right.'

I pointed my index finger to my chest. Stabbed the tip against my heart for emphasis.

'It's *me* objecting. Don't you see?' I gave a bark of mirthless laughter. 'There is no *you and me*. There is no *us*. Jen and Stu have been having a wonderful romantic time together. Something we were meant to do. It was the sole purpose of you booking Penwern Lodge in the first – for you and me to finally have some time together without the usual interruptions.'

'And now we are alone,' he said, coming towards me.

I quickly moved away. Over to the kitchen area. Made sure the table was between us.

'Things have changed,' I said quietly.

'Yes, I know,' Ryan nodded. 'You've gone all gooey over Mr Fancy Man.'

No mention of the handholding. Ryan hadn't clocked that. Not that it mattered, because I no longer cared. However, I didn't want to rub Ryan's nose in it by admitting Fin and I had feelings for each other. Hurting Ryan was to be avoided. And anyway, there wasn't anything going on with me and Fin. Well, not yet. So far, all we'd done was admit we liked each other. Nothing physical had happened. We hadn't even had a stolen kiss, for heaven's sake.

'Let's leave Fin out of the equation,' I said levelly. 'I'd rather talk about you and Heather.'

Ryan's eyes flickered.

314

'What about me and Heather? I told you ages ago that she and I are finished. What more is there to tell you?'

'You both behave as if you're still very much enmeshed. Very involved. Very *married*.'

'My son wasn't well. If this is about Joshua interrupting our Cornish weekend, then you need to park your bitter feelings to one side.'

'Bitter feelings?' I repeated. I blew out my cheeks. Wow, the accusations were all coming out now, weren't they! 'On the subject of Joshua' – I said quietly – 'one way or another, it strikes me that your boy is very keen to keep his dad and mum together.' Ryan suddenly couldn't meet my eye. 'And how is Joshua after his emergency trip to hospital?'

'Absolutely fine. But that's youth for you.' Ryan's tone was defiant. 'Youngsters have excellent resilience.'

'Exceptionally so, in your son's case.' My voice dripped with sarcasm. 'An astonishing immune system, indeed. From meningitis victim on Friday to not even a sniffle forty-eight hours later.' I put my hands on my hips, not in the mood for nonsense. 'You're being played, Ryan. And if it's not Joshua, then it's Heather. There's always one drama or another. All I know is that during our brief time together, there's been more interruptions than the adverts in a TV programme. I don't know the dynamics of your relationship. And frankly' – I held up a hand to stop him interrupting – 'I don't want to know. It's now irrelevant. For me, this weekend was the last straw.'

There was the sound of a key in the lock. A second later, Fin walked in.

'Oh, sorry,' he said. For a moment, he looked as if he might reverse back out. 'I didn't realise the two of you were in.' He turned to Ryan. 'I expect Lottie has told you what time the dining room opens. Will you both be eating with your friends this evening? If so, I'll make sure a table is reserved for four people.'

I blinked. Fin had switched into *professional* mode. Ryan frowned, momentarily thrown after accusing me of having taken Fin as a lover.

'Er, thank you,' said Ryan stiffly, before turning back to me. 'I think, Lottie, we will continue this conversation in our room.'

'Top floor,' said Fin pleasantly. 'In the meantime' – he said politely to Ryan – 'I'll be down here having a cuppa before I'm back on duty. I hope my presence won't be an inconvenience.'

'Of course not,' mumbled Ryan.

He'd been tactfully reminded that this was Fin's home. Not the hotel. I'd also picked up on something else. An unspoken message for me. *Any funny business, just shout. I'm here for you.* Which was reassuring.

'Lottie, could you lead the way, please,' said Ryan.

Reluctantly, I moved towards the staircase. We needed to finish this conversation, and not with an audience. I owed Ryan that much. And anyway – I reasoned, as he followed me up – I was perfectly safe. Any nonsense, and I'd scream.

Fin would hear.

Upon reaching the second landing, we both paused. The pair of us were slightly out of breath after climbing two flights of steep steps.

I opened the door to the turret bedroom and stepped inside. Ryan started to follow me in, but abruptly stopped.

I walked over to the dressing table and pulled out the stool. Ryan remained in the doorway.

'What's the matter?' I asked.

He didn't reply. For some reason, his face had drained of colour. He put out a hand. Clutched the doorframe. Almost as if to steady himself. I frowned, sat down, then crossed one leg over the other. Ryan continued to glance around the room. A strange look had settled over his ashen features. His eyes snagged on mine as I sat there. One leg crossed. One foot dangling. Both feet still encased in my hiking boots. He went to say something, but all that came out was a strangled gurgling. And in that moment, I knew. My eyes widened as I stared at his shocked face, my own expression now surely mirroring his.

'Omigod,' I whispered, appalled. 'You're Mr Muppet.'

Chapter Sixty

There was a moment where neither of us said anything.

We continued to stare at each other. Ryan was now gripping the doorframe as if his very life depended upon it. We were both slack jawed and horrified, as shockwave after shockwave crashed through our respective bodies.

Ryan was the first to speak.

'*You*?' His voice was hoarse. '*You* are *Fifi Footsy*?'

My heart was pumping wildly. What if Ryan spilt the beans? Revealed my identity? I blanched. What if he told my daughter? My friends? What if he rushed downstairs, found Jen and Stu, and shouted this revelation to the rooftop? Even more horrendous, what if he told Fin?

'Don't say anything to anyone,' Ryan implored. His voice was little more than a whimper. 'Please. Promise me, Lottie. Otherwise, I'll be ruined. A laughingstock.'

'N–No,' I shook my head. 'I promise. I'll never tell a soul.' As if. Why would I? The last thing I wanted was all and sundry finding out about my alter ego. 'Your secret is safe.'

Ryan let go of the doorframe. Slowly, he came into the room. Collapsed down on the bed. He leant forward and put his head in his hands. For a moment his shoulders shook. I wondered if he was crying. I didn't go to him. I was still reeling with horror. As a result, my backside remained welded to the dressing table stool.

Ryan dropped his hands into his lap. He stared unseeingly at the carpet.

'That's why she said she could no longer be with me,' he whispered. I straightened up. Strained to hear his words. 'Heather,' he clarified. 'When everything kicked off between us, she thought it was because I was having an affair. You see, she went through my phone.'

His voice was barely audible, and I struggled to make out what he was saying. Taking a deep breath, I stood up. My knees cracked like two pistol shots. The sound seemed abnormally loud in this tense, surreal atmosphere.

Ryan's Adam's apple bobbed as he gulped down emotion, ready to unburden. Confess. A man determined to deliver an explanation to the bitter end.

'Heather found the messages. The texts. Pictures. Voice notes. Everything. She went ballistic. Demanded to know if I was visiting call girls too.'

I flinched at his words.

You're not a call girl, Lottie, said my inner voice. *Chill.*

But – I silently answered – I was still providing a service. Doesn't that make me–?

No! You didn't have sex with anyone. End of subject. Got it?

Got it.

Ryan rubbed his face with the heels of his hands.

'I told Heather that it was just a harmless pastime, but she didn't understand. My wife didn't like that I'd spent money on it, you see.'

Understandable. Mr Muppet had been my best client. He'd spent over eight hundred pounds on yesterday's video, for crying out loud! Ryan shook his head imperceptibly.

'I tried to make Heather understand that hobbies cost money. I mean' – he spread his arms wide, eyes still on the carpet, firmly addressing the floor – 'she goes to the gym. Spends a fortune bouncing up and down on a plastic box. She takes pictures. All those women – sometimes men – in their itty-bitty shorts. Their backsides hanging out. Tattooed butt cheeks, for heaven's sake!' He shook his head. 'It's positively indecent. And yet *my* pictures aren't acceptable.'

'I understand,' I said quietly.

'Do you, Lottie?'

He looked up at me, and I could see that his cheeks were wet.

'The thing is, Ryan, your logic is somewhat…' I struggled to find the right words. 'Well… off. There's a world of difference between Heather's photographs and yours. After all, she's not getting her thrills out of them.'

He looked away. Stared at the floor again.

'We could have mutually thrilled each other,' he muttered. A touch of belligerence peppered his tone. 'But she wouldn't entertain the idea. Heather flatly refused to let me suck her toes. She said it was weird. But lots of couples have some kink in their sex lives.'

That was true enough. I thought of Jen. She loved not just energetic sex but also outdoors sex and got a huge buzz taking bizarre risks.

I gazed at one of the framed prints on the wall over the bed. A donkey. I now realised it was a photograph of Penny. Was it really less than an hour since I'd been at the sanctuary? It felt like a lifetime ago.

'Heather wouldn't budge,' Ryan continued. I dragged my eyes away from Penny. Looked at Ryan again. Somehow, he seemed smaller. Almost pathetic. 'Heather insisted that everything below the ankles was off limits.' He sniffed. Wiped his face with the back of one hand. I took this as a cue to offer my own explanation.

'I'm sorry you had to find out about me like this,' I said gently. 'For what it's worth, I'm not a thrill seeker. I wasn't getting any personal pleasure from being *Fifi Footsy*. It was a way of getting myself out of debt. I was sinking. Drowning. My ex-husband…' I trailed off awkwardly. 'It was tricky. My situation was dire.' I held out my hands. A gesture of helplessness. 'It was simply a means to an end. That video I made for you… along with the exorbitant fee… it cleared the last of my debt. For that, I am so very grateful. I thank you from the bottom of my heart.'

He nodded.

'It was a lot of money. The most I've ever spent. And totally a one-off,' he added hastily. 'Perhaps Heather and I should have marriage guidance counselling. After all, there's still a lot of affection between us. Maybe Heather could be persuaded to compromise. Let me massage her toes, rather than lick them.'

'Er… right,' I said, suddenly feeling slightly hysterical.

It's nerves. All that shock combined with relief has caught up with you, my inner voice assured.

Maybe, I silently agreed, as a giggle-snort landed in my nasal passages.

Think of something serious. Quick. I know, politics! Rishi Sunak congratulating the Lionesses after their Women's World Cup defeat… him asking a homeless man what he did for a job… or that time he appropriated an RAF jet to go to Scotland to announce two new "green freeports" … actually, I'll stop right there, Lottie, because you're starting to look furious.

'Bloody pillock,' I snarled.

'What?' Ryan startled. 'Do you think marriage guidance is a bad idea?'

'Sorry, sorry. I was thinking about someone else,' I soothed. 'The Prime Minister. He had a spot of bother with er, Mrs Sunak. I heard that she didn't know how to open a tin of baked beans. Astonishing, eh? In these modern times. Especially when can openers have been around for so long. I wonder what a marriage guidance counsellor would make of them,' I laughed. Slightly manically, it had to be said.

We were silent for a moment. Ryan no doubt thinking about Heather's feet, while my own thoughts veered towards throwing one of my hiking boots at a certain Tory's head.

'I'm sorry to hear you've suffered financial hardship,'

said Ryan eventually. 'It must have been very serious for you to… you know.'

'It was,' I murmured.

'In a perverse sort of way, I'm glad it was me who was instrumental in helping you resolve it.'

'Me too,' I nodded. That much was true.

Ryan gave me a watery smile. I returned it with a sad one. He took a deep breath. When he exhaled, it was as if he'd released all that previous upset and tension. His face suddenly looked lighter. Relief. He stood up.

'I won't join you, Jen and Stu for dinner,' he said, smoothing down the creases in his trousers. 'I'll head home. I'll give Heather a call from the car. Tell her I'm on my way back.'

'It's an awfully long drive, Ryan. Why don't you go back tomorrow? You can have my bed in the turret tower. I'll insist that Jen and Stu forfeit their night of passion and let me sleep on the pull-out.'

Ryan shook his head.

'No, Lottie,' he said quietly. 'If I leave now, I'll be home soon after midnight. It's early evening and there's very little traffic on the road.'

'Well, if you're sure,' I said, trying not to show my relief.

'I'm sure,' he said. 'Thank you for everything. You're a lovely girl, Lottie. You deserve happiness. I hope you find it with Fin. He's a lucky guy.' I opened my mouth to protest, but Ryan held up one hand. 'Don't,' he said. 'I may be a foolish sixty–year–old man, but I'm not stupid.'

He gave me one last look. Then he walked out of the bedroom, and out of my life.

Chapter Sixty-One

I don't know how long I sat in my turret room after Ryan had left. I was in a daze. Eventually I became aware that Fin was standing in the still open doorway.

'Lottie?' he said gently, hovering uncertainly. 'Are you okay?'

'I'm fine,' I sighed.

'I saw Ryan go. He said he wouldn't be staying for dinner. In fact, he said he wouldn't be staying at all.'

'Indeed,' I said quietly. 'He knows we're over. But, as I told you earlier, our relationship never got off the ground.' I shrugged. 'Anyway, it turns out he still has feelings for his ex. Who knows. There may be a grand reconciliation. I hope so. Meanwhile, I feel nothing but relief.'

I was still reeling – if truth be told – from the discovery that Ryan had also had an alter ego. I'd often wondered about Mr Muppet. Who he was. Whether the anonymous name belonged to a nutter. At times, when my imagination had been fanciful, I'd conjured up a creepy man. Jaw unshaven. Wearing a grubby mac. Sitting in a shadowy room. Swigging from a whisky bottle. A cigarette butt pinched between nicotine-stained fingers.

The image couldn't be further from the truth. Instead,

I'd been dealing with a respectable accountant. One who commanded authority. A distinguished looking guy. A husband. A father, no less.

I wondered about the other men who'd looked at *Fifi's* pictures. I had no doubt they were of similar character. Going about their respectable day jobs. Maybe having a beer on a Friday night with the lads. Going home to the wife and the two point four children. Washing the family car on a Sunday morning after taking the dog for a walk. Putting the bins out on a Monday morning.

I was also experiencing another type of relief. One that was running in tandem with ending the relationship. That of having finally been found out. Perversely that had been liberating. As if I'd been absolved from sin. And yet, my secret remained safe. One way or another, both Ryan and I had had a lucky escape.

'Jen came by earlier,' said Fin, scattering my thoughts. 'She saw Ryan's car outside, so knew he was here. She wanted to know if you were joining her and Stu for dinner. I said you'd get back to her.'

'Ah,' I nodded. 'I'd better go and see her. Explain what's happened. After all, I need Stu to drive me home tomorrow morning.'

'You know, you don't have to go,' he said softly.

'I know. But' – I hesitated, choosing my words cautiously but also honestly – 'right now, after…' I waved one hand helplessly. I wasn't about to spill the Mr Muppet beans. 'Let's just say that it doesn't feel like the right moment to start something new. So much has happened in such a short space of time. When I arrived on Friday evening, you and I were coupled-up with other people. Yesterday you ended your relationship with Marina. Today I ended mine with Ryan.'

'But not because of each other,' Fin pointed out. He was looking at me intensely. 'You were nothing to do with Marina and I parting company. Likewise, you said you'd already made up your mind about Ryan. Let's both be clear about that.'

'Of course,' I agreed.

'But I understand what you're saying about having some space,' said Fin carefully. 'About drawing a line under our previous relationships. Taking a pause.'

'Exactly,' I said, relieved that he understood. 'Otherwise, it would feel too much like a rebound. And that's the last thing I want.'

I knew to my cost – literally, with Rick – about rushing into a relationship. Throwing caution to the wind. And then, when Ryan had come along, I'd gone from one extreme to the other. Nothing much had happened, thanks to all those interruptions from Heather and Joshua, but there had to be a balance. A wiped slate. A clean start. Fin and I were both now single. Two free agents. We'd known each other for forty-eight hours, even if it did – peculiarly – seem more like forty-eight months.

'Apart from anything else' – I said softly – 'you're too special to risk being a rebound.'

He grinned, and his whole face lit up with joy.

'What about an old-fashioned courtship?' he suggested, his eyes twinkling with both merriment and mischief. 'So, no rushing in like Tarzan beating his chest before bedding Jane.'

'Quite,' I laughed. It was a good thing Jen wasn't here listening to this. A bit of role-playing would be right up her street. I could see her now, beating her fists against her bosoms before swinging from the chandelier. Although I wasn't sure Stu would like to play the part of Jane.

'In which case' – Fin had adopted a teasing tone – 'can I interest you in making a reservation at a very nice hotel I happen to know? It's called Penwern Lodge and can be found in a tucked-away pocket of Cornwall. The hotel itself is full, but there just happens to be availability in my guest room in the run-up to Christmas. The lodging would be totally free of charge, although there would be one non-negotiable stipulation.'

I arched an eyebrow.

'And what might that be?'

'That you, Miss Lucas, escort Mr Trewarren to the annual Christmas ball' – we seemed to have suddenly slipped into a regency romance scene – 'where there will be much merrymaking, fine dining, and music for dancing the night away.'

'That sounds most agreeable,' I said, getting to my feet. I walked slowly over to him. 'Miss Lucas assumes that she must dress to impress. Would that be correct, squire?'

'Your finest gown,' he concurred. 'Bonnet optional.'

'Any other stipulation?' I gave him a winsome look. 'Something that Mr Trewarren might possibly have overlooked?'

'Yes,' he said, his hands slowly encircling my waist. 'There is the small matter of a deposit. Mr Trewarren insists Miss Lucas pays this upfront. It is non-refundable.'

'Miss Lucas is bemused.' I flicked imaginary skirts. 'What is this downpayment that Mr Trewarren speaks of?'

Fin pulled me closer.

'A kiss,' he whispered, as his mouth met mine.

Chapter Sixty-Two

Six months later

I shut the door on the turret apartment. Leaning back against the wooden panels, I looked around in delight. Home.

When the rental had expired on Catkin Cottage, I hadn't renewed. Between Fin and I, there had been much toing and froing between Little Waterlow and Cornwall. Finally, I'd succumbed to the delights of Falmouth. Jen had been sad about me moving away, but also delighted at my newfound happiness.

'Stu and I will visit you often,' she'd assured. 'Fin's turret guestroom holds distinct romantic possibilities,' she'd giggled.

The apartment looked a little different to when I'd first seen it, last November. Feminine touches had been added. Only yesterday Pru had complimented me on one of the changes.

'I love the new sofa cushions,' she'd gushed. 'The colours are gorgeous – baby pink, the softest of greens and a dash of yellowy cream. So pretty!'

'Hm,' Fin had mock grumbled. 'They remind me of those sweets from our childhood. Fruit salads.'

My thoughts were interrupted by the pitter-patter of tiny paws coming down the stairs.

'Meow,' said Audrey. She hastened over and immediately weaved around my ankles.

'Hello, sweetheart,' I said, scooping her up. I hugged her to me tightly.

She'd settled in so well and was now living her best life. Audrey liked to spread largesse about. If she wasn't in the turret apartment, she was out on reception, greeting new arrivals. Anna – who'd since joined the staff as a permanent receptionist – was dotty about cats. Indeed, she had four of her own. She'd bought Audrey a snug fluffy basket which was now stationed on the reception counter's upper tier. A biro on a chain was positioned nearby. Guests used it to sign in. Audrey always took pleasure in watching guests deliver their signatures with a flourish. She'd then lunge forward, knock the pen from their fingers, and proceed to pat it back and forth as it dangled from its chain.

I now kissed Audrey's fluffy head.

'Let Mummy feed you,' I said, moving into the kitchen area. I parked her on the worktop. Yes, I know, not terribly hygienic. However, Fin and I were rather laid back in that department. I moved over to the cupboard where cat food in every flavour was kept. 'Talk about having the best of everything,' I prattled on, selecting a tin. 'Yum. Beefy chunks.'

'Oooh, is that what's for dinner?' said Fin, coming in through the front door. He sniffed the air theatrically. 'In which case, I can't wait.'

I set the dish down in front of Audrey, then walked into Fin's arms.

'I'm afraid I've been holed up in the staffroom for the last two hours,' I apologised. 'The Zoom call with my editor went on and on. As a result, cooking has been the last thing on my mind – which is a nuisance, because I'm famished.'

'Damn' – Fin gave an exaggerated eye roll – 'we'll have to eat in the restaurant again.'

'Such hardship,' I grinned.

He hugged me tightly.

'You're worth it.'

Oh, how I loved this man.

'How did the meeting go?' he asked.

'Sensationally,' I beamed. 'Sales are going brilliantly. Maxine gave me an update on the stats. All three books have, between them, sold nearly half a million copies *and* – my eyes were now shining – 'I've been offered another contract with Guns and Holsters Publishing. This time it's a ten-book deal. DI Denise Draper is on the case!'

'That's incredible,' said Fin, kissing me hard on the mouth. 'I'm so proud of you, Lottie. I think we'd better have a celebration. I shall ask the maître d' to provide champagne with our meal tonight.'

'Will he agree?' I asked, stifling a giggle.

'Let me ask him.' Fin released me, then plucked an imaginary phone from mid-air. 'Hello, is that Mr Trewarren?' He took a large step to the left. 'Yes, it is. Can I help you, Sir?' Fin took another huge step, this time to the right. 'You can, indeed. My fiancée, Miss Lottie Lucas, will be dining at the restaurant this evening. Please ensure there is a bottle of your finest champagne at the ready. She's celebrating being a best-selling crime fiction writer. Got that?' Fin took a big step to the left again. 'Absolutely, Sir. See you soon, Sir.'

Fin hung up the imaginary phone.

'Sorted,' he grinned.

'Thank you.'

I threw my arms around him and hugged him tight. His aftershave flooded my senses, and I inhaled it down to my soles. Lovely. Just lovely. This wonderful man was mine. All mine.

'Come and sit down for a minute,' he said, leading me over to the sofa. 'Let's have five minutes to ourselves before we go to dinner. I feel like I've hardly seen you today.'

We flopped down together on the couch. Seconds later, Audrey, having finished her meal, appropriated Fin's lap.

'Traitor,' I said to her, leaning over to stroke her silky ears. I looked up at Fin. 'I think my cat loves you more than me.' I eased my feet out of my summer sandals and, nudging the shoes to one side, swung my legs up onto the coffee table. 'That's better,' I sighed. I crossed them at the ankle. 'I also managed to speak to Sally this morning.'

'That's nice. How is she?' asked Fin.

Sally, having now met Fin a few times, was delighted her mother had a sane and sensible partner in her life.

'She's good,' I said, wiggling my toes. I'd recently visited one of Falmouth's nail technicians who'd made my feet look almost presentable. Certainly, I loved the glittery red polish that had been applied to my toenails. 'Also, Sally can't wait for us to meet her new boyfriend. Apparently, he's an absolute honey. Sal said she'd visit us this weekend and bring him with her. His name's–

I broke off. Frowned. Fin was staring at my toes.

'What's the matter?'

'Hmm?'

'Oy, mister. Are you even listening to me?' I thumped him playfully on the arm, which made Audrey flick her tail in annoyance.

'Sorry, Lottie. I *was* listening but…' – he looked back at my toes again, distracted. 'I don't think I've ever told you–'

'Told me what?' I said in bemusement.

'Well' – Fin hesitated – 'this might sound a bit weird, but you have the most amazing feet…'

THE END

A Letter from Debbie

I visited Cornwall with my husband in 2020 just as the UK was coming out of lockdown.

We took my parents with us. As both Mother and Father Bryant are physically disabled – and Mother Bryant has severe dementia – it was challenging. But the hotel was beautiful, the grounds exquisite and the staff so very kind. Penwern Lodge is fictional but based upon the hotel we stayed at.

At the time of Lottie visiting Cornwall, there was a rock festival going on and all the hotels were booked for miles. Such a rock festival is also fictional. However, I took the concept of this musical event from another, later, chapter in my life. Earlier this year, we tried to make a reservation at a hotel in Oldham to visit my mother-in-law. However, everything was booked solid in a twenty-mile radius – even B&Bs – due to *Parklife Festival*, Manchester's biggest music gig which takes place at Heaton Park.

So, for the purposes of Lottie's story, I took that event and transported it to Cornwall. After all, writers have free licence to do such things. More importantly, I needed a reason for Lottie to end up in Fin's apartment!

Audrey, Lottie's fluffy black-and-white cat, is based

upon my very own HRH Dolly. I do love letting our four-legged family members make cameo appearances in my novels! However, unlike Audrey, our Dolly is rather antisocial and prone to regal hissy fits.

The idea for this novel came to me after I innocently uploaded to Instagram a snap of my new, pink, high-heeled shoes. My daughter jokingly commented about me starting a foot pic side hustle.

Obviously I didn't! But instantly my head began to buzz with ideas. I started to research the subject and Lottie, my leading lady, began to take shape. You wouldn't believe how many people take photographs of their feet and GET PAID FOR IT! Someone I know – who shall remain anonymous – told me that *they* know someone else who is earning several thousand pounds every month. Straight up. Shall we start a consortium? Jokinggg! Tempting though, eh!

The subject of debt features in Lottie's story. Debt is horrific. The character Rick is loosely based on someone I once knew. He put his wife through financial hell. Having met the real-life guy, I needed to do very little research on the deviousness of his mind. I hasten to add that his wife didn't take pictures of her feet to resolve her debt! Instead, she took financial advice regarding the loans fraudulently put in her name, lumped everything into a single interest-free loan, then worked her socks off (no pun intended) to pay the wretched thing off.

Anyways, *Lottie's Little Secret* is my nineteenth novel. It sees a return to the fictional village of Little Waterlow. This is a small Kent village not dissimilar to my own stomping ground.

I love to write books that provide escapism and make a reader occasionally giggle. You will also find some drama – like debt – and sometimes that can be uncomfortable. I let my characters decide how a story is going to unfold, but its best to buckle up in case there's a tense moment.

There are several people involved in getting a book "out there" and I want to thank them from the bottom of my heart.

First, the brilliant Rebecca Emin of *Gingersnap Books*. Rebecca knows exactly what to do with machine code and is a formatting genius.

Second, the fabulous Cathy Helms of *Avalon Graphics* for working her magic in transforming a rough sketch to a gorgeous book cover. Cathy always delivers exactly what I want and is a joy to work with.

Third, the amazing Rachel Gilbey of *Rachel's Random Resources*, blog tour organiser extraordinaire. Immense gratitude also goes to each of the fantastic bloggers who took the time to read and review *Lottie's Little Secret*. They are:

Kirsten Bett's book reviews; Splashes Into Books; @webreakforbooks; Tizi's Book Review; InsomniacBookwormBookreviews; Little Miss Book Lover 87; Captured on Film; Storied Conversation; Sharon Beyond The Books; Ginger Book Geek; Books, Life Everything; Scotsbooksworm; Tealeavesandbookleaves; Rajiv's Reviews; iheartbooks.blog; Eatwell2015; Proud Book Reviews; My

Reading Getaway; @anitralovesbooksanddogs; Bookworm 86; and last but not least, *CelticLady's Reviews.*

Fourth, the lovely Jo Fleming for her sharp eyes when it comes to typos, missing words, and the like.

Finally, I want to thank you, my reader. Without you, there is no book. If you enjoyed reading *Lottie's Little Secret,* I'd be over the moon if you wrote a review – just a quick one liner – on Amazon. It makes such a difference helping new readers to discover one of my books for the first time.

Love Debbie xx

Enjoyed *Lottie's Little Secret*?

Then you might also like *Wendy's Winter Gift*.

Check out the first three chapters on the next page!

Chapter One

I stumbled over a tree root, arms briefly windmilling, before recovering my balance.

'Careful, Wends.' The caution came from my canine-walking partner-in-grime, Kelly. Her breath made clouds in the early morning November air. 'You're lucky you didn't slip on that pile of doggy-do over there. It's bang out of order that some owners can't be bothered to pick up after their pooches.'

'Perhaps the person had run out of poo bags,' I said, automatically fishing for one from the pocket of my Barbour.

'You're never going to pick up after someone else's dog, are you?' Kelly asked incredulously. Her huge brown eyes widened. She looked like a middle-aged Audrey Hepburn, but with swishy long hair.

'Absolutely,' I replied, bending to the task.

'*Ewww.* Rather you than me.' Kelly wrinkled her nose.

'Surely it's no different to picking up after Alfie,' I countered.

Alfie is Kelly's ancient German Shepherd – not an incontinent husband, in case you're wondering.

I stooped and scooped, then knotted up the chemically perfumed little sack. A moment later and it had been deposited in one of the handy red waste bins, dotted throughout Trosley Country Park.

'It's different picking up after your own dog,' said Kelly, as we resumed our pace. 'It's like when your kids are babies. I never thought twice about changing my sons' nappies, but could never do the same for my niece. My sister used to get really annoyed with me. She'd say, "For heaven's sake, Kelly. Poo is poo!" But it isn't really, is it? I mean, it's like wiping one's bum. You just do it. But you wouldn't do it for anyone else, would you?'

'Erm…'

I tucked a strand of blonde hair behind one ear. How on earth had we got on to this subject?

'I mean' – Kelly persisted – 'you wouldn't stroll over to a stranger – like that guy coming towards us – and waggle a pack of wet wipes at him while saying, "I'm offering a bottom wiping service. One wipe for a quid or a polish for a fiver."'

'No,' I agreed.

So far, our Friday morning conversation had been a far cry from the usual topic; namely, our husbands. And whether to stay with them or leave.

Like me, Kelly had been married for twenty-seven years. And also, like me, she insisted there was little companionship and a lack of marital bliss. But – *unlike* me – she was having a terrific flirtation with a married man. She'd met Steve in Costco, of all places. At the time, he was being publicly rebuked in the bread aisle by a sergeant major wife. This had been seconds after Kelly had had a public row with Henry. She'd left him sulking in *Beers and Wines* because she wasn't prepared to blow the housekeeping on twenty crates of the store's Whisky of the Week.

Henry's drink consumption was a topic that frequently caused huge arguments. As Kelly had swung past shelves stacked with seeded loaves, she'd locked eyes with the henpecked man, and something unspoken had passed between them.

He'd made his move just after his wife had declared him useless. She'd ordered him to stay put while she, and she alone, went off to source the next item on the shopping list. A hasty conversation had taken place between Kelly and Steve and numbers had been furtively exchanged.

Flushed with excitement and derring-do, they'd been secretly meeting in various supermarkets ever since, enjoying peaceful shopping excursions and sparky conversation.

However, at their last meeting, things had taken a different turn. While the pair of them had lingered in *Breakfast Cereals*, Steve had dared to lean in and drop an impromptu kiss on Kelly's lips. Flustered, she'd put out a hand to steady herself and sent several boxes of porridge cascading everywhere. She was now in a continual state of overexcitement, wondering if this was the universe's way of saying that Steve should have his oats.

'Anyway' – I hauled my mind back from its meandering thoughts – 'I don't have any truck with poop scooping. After all, as a professional dog walker' – I affectionately glanced down at Sylvie, a sweet Golden Retriever, at my heel – 'it's something that sometimes has to be done.'

Sylvie belonged to Jack and Sadie Farrell who were occasionally overtaken by their respective work commitments and needed a hand exercising their two dogs. Sadie was a talented potter who mostly worked from home, but this week she'd been involved in an arts and crafts pre-Christmas exhibition at nearby Paddock Wood's Hop Farm.

'Sylvie isn't mine' – I reminded Kelly – 'but nonetheless I love her to bits and am happy to do the right thing by her.'

'She is a lovely dog,' Kelly agreed.

Sylvie was one of the calmest dogs I'd ever had the joy to take out. Unlike William Beagle who – along with Kelly's dog – had long disappeared amongst the woodland in search of hares and squirrels.

'ALFIE!' Kelly fog-horned, making Sylvie and me jump. 'ALFIE, WHERE ARE YOU?' She stopped and did a three-hundred-and-sixty-degree turn, scanning the undergrowth. 'Where has he gone?' she tutted. 'He's far too old and arthritic to keep up with William.'

'He'll be back,' I assured.

'Yeah, hopefully not with a dead squirrel hanging out of his mouth. I'm not good with bodies. Every time the cat dumps a mouse on the doorstep, I end up asking my neighbour to dispose of the body.'

'Doesn't Henry do it for you?' I asked in astonishment.

Kelly rolled her eyes.

'Henry doesn't "do" anything other than make me

gnash my teeth. He's drinking way too much, blaming his excessive alcohol consumption on work and stress.'

'I know,' I soothed.

'I should leave him.'

'And I should leave Derek.'

'Do you think we'll ever be brave enough to take the plunge?' she asked gloomily.

But before I could reply, William Beagle shot out of a side path. He powered towards us with Alfie in stiff pursuit.

'Oh no,' I moaned.

'Bugger,' Kelly hissed.

William had a dead hare swinging from his jaws, while Alfie had found Mr Fox's calling card and had a marvellous time rolling in it.

'Never mind our husbands,' Kelly muttered. 'Right now, we have a far more pressing problem. How am I going to clip the lead on Alfie's slime-green collar, and how are you going to persuade William to drop that furry corpse?'

Chapter Two

'*Ewww,*' wailed Kelly.

She attempted wiping her hands on a small tissue I'd found in the depths of my coat pocket.

'DON'T RUB YOUR FACE ON MY LEGS!' she shrieked at Alfie, as he proceeded to wipe himself against her denim-clad thighs. 'Oh God,' she gasped. 'Why did I ever get a dog?'

'Because they're great company,' I said, snapping the lead on William's collar.

Feeling like a murderer's dodgy accomplice, I swiftly hurled the little beagle's "gift" into the undergrowth.

Don't think about your actions, Wendy. It's not a cute bunny. It's a dead body.

'I can't believe you just did that!' Kelly blinked in horror.

'What else could I do?' I asked helplessly.

'Well, I don't know. Shouldn't we have buried it, or something?'

'Unfortunately, when I left home, I didn't think to pop a shovel in my handbag.'

'No need for sarcasm,' my bestie tutted. She dropped the soiled tissue on the woodland floor, then kicked some dead leaves over it. 'Let's turn around and head to the public toilets. I need to properly wash my hands. I'm not looking forward to going home. There's nothing I loathe more than wrestling an enormous dog into the bathtub and trying to remove the stench of fox crap.'

'I've heard that tomato ketchup is a must when it comes to getting rid of the pong.'

'Really?' said Kelly hopefully as we headed back to the visitors' area. 'I'll give it a try. And then I'll have to wash my clothes and deep clean the bathroom before I can even *think* about bathing myself. That's ninety minutes of my life gone on a joyless task.'

'Text Steve,' I said slyly. 'See if he's able to skive off work and wash your back.'

Kelly's eyes lit up.

'I'd like nothing more than that.' She flashed me a furtive look. 'Lately, I've been fantasising about what he looks like without his clothes on. He seems to be in good shape for someone not far off fifty. Probably because of his job.'

Steve had his own construction company but wasn't averse to mucking in with the labourers. Consequently, he had broad shoulders and big biceps – from what Kelly had glimpsed when Steve had been wearing t-shirts.

The guy sounded very different to Kelly's husband. Henry had a blue whisky-nose, the paunch of a drinker, and spaghetti-skinny legs.

'Do you think it's wrong to daydream about another

man?' Kelly whispered as we passed a pair of joggers.

My answer was immediate.

'No.'

Heavens, I'd fantasised enough about men myself. Mostly actors in their heyday. Brad Pitt. Bruce Willis. George Clooney. More recently my thoughts had turned to my hunky neighbour. Ben was a whole decade younger than me with a wife who was rapidly going to seed. Lately, I'd been running a mental scenario on repeat. Ben saying, "You're locked out, Wendy? Why of *course* I'll shimmy up a ladder and climb through your bedroom window. Thank goodness you left it open." And then, when Ben reappeared downstairs, flushed and triumphant, me flashing him a smile and asking if he'd like a cuppa and a slice of cake by way of thanks. Except this was the point he'd waggle his eyebrows and say, "I have a far better idea about how you can repay me." And naturally I'd oblige. Energetically. Joyfully. Enthusiastically. Him sweeping me into his arms. Me swooning prettily. Him lowering his mouth to mine. Me closing my eyes as the tip of his tongue–

'Why are you panting?' asked Kelly.

My thoughts scattered like confetti.

'Er, because we're walking faster than usual. It's making me a bit, you know, out of breath.'

Kelly narrowed her eyes.

'Hm.'

'Anyway,' I chirped, keen to avoid her scrutiny. 'I expect sooner or later you and Steve will take things to the next level. I mean, you can't keep lurking in Lidl or skulking in Sainsbury's.'

My friend was instantly distracted, as I had known she would be.

'You're right,' she sighed. 'But it's one thing to keep flirty company and have a stolen kiss. It's quite another to do the deed. And anyway, where would we go? I daren't risk inviting him back to my place. I have two savvy teenagers who have a habit of turning up when least expected.' Kelly momentarily stared up at the sky as she visualised a scenario. 'Imagine. Ten o'clock in the morning. Henry safely ensconced behind his desk at the office. The boys at their respective universities and conveniently out of the way. And then, just when I'm stripped down to my undies and my lover is admiring the way my boobs haven't quite yet reached my navel, my sons bursting into the bedroom and reminding me they're home for study days and' – she adopted a shocked accent – '"Good GOD, Mother! Why are you breastfeeding a strange man?"' She tore her eyes away from a flurry of cumulus clouds. 'No, it would never work. Anyway, I have nosy neighbours.'

'Everybody in Little Waterlow has nosy neighbours,' I pointed out.

'True,' she agreed.

'What about going to Steve's place?' I suggested.

'Definitely not.' Kelly gave a mock shudder. 'Caroline is a full-time stay-at-home wife who is kept *extremely* busy supervising the cleaning lady, overseeing the gardener, and standing over the ironing lady who apparently even presses the family's pants.' She looked at me incredulously. 'I mean, *who* irons pants?'

'I have no idea,' I said, flushing slightly as I recalled another fantasy. Me standing over the ironing board. Blasting steam everywhere as I ironed black cotton briefs belonging to Yours Truly. The radio playing. Tom Jones belting out *Baby You Can Keep Your Hat On.* Me changing the lyrics and singing, "Wendy you can take your pants off," just as Ben magically appeared in front of the ironing board and hooked his fingers through the belt-hoops of my jeans... zipper going down... top coming off... until I was standing before him in nothing but my one good lacy bra and a pair of pristine briefs – not a crease to be seen – which miraculously also reflected my face on this occasion. Yes, I thought fervently, recalling my ironed pants. Best to be on the safe side. These days one needed all the help one could get to look good at forty-eight. If that meant ironing one's pants, then so be it.

'Wends? Are you listening to me?'

'Of course I'm listening to you,' I said, snapping to. 'Caroline sounds like a complete nightmare.'

'She is.' Kelly nodded fervently. 'I reckon if she caught me and Steve at it, instead of bawling him out for adultery, she'd more than likely march over and yell, "Not like THAT, you stupid man!" Apparently, she is a complete control freak in all areas, so I can't imagine her being any different in the bedroom.'

'Are they still sleeping together?' I asked carelessly. Kelly's face crumpled, and I realised I'd fluffed up by asking such a stupid question. 'Sorry, that was insensitive of me.'

'It's fine.' Kelly did a few rapid blinks and composed herself. 'Steve says not. He says they haven't done anything for yonks.'

'And do you believe him?'

She shrugged.

'I want to. He's asked me too. You know… whether Henry and I are still active under the duvet.'

'And are you?'

She looked anguished for a moment.

'Well, generally, no.'

'What do you mean *generally* no?'

'I mean, definitely no. Not for ages. Until two nights ago.'

'What happened two nights ago?'

'Something crazy. We're talking totally whacko. I'd eaten a load of blue cheese before bedtime and… did you know that cheese consumed in the evening can make you vividly dream?'

'I didn't.'

'Well, it does. And it did. And…' Kelly trailed off awkwardly.

'Ah.' Realisation dawned. 'You'd eaten blue cheese and found yourself having *blue* dreams.'

'Exactly!' she said, grateful for me cottoning on. 'So, there I was. In bed. Fast asleep and having the most *incredibly* heightened dream starring the delectable Steve and moi. Unsurprisingly, cheese featured. Steve wanted to play silly games. He'd dressed up as a pony with a mask on and I had to guess which cheese he was.'

'Mascarpone?'

'Very good, Wends! Well, the dream progressed, and we were having this bizarre conversation about what sort of music a cheese would listen to-'

'R & Brie?'

She nodded.

'And then Steve was whispering in my ear – which seemed incredibly erotic at the time – and he was saying that the Big Cheese had turned up and needed handling-'

'Caerphilly?'

Kelly gave me a sharp look.

'Were you having the same dream as me last night?'

'Absolutely not,' I said hastily.

'Anyway. Steve began nuzzling my neck and I let out a blissful sigh as he cooed, "I'm right brie-hind yoooo!" But… but…'

'But what?' I prompted.

'But it wasn't Steve behind me. It was Henry. In real life. My eyes snapped open in the dark just as Henry – boozy breath billowing – took advantage of his conjugal rights with a compliant wife who'd apparently woken him up moaning, "Do it! Do it! I Camembert it any longer." Henry has since stocked up the fridge with three vast blue cheeses and spent yesterday evening encouraging me to have a bedtime snack.'

'Oh dear,' I said, trying not to giggle.

'Do you think that counts as cheating?' she asked fretfully.

'Hardly. After all, Henry is your husband.'

'Not with Henry,' Kelly tutted, rolling her eyes. 'I meant with Steve.'

'No,' I said, telling her what she wanted to hear. 'You're not in a proper relationship with Steve, so how can you have cheated on him?'

'Yes,' she said, sighing with relief. 'You're right. Phew.'

'We're here.' I pointed to the Bluebell Café and the public loos alongside. 'Let's clean up and then have a quick cuppa before heading home.'

'I don't think I have the nerve to go inside the café reeking of *Eau de Monsieur Renard*.'

'I'll do it,' I said, stooping to the task of looping three sets of dogs leads around a nearby post-and-rail fence. 'Let me quickly wash my hands first. Do you want a Cheddar toastie too?'

'No thanks,' said Kelly. She flashed me a grin. 'Right now, I'm all cheesed out.'

Chapter Three

Ten minutes later, we were sitting outside the café, bums on a bench seat, drinks resting on one of the country park's trestle tables and doing our best to ignore the stiff November breeze.

We huddled into our coats whilst admiring the surrounding woodland which was a stunning backdrop of red, orange and gold. The grassy area around our table was heavily coated in leaf fall, indicating winter was just around the corner.

The three dogs sat together, looking on. Alfie and Sylvie were behaving impeccably, but William was having none of it. He kept up a steady stream of barking, baying his displeasure at being excluded from sampling a slice of carrot cake.

'*Arrrooooooo!*' he wailed repeatedly.

We'd already received some pained looks from other walkers who'd paused to enjoy an al fresco coffee and snack.

'Ignore,' I said to a rattled Kelly.

'Who? William or that cross looking elderly couple sitting over there?'

'Both,' I said firmly.

'I know those two,' she hissed, leaning in.

'Me too,' I whispered back.

'Fred and Mabel Plaistow. Little Waterlow's oldest residents who think they're entitled just because they're days away from receiving the Queen's telegram.'

'You mean the King's telegram,' I pointed out. 'Anyway, I don't think they're *that* ancient.'

'Mabel is giving us absolute daggers,' Kelly muttered. She turned and gave them her own ferocious scowl. 'There,' she said, smirking with satisfaction. 'That'll teach them to glare. Now then' – she took a sip of her drink, a regrouping gesture – 'this morning all I did was moan about Henry. Now it's your turn to moan about Derek. Tell me what's going on.'

I took a slurp of my own drink before replying.

'Nothing,' I sighed. 'It's the same old same old.'

'He's still picking his nose?'

'Yes.'

'And hogging the remote control?'

'Yes. But it's not his habits that rattle the chains of our marriage, Kelly.'

'Ah. In other words, he's still a self-opinionated, arrogant prat who treats you like the dog poo you pick up.'

'Yes,' I sighed again.

'Why don't you leave him?'

'Why don't you leave Henry?' I countered.

'I will when the boys have graduated from uni. I can't risk jeopardising their exam results. Do you *really* think you'll ever leave Derek?'

'One day,' I said, but my words lacked conviction.

'When exactly is *one day*?'

'Not sure. Anyway, an escape needs proper planning. After all, I have responsibilities.'

My friend rolled her eyes.

'You mean being a doormat.'

'That's a bit harsh,' I winced, trying to not look hurt. 'Ruby might not be at uni like your boys, but she's still living under our roof. Having unexpectedly made us grandparents, I can hardly turf her out along with my granddaughter, can I?' I felt upset at the very thought. 'I know your lads gave you the run-around for a while, but at least they got through their early teenage years without falling in with the wrong crowd and ending up pregnant at fifteen.'

'Well, being male, they could hardly get pregnant,' Kelly pointed out.

'No, but they could easily have got someone else's daughter up the duff, and how would you have felt then?'

'Awful,' Kelly admitted. 'I'm sorry. Now it's my turn to have dropped a clanger.'

The subject of Ruby was hardly a fresh one between me and my bestie. A little after her fifteenth birthday, my daughter had announced that her pal Simon was more of a mate than Derek and I had realised. Discovering that a missing ten-pound note from my purse had paid for a pregnancy test – one that showed two blue lines – had given me an instant out-of-body experience.

At the time my mind had splintered in two. I'd watched, from somewhere around ceiling level, the scenario that had gone on to unfold in the kitchen.

There was Ruby in her school uniform. And Simon, tall and gangly. Derek, mercifully, had not yet arrived home from work, so was not around to punch Simon's lights out.

On that lifechanging morning, Ruby had left for school with her hemline too short, eyes defiantly outlined in kohl, and her newly dyed hair an interesting shade of purple. Her attitude for the last twelve months had seesawed between truculent and sneering.

Back then, she'd looked down her nose at me. Her expression could shift from pity to disgust faster than a Tesla's acceleration. I was aware that raging hormones were behind the transformation in my previously sweet girl. Almost overnight she'd morphed into a spotty, bad-tempered adolescent with unexpected tantrums fuelled by pre-menstrual tension. Suddenly everyone was an idiot. I was an idiot. Derek was an idiot. Even the cat next door was an idiot.

On this particular day, she'd returned home from school with Simon. Ruby had revealed an emotion never witnessed before. Fear. She'd tried to disguise it by carelessly tossing the plastic tester across the kitchen table but had then slumped down on a chair. I'd not needed any further explanation.

'I'm not having an abortion,' she'd shrieked into the shocked silence. 'Simon and I have already discussed it. We want to be together. If we have a boy, he'll be called Sunshine Lord, and if it's a girl, she will be named Moonbeam Fairy.'

I'd been unable to reply on account of my essence bobbing somewhere around the kitchen's lightshade. I'd looked on – like a member of the audience at a play – as the drama played out.

Ruby's boyfriend had decided not to sit down at the table – possibly in case Derek came home early and Simon needed to make a quick getaway. The kitchen was too small to pace around, so instead he'd had a complete outbreak of the fidgets, shifting his weight repeatedly from one foot to the other.

'SAY SOMETHING!' Ruby had roared, making Simon visibly jump.

Her outburst had catapulted my mind back into my body which had been leaning against the worktop. The edge had dug painfully into the small of my back.

'Erm,' I'd croaked, before hastily clearing my throat. 'Nice names.'

I hadn't dared say otherwise. Who knew what wrath my disagreement might have caused? Yes, I admit it. I'd been a little scared of my teenager. Keeping the peace had been paramount. Avoiding rows, essential. Deflecting temper outbursts had been all. And trying to keep Derek and Ruby at arm's length from each other had been crucial because, if father and daughter went head-to-head, I'd inadvertently end up as whipping boy for the pair of them. Pathetic? Yes, maybe. But unless you've shared your home with a human box of fireworks, you won't know what it's like being permanently on edge. Waiting for one of them to light the emotional fuse – BOOM! – leaving you trembling at the vileness. The hateful words. The breathtaking ugliness of it all.

Want to know what happens next?
You can download the book from Amazon

Also by Debbie Viggiano

Wendy's Winter Gift

Sophie's Summer Kiss

Sadie's Spring Surprise

Annie's Autumn Escape

Daisy's Dilemma

The Watchful Neighbour (debut psychological thriller)

The Man You Meet in Heaven

Cappuccino and Chick-Chat (memoir)

Willow's Wedding Vows

Lucy's Last Straw

What Holly's Husband Did

Stockings and Cellulite

Lipstick and Lies

Flings and Arrows

The Perfect Marriage

Secrets

The Corner Shop of Whispers

The Woman Who Knew Everything

Mixed Emotions (short stories)

The Ex Factor (a family drama)

Lily's Pink Cloud ~ a child's fairytale

100 ~ the Author's experience of Chronic Myeloid Leukaemia

Printed in Great Britain
by Amazon